SAM CURTIN, THE JUDGE

The town marshal was on the scene shortly. Sam handed the wanted poster to him and pointed to the body, saying, "Willie James Cook. He raped, tortured, and killed a teenage girl in Robertson County."

"Do you know for sure that he was guilty?" Jordan did not wait for Sam to speak, choosing to answer the marshal's question himself.

"Hell, yes. He stood right here on this walk ten minutes ago bragging about it. The Judge, here, gave him a chance to go back and stand trial, but Cook wouldn't have it that way. He wanted to play gunfighter. When he tried to outgun the judge, he plain committed suicide." The Judge. Sam Curtin had just picked up a nickname that he would carry for life.

By Doug Bowman
from Tom Doherty Associates, Inc.

Gannon
Sam Curtin

SAM CURTIN

DOUG BOWMAN

A TOM DOHERTY ASSOCIATES BOOK
NEW YORK

SAM CURTIN

Cover art by Carl Cassler

A Forge Book
Published by Tom Doherty Associates, Inc.
175 Fifth Avenue
New York, N.Y. 10010

ISBN: 0-812-53453-0

First edition: October 1994

Printed in the United States of America

0 9 8 7 6 5 4 3 2 1

In memory of Kirby, Estelle, and Singing John: my father, my mother, and my grandfather.

One

Sam Curtin sat in the shade, astride his big chestnut gelding. For some time now he had been watching his nephew, seventeen-year-old Bud, practice with his handgun. The blond, blue-eyed youngster was small in stature, with a fine-featured face that was so handsome he almost looked girlish. Last year, after deciding that the big forty-four was too large for his small hands, he had paid the gunsmith to mount the same caliber on a smaller frame. He had learned early on that he could get the weapon into action quicker by tying the trigger down with rawhide and fanning the hammer with his left hand. Today, as he did every day of late, he was burning ammunition at the several small wooden blocks he had set up along the top pole of the old, seldom used corral. Bud made no secret of the fact that he wanted to be the fastest gun in Texas.

Sam stabled his horse and walked to the house. His

older brother, Hamp, father of young Bud, sat on the porch in his rocking chair, spitting tobacco juice into a small bucket he held on his knee. Pointing down the hill to his son, Hamp spat the brown cud into the yard.

"That boy any good with that thing?" he asked.

"He's fast."

"Fast as you?"

"Could be. He does have one problem, though, that might get him hurt some day."

"Yeah?"

"He can't hit the broad side of a damn barn!"

Sam walked into the house to find that his sister-in-law, Lula, had seen him come up the hill, and had put food on the table. The sowbelly, turnip greens and cornbread that she served apologetically disappeared quickly.

"I hate to keep fixing the same old thing every day, Sam, but there just ain't nothing else. I can't see why Hamp don't butcher a steer."

"He would if he had a steer, but he only has the bull and a few heifers that will drop calves pretty soon. He sold every steer he had last fall to meet the mortgage. I understand his situation, he's afraid he'll lose the ranch if he can't come up with three hundred dollars more for the fall payment." Sam walked to the water bucket and drank from the dipper that had been made from the dried shell of a gourd. He wiped his mouth on his sleeve and continued talking. "Two goats down at the barn, but nobody around here will eat them. I'll see if I can get a deer early in the morning."

"That'll help a lot, Sam," Lula said. "Seems like Bud can't be quiet enough to get one, and Hamp's got that bad foot that hurts him all the time." She then went to another room, continuing her housekeeping chores. Hamp's "bad foot" she had referred to had been run over by a wagon last winter and had never healed properly. The doctor in town had finally left the foot to nature's healing process, saying he could do no more. Hamp had mentioned having the foot amputated at the ankle and fitting himself with a peg. He believed that in doing so, the stump would heal and become tough and he could walk without pain. Sam thought that was probably true, but had offered no advice to his brother.

Hamp Curtin had bought the three-section ranch six years ago, and if he could just keep his nose above the water for the next four years he would own it outright. As of now, he had only two hundred dollars, and on November first a payment of five hundred would be due. How he could come by the additional money was a matter of great concern to him. Lula worried just as much, but was better at hiding it. She was constantly reminding Hamp that they had been down before, but had always bounced back. Things just naturally had a way of leveling out, she told him almost daily, and in the end most folks got as much as they deserved. She believed Hamp deserved the ranch free and clear, and was confident that it would turn out that way.

Hamp was quick to tell anyone who would listen that marrying Lula was the best decision he had ever made. The two had been classmates in school, and had married as teenagers in Pass Christian, Mississippi. They had come to Texas that same year in a covered wagon, trailing a milch cow and two redbone hounds. Many was the time that the cow's milk had been their main source of nourishment. The hounds took care of themselves, for they were good hunting dogs. With regularity, when the day's traveling was done, each of the canines would trot into camp with a rabbit or some other small animal clamped tightly in its jaws.

Shortly after their arrival in Texas the young couple

had been lucky in meeting Ed Haynes, who had put them to work on the same ranch on which they now lived, growing hay and vegetables and tending cattle. Haynes had been well pleased with the hardworking Curtins and had kept them on year after year. At Haynes' untimely death his heirs had sold off the cattle separately, then sold the ranch to Abe Martin, who had resold it to Hamp Curtin.

The house and outbuildings were now in top condition, for prior to his accident Hamp had kept them so. He was a man well acquainted with hard work, and Sam had often made the remark that his brother covered more territory in a day than most men did in a week.

The Curtin ranch was a fine one indeed. Located in east-central Texas near the town of Calvert, it was watered by three clear-running creeks that flowed year-round. Several springs dotted the landscape and the soil would grow almost anything. The Curtins had fallen in love with the place at first sight. Young Bud had been born in the cabin down by the hay meadow, and the family had lived there until Haynes' death. Sam had also been raised in the cabin till he had gone to work breaking horses for an outfit in Fort Worth that supplied animals for the army. Now, Sam sat on the doorstep, looking down the hill to the stock pond.

"Abe Martin is not gonna get this ranch, Hamp!"

"Lord, that sounds good, but I sure don't know anything I can do to stop him. Lu's got that two hundred salted away somewhere but I'm three hundred short, with nothing coming in. The cattle wouldn't bring anywhere near that much."

Sam continued to stare down the hill because he could not bear to look at the worry and weather lines on the face of his brother, who was beginning to look stoop-shouldered and old before his time. The remembrance that Hamp had literally raised him after the deaths of their parents, often giving up things that he needed for himself so his younger brother could have more, was never far from Sam's mind.

"The cattle are not for sale, Hamp. You just keep your weight off that foot, I'm gonna get the money for you." Sam got to his feet and walked to the barn. A few minutes later he rode the chestnut through the gate and down the hill toward Calvert.

Located in Robertson County, the small town of Calvert had grown up almost overnight when the Houston and Central Railway, one of Texas' first, reached the crossroads of the bald Texas prairie in 1868. At times, as many as a hundred wagons loaded with goods bound for the coast would await the train's arrival. More than thirty thousand immigrants rode the rails as far as Calvert, then fanned out across the state by wagon, stage or mule during the railroad's first three months of operation. Population swelled to ten thousand, and Calvert was soon the fourth largest town in Texas. Honorable businessmen built Victorian homes, hotels, opera houses and theaters to impress the newcomers as they stepped off the train.

But, like all boomtowns, Calvert had another face that was much less apparent to the travelers. There were places in the area where a man could get shot simply for speaking out of turn. Sam Curtin had firsthand knowledge of the town's wild side. Four years ago he had shot a gunslinger dead in front of a dozen witnesses at a saloon across the tracks. All who saw the shooting testified that the draw had indeed been a fair one, that the young gunfighter had simply been unable to match the quick hand and marksmanship of Sam Curtin.

Today, Sam was in town to talk to Abe Martin. He knew Martin only slightly, but folks around town who knew him better seemed to think that he was no better or worse than any other businessman. When a note came due he expected his money, with no excuses.

Sam had heard it said that Martin had come to Calvert from St. Louis, but nobody seemed to know for sure. In this country that question was rarely asked of a man. One thing was obvious to all: he was a man of means. Martin had begun to buy up land in all directions upon his arrival, and now held mortgages on half the farms and ranches in the area.

Sam paused at the office door, over which hung a neatly painted sign: A. MARTIN—LAND CONSULTANT. Dressed inexpensively, with no hat on his graying head, the grossly overweight man sat behind a plain brown desk. At Sam's entrance, he was on his feet quickly.

"Good afternoon, Mr. Curtin. What can I do for you?"

"I want to talk about my brother's ranch." Martin walked to a filing cabinet and soon was explaining to Sam that he could extend the due date on the mortgage till the first of the year, but no further. Sam thanked him for the sixty-day extension, and was about to leave the office when Martin spoke again.

"How would you like to earn the money to pay off your brother's mortgage?" Sam stood motionless for a moment. Then, with the slightest hint of a smile playing around his mouth, he turned to face Martin.

"Who do I have to shoot?"

"Nobody. I mean . . . maybe nobody. I suppose you remember when little Kelly Ryan was raped and murdered between here and Hearne last year." Curtin nodded, and Martin continued, "The girl was my wife's cousin. Sadie took it mighty hard, and has literally been wasting away ever since." Martin reseated himself and pushed a chair forward with his foot, which Sam accepted. "There is a two-hundred-dollar reward on Curly Cook," Martin continued. "Everybody thinks he's the killer, but nobody wants the money bad enough to tangle with him. It's common knowledge that he's fast with a gun, and not terribly selective about who he points it at. I figure it'll take a man like you to bring him back to Calvert. These damn lawmen ain't gonna do it, they tremble like frightened animals when somebody mentions his name.

"I'm offering you a deal, Sam: you bring Curly Cook down that street out there sitting up or lying down, makes no difference to me, and I'll hand you a clear deed to Hamp's ranch."

"How do you know he's guilty?"

"Hell, that's what it adds up to. Marshal Pond had him in jail that same night, and he had blood on the front of his pants. Cook told the marshal the blood came from a fistfight he had been involved in. He was only charged with being drunk and disorderly, so he paid his fine and skipped the country before the girl's body was found." Martin, who had already smoked two cigarettes during the short time Sam had been in the office, now rolled and put a match to a third. "Cook was seen by two line riders that same day, less than a quarter mile from where the body was found," he said, coughing out a billow of smoke. "If he's innocent, why did he run? Why won't he come back and stand trial? He ran off and left a wife and young baby. That ain't normal, Sam."

"It might not be normal, but men do it all the time," Sam said. "When you put it all together, though, it does put Cook in a pretty bad light. I might just see if I can persuade him to come back and tell his side of the story. I'd be needing some expense money up front, Abe."

"Of course you will. I'll take care of it." Sam got to his feet and headed for the door.

"Keep this conversation between the two of us, Abe, and put the deal in writing, along with your guarantee that you won't foreclose on Hamp's ranch as long as I'm on Cook's trail, no matter how long it takes. I'll sleep on it and let you know tomorrow."

"That's fine, Sam. I'll be here at the office."

Sam Curtin's prowess with a six-gun was well known throughout Texas. He had traveled with a trade show for more than two years, demonstrating the quick draw and trick shooting. He had tried most of the short guns on the market, and had settled on the weapon that now hung from his belt in a cutaway holster that was tied to his leg with rawhide: the Colt single-action army revolver.

The "Artillery" model, so styled from its five-point-five inch barrel with six-groove rifling, was rapidly becoming the most famous handgun of all time. Among other names, it had been called the "New Model Army" and the "Frontier." Firing forty-five caliber ammunition, the revolver had a relatively slow muzzle velocity, but was prized by most Western men for its "knock-down-and-keep-down" shooting power. Texans simply called it the "Peacemaker."

Nodding to several acquaintances, Sam rode down the street and took the road to Hamp's ranch. Holding his horse to a walk, he was enjoying the cooling evening. He was thinking that with the ranch paid off, Hamp could take it easy and let nature build up his herd. He was expecting a good calf crop, then they themselves would drop calves and the cycle would continue. Within a few years he would have the herd he had worked so hard to obtain.

Sam always enjoyed this ride, viewing the creeks and

hillsides, and the beautiful bluebonnets that grew everywhere. He knew of no place better suited to the raising of cattle, hay and grain.

His immediate problem, however, was how to bring Cook back to the county to face his accusers. He had seen Cook on several occasions, and would have no problem identifying him. Even though he might resort to disguises, the deep scar across the wanted man's nose would be difficult to hide, as would the dark hair that was so curly that even getting a comb through it was surely a problem for him. Sam doubted that Cook would come back without a fight. If that turned out to be the case, then so be it. He had decided to hunt the man down and bring him to Robertson County—one way or another.

Asking his brother to keep the information from Lula and Bud, Sam explained to Hamp what he had decided to do. Hamp objected loudly, then limped off to the barn, where he began to assemble the harness Sam would need for his pack animal. Later, Hamp went to bed without speaking to anyone.

One hour after sunrise the following morning Sam unloaded a large deer at the meathouse, asking Bud to butcher the carcass. The venison, along with the one hog that remained down at the pen, should sustain the Curtins till Sam's return, he thought. It was now time for him to be on his way. Half an hour later he rode into the yard, leading the small black mare that he would use for packing. Unhurriedly, he began to load the pack with the things he would need for what might turn out to be a long journey. Lula stood watching, but said nothing. As he rode out of the yard, she yelled to him, "You do be careful, Sam, you hear?"

He waved his hat and rode down the hill. An hour later he was in Abe Martin's office. Martin quickly handed him two hundred dollars and the agreement he was asked to put in writing. Abe said he had heard that Cook was living below the Mexican border, where he crossed the river into El Paso whenever he wished. Sam had heard the same thing, and intended to start his search there. As he neared the door, Martin called to him, "Just remember, Sam, he's a mean sonofabitch. Folks who saw the body said it appeared that the girl had been tortured before she was killed."

As Sam rode toward the livery stable many people who knew him took a second look, for they had never seen him leading a pack horse before. His loud knock on the barn door was answered by a man the townspeople called Arkansas, who went about filling Sam's order. The grain bags Hamp had fitted to the mare's back were now being filled with oats. As he worked, Arkansas began to ask questions.

"Goin' huntin'?"

"Maybe."

"Thought you might be goin' after Curly Cook. I saw ya goin' in an' out of Martin's office. I know he wants Cook real bad."

"Would you happen to know where Cook is?"

"No, an' I c'n tell ya right now, I don't wanna know. That man is sumpin' else. Why, once I seed him roll a can all th' way 'cross that corral pumpin' shots into it."

"Yeah, some fellows can do that," Sam said, mounting the chestnut, "especially if the can is not shooting back." After stopping at the town marshal's office to pick up some wanted posters on Curly Cook, Sam forded the Brazos River and continued west. In the boot of his saddle rode the 1873 model Winchester rifle he had traded into just a few months before. Its magazine was loaded, but he never carried a shell in the chamber unless he was hunting game. The same was true for the

Peacemaker on his hip. With no shell in the chamber, the gun could not fire accidentally. He, like most men, only carried five shells in the cylinder. However, if a man was expecting trouble in the immediate future he might add a sixth shell.

Knowing he might be in the saddle for weeks, Sam set a leisurely pace for El Paso. He knew it would be a long, hot ride. As he rode along, his mind wandered to some of the sad stories Hamp had told him about the Civil War. Young Sam had not been old enough for the fight, but his brother had vainly devoted almost three years of his life to the Confederate cause.

Sam Curtin had just recently turned twenty-five years old. Considered a big man by most standards, he stood well over six feet, and weighed a very muscular two hundred pounds. With brown hair and eyes and a ruddy complexion, he was a handsome man. Although he had near-perfect teeth and a disarming smile, he seldom used it. Most of the time he was a serious man who tolerated little nonsense. Though he did have a sense of humor, and occasionally laughed heartily, his humor was subtle and dry.

He had taken up prizefighting at age twenty, and though he had won each and every contest, he had earned very little money. Purses had been small, and bouts very hard to promote. He had given up the fight game after two years, and had gone back to breaking horses for the army in Fort Worth. Any fat that had attempted to accumulate on his body had quickly been discouraged by the bucking broncs he fought on a daily basis. Physically, Sam Curtin was cat-quick and tough as nails.

His parents had died together in a boating mishap on Mississippi's Gulf Coast, where they had had their own small commercial fishing operation. His mother's body had been found within a few hours, but it had been more than a week before John Curtin's body washed up on Biloxi Beach. Hamp had married Lula shortly thereafter, fearing that without a wife he might lose custody of his younger brother, Sam, who was seven years old at the time. Lula had mothered and educated Sam as if he had been her own son, and today he was on a journey that he hoped would repay her for some of the hard work she had put into his upbringing.

Sam had no desire to be a bounty hunter, an occupation loathed by many, and he thought this would be the one and only time he took up a wanted man's trail. Though spurred by the chance to rid his brother of debt, that was not his sole reason for making this trip. He had as much sympathy for young Kelly Ryan's plight as did anyone else, and if Cook was guilty, only one penalty would satisfy the people of Robertson County. If the county could not prove his guilt, Cook had nothing to fear by standing trial. The jury would be composed of good, solid men who were reasonable, and if the county could present no more than circumstantial evidence, Cook would walk free. Sam expected to explain that to him in the near future.

Just before sunset, he picketed his horses on good grass and set about making camp for the night. After heating his supper and making coffee, he sat beside the small stream, eating and watching the jumping fishes. He knew that come daylight he would have a hook in the water, for he was hungry for fish. Shortly after dark, he rolled into his blanket and was quickly asleep.

Two

He replenished his food and grain supplies at Brownwood, and one week later rented a hotel room at Fort Stockton. The town had developed around a military post of the same name at the crossing of Old San Antonio Road and the Comanche War Trail. Sam had decided to rest himself and his horses for two days before taking on the final trek of Texas desert.

He had crossed most of West Texas, and had been unmolested by Indians. A few times he had encountered parties of Comanches numbering four or less, who sat their horses and eyed him with curiosity. Each time, he had unsheathed his rifle and laid it across his saddle, hoping they might plainly see that he was armed with the gun they feared most. Each time, they had turned their horses and headed elsewhere, not wishing to take on the repeating firepower of the Winchester '73.

Today, he had bought some thin paper, and was sitting in his hotel room tracing Curly Cook's likeness from the wanted poster. Knowing that some people would be reluctant to give information to a bounty hunter, he would claim to be searching for a friend, showing only the tracing, and not the poster itself.

In the afternoon, he sat in the Grey Mule Saloon, the town's leading dispenser of red-eye. The bartender had been out of beer, and Sam had settled for the short glass of whiskey he was now nursing. As the day wore on, he began to tire of trying to follow the many conversations that were going on in the room, though no one had spoken to him directly. He had tossed off the remainder of his drink and was about to leave, when a tall man who appeared to be several years past his prime approached his table. Though his hair was gray, some of its original sandy coloring could be seen. Scratching his red beard, first on one side, then the other, the stranger spoke in a heavy baritone voice.

"Ain't seen you around, young fellow," he said, pulling out a chair for himself without being invited, "but I couldn't help noticing that you seem to be alone. I thought maybe you might like some company." He laid his Sharps rifle across a nearby table, offering a handshake. "My name is Joshua Jordon, but not many people know it. Folks just call me Red." Sam took the outstretched hand and introduced himself.

"Oh, then," Jordon said, "us both having Biblical names, we should get along just fine."

"My name is not Samuel. My pa just named me Sam, and he obviously felt that I needed no middle name." Jordon shrugged, and said nothing. He wore unseasonably warm clothing, and though no holstered weapon was visible, Sam had the feeling that the man was armed to the teeth. Sam ordered drinks from the bartender.

"No, no, Mr. Curtin. Since I sort of invited myself to your table, I'll do the buying." Over drinks, Sam learned that Jordon had come west from Virginia in 1851. He had trapped in the Northwest and prospected for gold in California and Mexico. Every place that was mentioned in the conversation, Red had been there. He talked as if he knew the West like the palm of his hand, and Sam was not surprised at the next question.

"Coming from Calvert to El Paso, you're a little farther south than was necessary, ain't you?"

"I turned south because I needed grain for my horses."

"Good idea. They'll find damn little to eat west of here except what you carry with you. I'll be headed that way myself in a day or so, makes sense that we travel together. Renegades, be they red or white, are somewhat slower to attack two men with rifles."

"That's fine with me, Red. Have another drink."

Red Jordon had been among the thousands of prospectors who had found more hard work than gold. Though he had picked and panned enough of the precious metal to sustain himself, his biggest strike had been the day he traded an Indian a small jar of Mexican bean dip and a plug of chewing tobacco for a hatful of gold nuggets. The gold had supplied his own needs and fed his horses for almost two years.

Like Sam, Jordon had stopped at Fort Stockton to rest and buy supplies. Several weeks ago he had been hired by three families to guide them from El Paso to Houston, and had been paid well for the chore.

Though the people had been equipped with good wagons, they had decided to quit a train headed west and seek their fortunes in Houston. Now, on his return to El Paso, Red had been loafing in Fort Stockton for the past week.

Curtin had never been this far west, and was glad that he would be riding with someone who knew the country. The miles ahead would surely be hot and dry, and Red knew where the water was. Though he had been around for more than a few summers, Jordon still moved around like a young man, and Sam had liked him immediately. He thought that Red would be plenty tough, and able to handle himself in any situation. After deciding to head west the day after tomorrow, the men parted at dusk, each heading for his own hotel room.

Two days later the pair rode due west toward the Mexican border, which Jordon said would take five days. El Paso was then a two-day ride northwest. Both men led pack horses loaded with grain and water. Jordon rode a big black gelding that any man who loved horses would covet. The animal's head and eyes, long, slim legs and sure, quick steps suggested that he had been sired by a thoroughbred.

"Don't know where he came from," Jordon said, in reply to a question from Sam. "I never saw that brand before, but I would suppose he came from back East somewhere. I got him from a Comanche Indian who had no further need of a horse."

After two days of steady climbing, both men and horses needed rest. They camped in the Apache Mountains at an altitude of more than six thousand feet. The night air was cool, and a nearby spring furnished them with good-tasting water. Their horses drank from the pool many times during the night. After nightfall, the men sat beside a small campfire, keeping their voices muted.

"Ever had any dealings with Apaches?" Jordon asked.

"No."

"If we meet any let me do the talking. I can talk sign."

"You got any more bean dip?" Sam asked.

"Bean dip won't work on Apaches," Red answered, extinguishing the fire and rolling into his blanket. Chuckling into his beard, he went to sleep.

Early next morning Red walked farther up the mountain and was back within the hour, saying he did not like the idea of crossing that plateau in broad daylight. Skylining themselves for such a long period of time would be asking for trouble, he said. Perhaps they should stay where they were throughout the day, and cross the plateau at night. Sam agreed, and went about moving the horses to a place of greater concealment. Afterward, he returned to his rock overhang and was soon asleep again.

He awoke at noon to find that Red was nowhere in sight. Grabbing his Winchester, he peeked around the rocks and up the hill. Seeing nothing, he moved to the ledge to check on the horses. They were standing just as he had left them. When he turned, Jordon was standing beside him. Sam was not an easy man to approach undetected, but Jordon had done it as soundlessly as a breeze.

"Dammit, Red, don't sneak up on me like that."

"Making noise can cost a fellow his hair," Jordon said. "I just saw three Apaches come across the mountain and go down the other side. I'm glad you moved the horses, they might have seen them."

At dusk, they rode over the mountain and out across the flat, treeless plateau. The only vegetation was an occasional mesquite bush that was shorter than a man. Jordon rode in the lead without being asked, for he knew the area. They made good time, and at daybreak, made a dry camp where the plateau ended. A narrow trail led down the other side of the mountain to the desert floor, a thousand feet below. They fed their horses and poured water into a frying pan for them to drink. Jordon knew the location of a spring they should reach by midnight, where they would refill their waterbags and canteens with enough water to see them across the remainder of the desert. Their camp was more than a mile high, with only a few cedars growing about that were too small to hamper their view.

"Good place to spend the day," Jordon said, "we can see any visitors we might have long before they see us."

"I like it too. First time I ever camped this close to the clouds."

They spent the morning resting, and talked little. Sam spent the better part of an hour killing horseflies that were pestering the animals and bringing blood to the back of his chestnut. He had heard talk of solutions that would keep the flies away, but nothing he had ever rubbed on his animals had done the job.

In the afternoon, while eating cold beans and biscuits, Sam began to question Jordon.

"You spend a lot of your time around El Paso and the Mexican border, Red, did you ever run into a man named Curly Cook?"

"Can't say that I have. You hunting him?" For an answer, Sam produced the tracing he had made from the wanted poster. Jordon studied it long and hard, then slowly handed it back.

"Looks a lot like Willie James," he said. Sam knew instantly that he had located his man, for Curly's full name was Willie James Cook. Sam decided to lay the whole story out for Jordon, who listened patiently. Detailing the crime against the Ryan girl, Sam added that Cook was the only suspect.

When told that Abe Martin would cancel the mortgage on Hamp's ranch for Cook's return, Jordon said, "I've been on that ranch, remember it well. Ed Haynes traded me a fresh horse for a tired mare several years ago when I was needing to travel fast. As for James, or Cook, they say he's fast with a gun, and he says so himself. He killed a drunk in El Paso last winter; claimed it was self-defense, but I've heard it said that the man didn't even have a gun. He never did give me any shit, but he's a cocky bastard. I've heard him mouthing off and bragging about his fast gun plenty of times."

"What does he do for a living?"

"I don't know, but it must be an easy job. He spends most of his time hanging out in saloons. I can't say that I've ever seen him drunk, though." Red scratched his beard and raised his eyebrows, adding, "You intend to meet him head-on?" Sam was busy uncorking his canteen. After taking several gulps of water, he wiped his mouth on his sleeve and spoke softly.

"Of course."

Two nights later they camped beside the Rio Grande. Across the river was Mexico, and neither man had any desire to go there. A small wagon train was camped close by, and the wagonmaster sold them oats for their horses. The animals had been on short rations of both feed and water, and the hot, mountainous travel had taken its toll. The men would rest the horses for two days, then follow the river northwest to El Paso, still more than a hundred miles away. They had a hindquarter from a deer Sam had shot just before sundown, and after eating their fill, sat by the fire till midnight.

Jordon said he had not fought in the recent Civil War for two reasons: he had been living and trapping in Canada and didn't even know there was a war going on till a year after it started. When he heard that all the shooting was about slavery, he returned to the mountains. He owned no slaves, but didn't care if someone else did, so he felt no calling to join either side.

Sam was glad that he had been too young for the fight, for he knew that he could never have condoned the enslavement of one person by another. But he also knew that issues other than slavery, on many of which he agreed with the Confederacy, had been contributing factors in bringing about the hellish war. He was happy that he had not been forced to make a decision, and said so to Jordon. The conversation died on its own, and the men turned in for the night.

On the third morning, they were in the saddle again, following the river. Water for their horses would no longer be a problem. They had seen no Indians since crossing the Apache Mountains, but Sam had the eerie feeling that many Indians had probably seen them. He had been uncomfortable the whole time, knowing that unseen eyes might be watching his every move. He knew that most of the Apaches had moved farther west, but some had remained in Texas. Comanches still roamed the state far and wide, and both tribes were fierce fighters.

He had been told many times that Apaches would not attack at night, but he knew from experience that Comanches would. In fact, they seemed to prefer night fighting. On this road up the river, however, it was doubtful that they would see any Indians, for it was much more densely populated. The red men knew that they traveled at great risk in this area, for there was always the chance that they would encounter a company of soldiers on patrol from Fort Bliss, against which no Indian party had been known to win a single skirmish. Since the fort had been established in 1848, Indians in general had given the areas of West Texas and southern New Mexico Territory a wide berth.

They rode all day, stopping only to water their horses and let them blow occasionally. They camped at sundown, each man thinking about the comfortable hotel bed he would sleep in tomorrow night. When night settled in, Sam took a walk into the desert. He wanted to loosen up his shooting arm and quick-draw hand, for without practice a man would lose some of his speed.

In total darkness, he walked several hundred yards from camp and stood listening to the night sounds of the desert, sounds of numerous small creatures scampering around that would never be seen in the light of day. Soon, the only sound was that of Sam slapping his leg as he brought the Peacemaker up to an imaginary target. If there had been onlookers, just as had been the audiences of the trade shows in bygone days, they would have been astounded at the speed with which he moved the weapon into firing position from its cutaway holster, which had been designed and built by his brother. Hamp was a master leatherworker, and everything Sam owned that was made of leather had been made by him. Belt, boots, bridles and saddle all beautifully bearing the unmistakable touch of Hamp's crafty hands. After an hour, satisfied that the speed was still there, he walked back to camp and rolled up in his blanket.

As Sam saddled his chestnut next morning, Jordon, who was already astride his blaze-faced black, decided to put on a show. Using only his knees, he had the big horse dancing to a cadence that looked almost human, first to one side, then the other, then back and forth. Sam was impressed; Red had never touched the reins with his hands. When the game was over, Red spoke.

"Comanches taught him. They play all sorts of games on horseback, and whoever can get his horse to do the silliest things is a big man around the village. There is no doubt in my mind that they are the best damn horsemen in the world. The same thing has been said of George Washington, but he never had to pit his horsemanship against them. He would have lost, Mr. Curtin."

They took the wagon road northwest at sunup. Riding side by side, Jordon was paying close attention to Sam's horse.

"That chestnut's got a mighty good step, Sam. You raise him yourself?"

"Got him when he was a year old. I finished raising him on oats and corn, and trained him myself." Then, half smiling, Sam added, "He can't dance worth a shit, but other than that he's a mighty good animal."

Nightfall found them at Socorro, one of the two oldest towns in Texas. Only one room could be had at the hotel, and Sam spread his bedroll on the floor, offering the bed to the older man. They were now no more than an hour's ride from El Paso. When Sam had blown out the lamp and stretched out on the floor, Jordon asked, "Would Cook recognize you on sight?"

"Probably, I'm pretty well known in Calvert. I've seen him around town several times, so I would have to suppose that he saw me at the same time."

Jordon turned on his side and lay still for a long time. Then, speaking into the darkness, he said, "It ain't gonna do for you to go walking around town looking for Cook, Sam. If he saw you first he'd get the drop on you."

"That has crossed my mind more than once, Red."

"I live across the border," Jordon said, "and I believe he sleeps over there. If you'll stay put in a hotel room, I'll seek him out and come for you when I've located him."

"You'd be doing me a favor, Red. I'm not going across the river, I don't want any problems with Mexican authorities."

"Good thinking. This whole area on both sides of the river seems to be one town, but since the treaty, it damn sure ain't."

The treaty Red had mentioned had been in effect for many years. In 1848, the treaty of Guadalupe Hidalgo established the Rio Grande as the boundary between the United States and Mexico. The river divided El Paso del Norte into two settlements. The north bank would later become El Paso, while the Mexican settlement on the south bank would retain the name, Paso del Norte.

Sam lay awake till the late hours of the night. He was wishing he had camped outside, where the ground was much softer than the floor. Though his present mission lay heavily upon his mind, the thought that he might be unable to find Cook had been put to rest. Red had said that the man made no attempt to carry a low profile. Maybe he thought he could hide forever behind a simple name change. He was here—and Sam intended to find him.

He felt that he owed Hamp and Lula much more than he could ever repay, but he was determined that they would have the ranch. With no mortgage to worry about, perhaps Hamp would eventually go public with his beautifully tooled leatherwork that was second to none. His saddlemaking ability was well known around Calvert, and only last month he had made a double harness for a neighbor's buggy team in exchange for a fine wagon. And the neighbor had furnished the leather. Sam was confident that, when word got around, Hamp would have more business than he could accommodate.

Lying on the hard floor with his eyes closed, he relived the gunfight that he had been involved in four years ago. He had walked into the situation completely by accident:

On a hot day in Calvert, he had decided to have a

cold beer, and had ridden across the railroad tracks to the saloon. After tying his horse to the hitching rail, he turned to see a man staring at him from the doorway, a dozen feet away. The man obviously intended to block the entrance. Sam would learn later that his name was Jack Pelt; that within the past few minutes he had pistol-whipped two bar patrons, then fired a shot through the ceiling of the saloon. Pelt continued to stare at Sam with a smirk on his lips. He wore a tied-down six-shooter low on his hip, and Sam could plainly see the notches filed in its pearl handle. A sizable crowd had gathered on each side of the men, anxiously awaiting the action. With his blond hair blowing in the wind, Pelt began to smile, then spoke.

"So you came over to stick your nose into it, huh?"

"I came over to have a beer."

"Well, they got plenty in there. Just take that gun out real slow and drop it on the ground, then you can have a beer."

"Slow, hell." Sam spat out quickly, "If it comes out at all, it'll come out in a hurry." Pelt began to move away from the doorway and out into the street. Sam knew immediately that he was in a dangerous situation, but he was neither nervous nor afraid. The onlookers had quickly rearranged themselves so as to be out of the line of fire. Every man except Pelt was well aware of Sam Curtin's skill with weapons, and each man thought that Pelt was about to meet his maker. Sam had long ago learned that a man who filed notches on a six-gun usually had very little between his ears. He decided to try to rile the man, hoping to gain an edge.

"Hey, I know you," he said, looking Pelt straight in the eye, "you look just like your sister. You know, the one who used to sell it over in Hearne. Hear tell she sure used to see to it that a man got his quarter's worth.

I guess she's giving it away, now, hear she takes on a dozen Indian bucks at a time." Having no way of knowing if the man even had a sister, Sam watched as his face turned from a pale tan to deep red. His green eyes seemed to be afire as he reached for his gun. He was just clearing his holster when Curtin shot him in the mouth. Sam had had more witnesses than he needed, and was not even arrested.

Hamp had taken the news of the shooting hard, fearing that his brother might become a target for would-be gunfighters seeking a reputation.

"I've seen it happen a dozen times," Hamp said. "You just mark my words: they'll be coming." Sam felt that Pelt had needed killing, and had lost no sleep over the incident. It was never determined what Pelt was doing in Calvert; Dallas County had been his stomping ground. He was well known there, and feared by many. Sam was aware of the fact that gunmen might seek him out, but he had long ago decided not to worry about things he could not control. He answered Hamp with a phrase he used often, "If it happens, so be it."

During the four years since, no man had come to test Sam's hand. He went to sleep feeling that his hand would be tested in the very near future.

After breakfast next morning, they began the short ride into El Paso. Sam commented several times on the scenery of the area, which was beautiful and interesting. Located in an ancient mountain pass from which the town's name derived, El Paso was surrounded by mile-high peaks. As they rode down the street, Jordon pointed to the hotel, saying, "Register there under the name of Smith. I'll come for you when I've found your man." Jordon rode on through town, never looking back.

Sam was given a room on the second floor. He ordered bath water, shaved his face and set about trying to straighten out his clean clothing, which had been rolled up and stuffed into a canvas bag. The blue shirt, his favorite, had been sewn by Lula. She had made all of his clothing when he was a child, and even to this day she occasionally made a shirt or jacket for him. He hung the garment across the back of a chair, hoping the wrinkles would disappear.

He stayed in or near the hotel for the next six days, leaving the establishment only to eat or to check on his horses. He was lying on his bed reading a newspaper when he heard the loud knock at his door.

"Cook's in the saloon just two doors down the street," Jordon said, entering the room. "I've had my eye on him for several days, but he never would light in one place. He's been out to Fort Bliss three times, and I can't imagine an honest man having that much business with the army. I figure he's peddling stolen cattle. The soldiers neither know nor care where their beef comes from."

Sam buckled on his gunbelt and added a sixth shell to the Peacemaker. "Coming?" he asked, heading for the door. Jordon followed him down the stairs and out into the street. Sam walked to the saloon and stood leaning against the building, only a few feet from the bar's swinging doors. Jordon walked farther on, finally leaning against a post in front of the windows, where he had a good view of the customers inside. An hour later, Red looked at Sam and nodded. When the batwing doors opened, Curly Cook walked through. He looked in both directions, then turned his back to Sam and began to walk away. He had taken no more than a dozen steps when Sam moved onto the walk behind him and shouted, "Willie James Cook!"

Cook stopped in his tracks, then slowly turned to face

Curtin. Obviously failing to recognize Sam, he asked, "Who are you?" Sam ignored the question and spoke again.

"Some folks in Robertson County want to talk to you about a girl named Kelly Ryan." Cook's poker-faced expression gradually changed to one of sneering, and he began to speak contemptuously.

"Then let them come to Mexico. That's where I live, and where I'm headed right now. Miss Fancy Pants got just what she deserved; always licking her lips and teasing, shaking her tits and ass at every man she saw. Then when somebody really takes her up on it, she decides it's something to laugh about. Last time I saw her she wasn't laughing. It ain't none of your business anyway, you ain't no judge."

"Wrong, Cook. Right now I'm the judge, and you just convicted yourself with your mouth. You're coming back to Calvert with me." Cook eased himself into his gunfighter's crouch, his right hand hanging close to his gun butt.

"The only way I'll be going back is with my toes turned up," he said with a smirk. Sam took the man at his word. He made his circus-type draw and shot Cook through the chest. Cook had made a defensive draw, but the shock of Curtin's forty-five caliber slug knocked the admitted murderer loose from his weapon and spun him around, where he fell on his face.

Both Curtin and Jordon walked forward, as Cook turned himself onto his back under his own power. He raised himself to one elbow, his eyes wide with fright at the thought of approaching death. A trickle of blood dripped from one corner of his mouth as he began to plead:

"Please . . . help me! I'll do anything. Don't let me . . . die. Lord!" Then with a quick jerk, he was dead. Jordon stared at the body for a moment, no sympathy whatsoever in his eyes.

"Typical tough ass," he said, "spent his lifetime big-assing and killing defenseless people. Then when his own number gets called, he starts whining like a broke-dick dog. He not only couldn't live like a man, the sonofabitch couldn't even die like one."

The town marshal was on the scene shortly. Sam handed the wanted poster to him and pointed to the body, saying, "Willie James Cook. He raped, tortured and killed a teenage girl in Robertson County."

"Do you know for sure that he was guilty?" Jordon did not wait for Sam to speak, choosing to answer the marshal's question himself.

"Hell, yes. He stood right here on this walk ten minutes ago bragging about it. The Judge, here, gave him a chance to go back and stand trial, but Cook wouldn't have it that way. He wanted to play gunfighter. When he tried to outgun the Judge, he plain committed suicide." The Judge. Sam Curtin had just picked up a nickname that he would carry for life.

Three

The town marshal, whose name was Higgingbotham, was a middle-aged man of medium height whose reputation for letting men settle their own disputes usually kept him out of sticky situations. He had arrived on the scene of the shooting with no gunbelt around his wide hips.

"Have you given any thought to how you're gonna get the body back across that desert?" the marshal asked. "Hot as it is, you won't have anything left to show."

"I'm hoping you'll write something for me to carry back; something stating that you witnessed Cook's dead body. I'll bury him wherever you folks put people like him."

"I'll write the letter for you, but the town ain't gonna bury him. That expense is yours."

"I understand, Marshal, and I'll appreciate the letter."

Sam paid the local undertaker to bury the body, even gave him money for a gravemarker that he doubted would ever be erected. A few hours later, having no more business to conduct in El Paso, he headed east. Red Jordon rode beside him, saying that he had some fish to fry in Waco and would ride as far as central Texas with him. They rode for two hours then camped for the night, building a fire to heat their supper.

They ate their meal in silence, and Sam read once again his "To whom it may concern" letter signed by Higgingbotham and two deputies. Neither Curtin nor Jordon had mentioned the shooting, and Sam was almost asleep when Red spoke.

"I've seen plenty of fast draws in my day and I didn't expect you to be slow, but I had no idea you were a damned magician." Sam said nothing, and both men went to sleep.

After riding for two hours next morning, they met a Mexican who obviously spent much of his time eating, for he appeared to weigh at least four hundred pounds. He was astride a small burro that weighed very little more than its rider, whose legs dangled almost to the ground as the diminutive animal plodded along under its heavy burden. Jordon dismounted quickly, signaling the man to stop. As he came alongside, Red began to speak.

"That animal's too small to carry you. Get down and turn him loose."

"Oh, but I cannot walk, senor; too heavy. See?" he laughed, pointing to his huge belly.

Jordon pointed his buffalo gun at the same place, saying, "I'm not gonna argue with you, fellow, you've got two choices: get your fat ass off that donkey or get it blown off." The man quickly unstraddled the animal and backed away. Jordon did not speak again. He tied the burro's reins to his horse's tail and rode away, leaving the fat man standing in the hot desert. He led the animal for many miles, then released it beside the river near good grass.

Curtin had not spoken during Red's exchange with the Mexican. He now rode beside Jordon, deciding that he liked the man's way of doing things. He had watched Red's eyes and facial expression closely, and had no doubt that he would have shot the man off the donkey.

More than two weeks passed before the men rode into the Brazos River valley. The river, separating the town of Waco east to west, was spanned by a suspension bridge that when built in 1870 was America's largest. The first white men to see the area were remnants of DeSoto's band in 1542. The Texas Rangers established a fort near the Indian village in 1837, and the first white settlers came in 1849. Great plantations prospered along the Brazos for a short period of time, but the Civil War wrecked the agricultural economy and scattered the population.

The Western movement and the Chisholm Trail through Waco brought another boom, and frontier wildness that nicknamed the town "Six-Shooter Junction." Very few of the town's inhabitants would have argued that the name was misplaced. Several gunfighters roamed the area, and even the traditional fistfight between otherwise normal men would often escalate to gunplay. Sam had been to Waco many times, and had performed his quick-draw and trick-shooting act here at least twice. As they neared the first saloon, Jordon stopped his horse.

"Ain't been this dry since I spent that year in Canada," he said, "what do you think about us having a drink?" Sam nodded, and soon both men were sipping whiskey. Curtin knew at a glance that the bartender had recognized him, but it was mentioned by neither man. Jordon inhaled his drink and ordered another. When his glass had been refilled, he quizzed the bartender.

"I'm looking for a fellow named Ike King; know where I might find him?"

"Sure do. You go out the front door, there, then turn left up the hill. He's been up there about three years. I think somebody finally put up a marker."

"You mean the cemetery?"

"Yep."

"Damn!" Red said. "He owed me two hundred dollars."

"He owed everybody two hundred dollars. Owed more'n fifty right here at the bar."

"Somebody shoot him?"

"Naw. I think somebody would have done it eventually, but he cheated them all out of the chance. He fell off a wagon drunk and broke his neck."

"Damn," Red repeated, "rode seven hundred miles for nothing."

When Curtin left Waco two hours later, Jordon still rode beside him. Red had said that since he was in the area, he had a hankering to see the old Haynes place again; that if Sam did not mind, he would ride along.

They followed the river south and camped on its bank an hour before sundown. Leaving Jordon to set up camp, Sam walked down the river with his Winchester cradled in his hands. Shortly after sunset Jordon heard the report of the rifle. He took a frying pan from his pack and began to smooth out the fire for cooking, seriously doubting that Sam had missed his target. Twenty minutes later, Sam stood beside the fire, holding a huge gobbler, on which the men feasted well.

They carried no grain on their pack horses now. Unlike the West Texas terrain, this area supported perennial grasses of many kinds. They traveled leisurely, giving their horses plenty of time to graze, and watered them from the river every few hours. The trail down the river was well traveled, and easy on both horses and riders.

On the third day, they rode down Calvert's main street, and Sam headed straight for Martin's office. Soon, he sat in his saddle, staring at the boarded-up doors and windows, and the CLOSED sign that hung from the office door. He immediately knew that something was wrong, for Martin's concern was much too prosperous to simply go out of business. He quickly found the town marshal.

"What's the matter over at Abe Martin's office, Leo?"

"Abe's been dead about a month, Sam. They found him sitting in his chair with his head lying on his desk like he was taking a nap. Doc said it was heart failure. He had a cigarette in his hand that burned a big blister on his palm; it's a wonder that it didn't burn the whole building down."

Curtin handed the lawman the letter that had been given to him by El Paso's marshal. After reading it, Pond shoved it back into Sam's hand, saying, "I knew you'd gone after Cook; knew you'd have to kill him, too. The reward is in a special fund over at the bank, but the sheriff is the only man who can release it. I'd say that letter is all you're gonna need to get it, though."

Not wishing to divulge the details of his transaction with Martin, Sam asked, "Do you know who's handling Abe's estate?"

"Yout, I suppose. I know he was Abe's lawyer; makes sense that he'd be handling things now."

"Yeah, thanks, Leo." Curtin had not introduced

Jordon to the marshal because he felt it was unnecessary. He headed for the lawyer's office with Red trailing along. Jordon waited outside as Sam took the steps leading to Yout's second-story office two at a time.

The attorney sat behind a big oak desk that was probably ten feet long. Sam almost smiled at the comical picture the man created. Yout was no more than five feet tall, yet he sat in a high-backed chair that was large enough for a giant. Sam wanted to peek around the desk to see if his feet touched the floor. Yout had a reputation for being as honest as a lawyer was expected to be, so Sam handed him both the agreement Abe Martin had written and the letter from El Paso. After reading both, the tiny man spoke.

"This looks to me like proof enough that Cook is dead; the marshal even writes that he confessed to the crime. As for this thing between you and Abe, I recognize his handwriting and signature, but I can't give you the deed. It could be that you'll have to take it to court. Even then, I doubt that you could win."

"I'm not taking anything to court, Mr. Yout, and if word gets around that I have this piece of paper I'll know it came from you."

"It won't get around, Mr. Curtin, and I resent your insinuation that I might discuss your business with another party." Yout had climbed down from his chair and now stood beside his desk. "There is only one way you can get that deed without going to court," Yout continued, "and I would advise you to listen closely: Sadie Martin is a good, unselfish woman, and she is the sole benefactress of his will. If you let her read what Abe wrote, she just might give you the deed. If so, she'll have to sign some papers. If she is unable to come here, I will be happy to carry them to her. Good-bye to you, sir."

Yout then turned his back to Sam, who hurried down the stairway feeling that he had been dressed down quite properly. When told that Sam intended to visit Mrs. Martin, Jordon politely excused himself.

"You don't need me tagging along, Judge. I'll hang out in the saloon till you've finished your business."

Mrs. Martin lived in a beautiful home at the top of the hill, six miles from Calvert. Sam covered the distance in half an hour. A large bulldog announced his arrival, and Sam stood at the gate of the fenced yard. A small, gray-haired woman opened the door and spoke to the dog, then to Curtin.

"Do you have business with me, sir?"

"I have a letter from your husband that Mr. Yout thinks you should read. My name is Sam Curtin; I grew up on the old Haynes place."

"Oh, yes, I've heard your name mentioned many times," she said, pushing the dog inside the house and closing the door, "come on up to the porch, Mr. Curtin." Sam sat in the chair he was offered and presented the folded piece of paper.

"This is not really a letter, Mrs. Martin, just an agreement between Abe and me." She read what her husband had written, then looked at Sam expectantly. He quickly produced the letter from El Paso. After reading it, she said, "Mr. Cook actually confessed to the crime, then?"

"Yes, ma'am."

"Such a shame. Little Kelly was going to study medicine, try to help the sick."

"I'm sorry, ma'am," he said. Wiping perspiration from her forehead, she looked at Sam through pitifully sad eyes.

"Mr. Cook won't be harming any helpless young girls now, will he?"

"No, ma'am, he sure won't."

She reread her husband's promise to cancel the mortgage, then said, "There is absolutely no doubt that Abraham wrote this. What seems to be Mr. Yout's problem with it?"

"He just thinks it's a matter that you should handle personally, Mrs. Martin. I wouldn't ask you to travel in this heat, I would be glad to bring Mr. Yout to you."

"You do that, and tell him to bring whatever papers he thinks are necessary. I'm quite proud of what my husband did, and his promise to you is written in plain English. It is obvious that you've held up your end of the bargain. I neither need nor want your brother's ranch, fine one though it is."

Curtin rented a rig at the livery stable, and one hour later was back at Mrs. Martin's house with the attorney in tow. Though Yout had exhibited a surly mood when asked to make the trip, he was smart enough to be gracious to Mrs. Martin, doing exactly as he was told. He did not speak directly to Sam during the entire transaction, but when he was delivered back to his office, he had a few words to say.

"You getting that deed was no skin off my nose, Curtin, but I'll tell you this right now: I do not like you!"

Almost breaking into a smile, Sam studied the tiny man momentarily, then said, "Well, if you don't like me I guess by god I don't like you. Get your ass off this wagon before I throw you off." Yout stepped down, the rear wheel narrowly missing him as the wagon sped away.

After collecting Red Jordon from the saloon, Sam headed home. He had bought a bottle of whiskey himself, for he had something to celebrate. He felt good about the world in general; felt good about himself, for he had finally been able to do something for Hamp and

Lula. They rode slowly, with Red commenting favorably on the quality of the ranch and the fat cattle that were standing knee-deep in grass. Riding up the hill toward the house, Sam could see Hamp sitting on the porch in his rocking chair, and Bud standing in the yard wearing his overalls. Then Bud started shouting.

"Momma! Uncle Sam's coming up the hill; he's got somebody with him, too." Lula bounded from the house and into the yard. When Sam had dismounted, she grabbed him in a tight hug.

"It's so good to have you back, Sam, we've all prayed that you would be all right." Hamp sat in his chair, smiling.

"Tell your friend to get down, Sam," he said, nodding to Jordon, who was still in his saddle. When Red had shook hands all around, Sam brought the whiskey from his saddlebag.

"I knew you had a drink occasionally," Hamp said, "but you never brought none home before."

"Occasionally is right, Hamp, and this is an occasion. We've got a fire to build and a mortgage to burn." Taking the deed from his pocket, he handed it to his brother, adding, "The old Haynes place does not exist anymore. From this day forward it shall be known as the Hamp Curtin Ranch." As Hamp looked at the deed, Lula was back into the yard with both her arms around Sam's neck, tears of joy rolling down her cheeks.

"You did it, Sam, you actually got us out of debt." He held her away from him, speaking to her as a man would his mother.

"It's a small thing, Lu, considering all you and Hamp have done for me. I'm just glad I got a chance to help."

When the men had taken their horses to the barn, Hamp called his young son to him.

"Bud, I want you to go down to the pasture and get

that spotted heifer. You know, the one that never does want to breed. Take her to the meathouse and butcher her. You heard what Sam said, we've got some celebrating to do." Bud had never seen a tear in his father's eye before. He cast his own eyes downward and headed for the pasture. And the spotted heifer.

Red Jordon stayed on the ranch for a week, then said that he had business in Dallas. The family had liked him very much, and each member had expressed regret at his leaving. He had been very helpful; when he saw something that needed fixing, he turned to it. Bud had especially liked listening to his stories of Indian fighting, and had him tell and retell the story of Sam's fast draw against Curly Cook. Hamp had shown no interest in the story, saying he knew all about Sam's fast gun, that he had been watching it since his brother was fourteen years old. As Jordon rode down the hill, the Curtins stood in the yard waving good-bye. Red stood up in his stirrups and waved his hat, then he was gone.

"I'll miss that old bird," Sam said, "I'll miss him a lot." Then he went to check on the spotted cowhide he had tacked onto the barn wall to dry. Hamp had said he would use it to make new seats for the kitchen chairs.

In the afternoon, Robertson County sheriff Wally Pate rode up the hill and stopped at the porch.

"Sam around, Hamp?" he asked.

"He's down at the barn; I'll send the boy for him."

"No use for that, I'll just talk to him down there." He rode to the barn, where he found Sam working on a wagon wheel. Sitting on a nail keg with a handful of grease, Sam acknowledged the sheriff's presence and laid the wheel aside. Wiping his hands on a grain sack, he walked forward.

"Haven't seen you lately, Wally. What brings you out?"

"Leo told me about your letter from El Paso, so I've brought the reward money to you. I'll be needing that letter, though." Sam produced the letter and told the sheriff that Cook had laughed about killing the girl. Pate shook his head disgustedly as he counted out the money.

"That don't surprise me at all, Sam; I've known too many men like him." Pate dismounted and sat down on a grain bin. "You know, Sam, I could use a man like you as a deputy," he continued. "Pays seventy a month." Having no desire to become a lawman, Sam declined the offer.

"No, thanks, Wally. I intend to shape up things around here, then I'll probably go back to Fort Worth. I can earn enough money to get by breaking horses for the army—three dollars a horse, and I don't get shot at." Pate dropped that subject, and began to speak from a different angle.

"A sheriff has a limited jurisdiction, Sam, and the small number of U.S. marshals throughout the state can't even come close to tracking down all the criminals that are on the run. They simply don't have the manpower.

"For every man like Cook, who finally got his due, there are hundreds that are living high somewhere, laughing at the law. If I were you, I'd be thinking about bringing some more of them to justice."

"People don't like bounty hunters."

"The hell they don't! Do they like killers and robbers better? You think it over, Sam; the only conscience you have to answer to is your own. None of those bastards can match that fast gun of yours, and they have prices on their heads that can make you rich. Besides, you'd be doing an honorable service for the great state of Texas." As the sheriff mounted, he added, "Let me know if you change your mind, I can give you some leads that will put you in business."

Pate's words rang in Sam's ears all afternoon. Even after he was in bed trying to sleep, the image of the laughing Curly Cook continued to dance before his closed eyes. Pate had said there were hundreds like Cook, living high and laughing at honest people, probably thinking of hard-working folks as no more than prey—suckers for the taking.

When he came in for breakfast next morning, Sam had made a decision. Life was about to become more difficult for a few men who had committed the heinous crimes described by Sheriff Pate.

Four

A few mornings later, Sheriff Pate stood in the doorway of his office, casually speaking with passersby. The lanky, brown-haired lawman knew most of the area's citizens on a first-name basis, and was well liked and respected by all. He had received his formal schooling in Tennessee, and his law-enforcement training in Ohio. He had come to Texas shortly thereafter, and had been Robertson County's sheriff for many years.

Though now past forty, Pate was thought by some to have ice water in his veins. Sam Curtin knew him to be plenty savvy and long on both nerve and ability. Most men who operated outside the law, not wishing to risk a showdown with Pate, simply rode around his county. Now, the sheriff smiled broadly as he watched Sam Curtin tie his horses to the hitching rail in front of the office.

"Good morning, Sam. Looks like you're all packed up and headed somewhere."

"I've been thinking about the things you said a few days ago, about some people getting away with murder."

"Glad to hear that, Sam. Come on into the office."

The pile of wanted posters on Pate's desk was neatly stacked, as if he had been expecting Sam. The sheriff referred to the posters as "dodgers," and handed them to Curtin, who began to look through them. The several sheets of paper, each one bearing the likeness of a wanted criminal, listed his crime and the reward that would be paid for his capture. A few of them frankly stated that the man was wanted "dead or alive." The charges against the men ranged from jail escape to robbery and murder, and the reward scaled upward from one hundred dollars, according to the severity of the crime. As Sam finished reading, Pate spoke again.

"Put all of them in your saddlebag, no telling when you might need them." Then, taking another poster from his desk, he handed it to Sam, adding, "Here's the big one. Tarrant County will pay five thousand dollars for him dead or alive, and I would suggest that you consider the former. He killed a deputy sheriff in Fort Worth three years ago, and he'll gun anybody else he thinks is a threat to him." Sam studied the picture thoroughly, deciding he had never seen the man. Born Jess Badger, he had also used the names Jess Brown, Jack Brown and Jack Little.

"I know enough about you to know that you fear no man," Pate was saying, "and since you're gonna go, why not go after the man who pays the highest reward?"

"Badger's top priority, Wally."

"Good boy. I think you'd do well to start snooping

around Fort Griffin. I know he has a sister who lives there; she's married to Joe Newton. Her name is Anna."

On the first day of September, Sam rode into the town of Fort Griffin. He had spent a week in Fort Worth, talking with lawmen and members of the Texas Rangers. All agreed that Jess Badger was indeed bad news, and as elusive as a prairie wolf. On several occasions the Rangers had thought they had him cornered, only to spring the trap and come up empty. Each time, Badger had been long gone. They assured Sam that the outlaw was both quick and deadly with handguns, and a long-range rifle expert. Rumors of his whereabouts abounded. The rumor that he had been sighted in the California gold fields, and another that he had been killed in a cattle stampede, had been discarded by the Rangers.

Another rumor, which was still under consideration, was that Badger had ridden with the notorious Sam Bass gang, which had been put out of business only six weeks ago. The gang had plagued stagecoaches, trains and banks, and had been the object of an intensive chase by the Rangers. An informer had warned the Rangers and Round Rock, Texas, lawmen that the Bass gang would soon attempt a raid on a local bank. The gang was ambushed there on July 18, 1878. Sam Bass died two days later from a gunshot wound he received during the battle. Curtin had spent several days in Round Rock, and had found no evidence that Badger had participated in the attempted robbery and gun battle. Nor did he give credence to the gold field and cattle stampede rumors, for Badger was known to detest both punching cattle and such hard work as would be necessary in searching for gold.

* * *

The community of Fort Griffin had sprung up around the military post of the same name, and now served as the trade center of the area. Rough and wild, the settlement was frequented by cavalry troopers, trail-herd cowboys, buffalo hunters and outlaws. Gunfights were common, and more than thirty men had already died in public shootings. Though many of the cavalrymen spent their meager wages there, the town's economy largely rested on the shipment of hides from the ever-increasing number of buffalo that were slaughtered daily by the hunters. Millions of prime hides had been shipped from this point in recent years.

As Sam rode down the street, he saw no man who was unarmed, and several carried rifles in their hands. A few men eyed him casually, but most paid him no mind as he rode to the livery stable and turned his horses over to the hostler. Walking back to the hotel, he passed a dry goods store with a sign proclaiming Joe Newton owner and operator. He made a mental note to buy something there. Fall, then winter, would be along soon and he needed a new hat anyway.

He climbed the stairs to his room after writing a name on the hotel register. He was now Mr. Sam Smith! The room was furnished much better than he expected, even had a mirror on the wall. He raised the window, which offered a good view of the street below, then tested the bed. It had a wool mattress and was very comfortable. He was pleased, for he knew he might be staying here for quite some time.

Curtin could easily understand the thinking of people who disliked bounty hunters, for only a short time ago he had been among those who would not give the time of day to any man who was on the trail of another. Watching Curly Cook laugh about killing the Ryan girl, the long talk he had had with Sheriff Pate, and the many briefings with lawmen and Texas Rangers in Fort Worth had completely changed his mind. Collectively, they had convinced him that there were men running from the law who were completely devoid of conscience, and had committed crimes so ghastly that they were frightful to look upon. Jess Badger was such a man.

An old couple had been butchered with an ax in West Texas, and Badger had been seen more than once riding the old man's horse. He had also sold some of the couple's belongings to a businessman who had turned the items over to the sheriff. A reward had been on Badger's head even before he shot the lawman in Fort Worth. He had gunned the deputy before the eyes of several witnesses when the young man tried to arrest him.

Sam had no doubt whatsoever of Badger's guilt, and intended to spend the reward money buying property adjoining Hamp's ranch and setting his crippled brother up in the saddlemaking business. Hamp's work was sure to fetch fancy prices. He was the only man Sam had ever known who tape-measured the buyer before starting a custom-made saddle. Sam felt that word of mouth would be the only advertising necessary; that the "Curtin" saddle would indeed be Hamp's ticket to financial security.

Two hours later, Sam stepped inside Newton's store. A bell attached to the top of the door rang as he entered, bringing a beautiful dark-haired woman to the front counter. Her well-proportioned figure was obvious in the tight-fitting clothing she wore, and her blue eyes seemed to dance as she smiled flirtatiously.

"May I help you?" she asked.

Sam looked around the store for another person, thinking that surely such a lovely creature as this would have a man around. He saw no one. Standing at the counter with hat in hand, he told her, "I need a new hat."

"Come this way," she said, leading him to a table that was stacked with hats of many shapes and sizes. "A good-looking man like you would want a nice hat, I'm sure." Sam said nothing and chose a black felt with a wide brim. Standing beside the woman, blocking the new hat with his hands, he asked about her husband.

"A man in Fort Worth told me that Joe would know where the fish are biting. Is he around?"

"Joe is dead, Mr.—"

"Smith," Sam interrupted, feeling like the imposter that he was.

"—Smith," she repeated. "Joe caught a bad cold swimming the Clear Fork on horseback last winter, and he never recovered. I am his widow; my name is Anna."

"I'm terribly sorry, Mrs. Newton, I—"

"Call me Anna, everybody in town does. Nobody called me Mrs. Newton even when Joe was alive."

"Well, thanks Anna, and I'm sorry about Joe." Still facing her, he continued to walk backward toward the doorway till he bumped the sharp corner of the counter, hurting his ribs.

"Good day, Mr. Smith. I surely hope to see you again."

"Sam," he corrected. She waved coquettishly as he walked past the window.

Farther down the street he stopped to lean against a small building, looking the town over and thinking about his recent encounter with Anna Newton. His ribs were still hurting, and he was thinking that he must have looked like a damn clumsy kid backing into that counter. Damn! what a woman. Never in his life had he come face-to-face with such a female. And were her last words an invitation? Maybe, but it could be that her friendly actions were no more than those of a smart businesswoman who knew how to sell her merchandise. He forced himself to push all thoughts of the woman out of his mind. Anyway, wasn't he here to carry her brother back to Fort Worth on a charge that would surely result in an appointment with the hangman? Yes, and he would allow nothing to deter him from his mission.

Walking back to the hotel, he had taken only a few steps when he met a smiling old man who obviously recognized him from his days with the trade show.

"Hey, I know you," the man said. "Is the show playing around here somewhere?"

Sam walked past him quickly, saying, "I know nothing about a show, sir." As he entered the hotel, Sam looked over his shoulder to see the man standing on the plank walk staring after him. The expression of recognition was still on his face as he stood scratching his head. Knowing he had not fooled the man, Sam was hoping the oldster would not be able to recall his name. Later, he sat on his bed thinking.

Knowing that his name and reputation had no doubt circulated around Fort Griffin, he must keep his identity secret at all costs. If the old man suddenly remembered the name, Sam would simply give him the lie, publicly. Someone important had once said that all things happened for the best, so with that in mind he decided to sleep away the afternoon. After dark he would get out among the town's inhabitants and listen.

It was past ten in the evening when he walked into the big saloon a few doors from the hotel. A forty-foot bar was on his left, behind which stood two bartenders. The room was filled almost to capacity with cavalrymen, cowboys and men who appeared to be full-time gamblers. Through the smoky haze, he could see several gaming tables in the rear, with some men playing cards and others watching. On his right, a dozen men sat around tables, drinking and talking. What Sam did not see was the man sitting in the far corner, sipping a glass of whiskey.

Sam walked forward and leaned against the bar as he waited for his eyes to adjust to the dim lighting. He was about to order a drink when he heard the voice of the old man he had met on the street today. Sam could see him pointing in his direction, and the room suddenly became eerily quiet. In a shrill voice that was piercing to the ear, the old man was saying, "That's him, I tell you!" He continued to point at Sam. "He's a show-off with that gun; I've seen it myself. I can't recall his name, but he used to go around the country doing a lot of gun tricks, and charging everybody fifteen cents."

Behind Sam, a man slowly arose from his chair, flipping the thong from his Peacemaker. He stopped suddenly when Red Jordon poked him in the ribs with his rifle. Red leaned forward, speaking softly into the man's ear.

"It's a fifty-caliber, fellow; it'll take about two pounds of meat right out of the middle of a man." As the man sat down, Red took the Peacemaker and shoved it behind his own waistband. He continued to stand beside the man's table.

A large man who wore no gun began to walk toward Sam. Weighing more than two hundred pounds and very muscular, he had a red, battle-scarred face that told Sam he was a brawler.

"What is your name?" the man asked, stopping ten feet away.

"That should be of no concern to you," Sam said, "I'm not running for office." A few men laughed in the background, seeming to set the big man off. He came running straight ahead with his fist drawn back, his other hand reaching for Sam's shirt.

"By god I didn't ask for no smart-ass answer, I'll—"

The brawler was quickly lying at Curtin's feet. Sam had thrown one punch to the charging man's chin—all that was needed. He had gone down as if he had been hit with a sledge. All eyes were upon Sam as he took one step backward, looking around the room. He bent over the prone figure on the floor and spoke loudly, so all could hear.

"The name is Smith!" he yelled to the unconscious man. He heard a single pair of hands applauding behind him, and turned quickly.

"Very convincing work, Judge," Red Jordon said, continuing to clap his hands. He put his foot against the back of the man he had disarmed and kicked him forward, adding, "I caught this sonofabitch trying to gun you in the back." He placed the gun back in the man's holster, then said to him, "He's looking at you now, fellow. If you still want to play, I promise you I won't interfere." The man hung his head awkwardly, then turned and walked through the front door. Sam stood watching the retreating man until he was out of the building, then turned to shake hands with Jordon.

"Thanks, Red," he smiled appreciatively, "don't know that I've ever been quite so glad to see somebody."

"No thanks necessary, come on to the table and I'll buy you a drink." Sam followed, and took a chair at the table. Red handed his rifle over, saying, "Hold this while I get a bottle." He bought whiskey at the bar and had a short discussion with the bartender. When he returned, he poured a drink for Sam and began to talk.

"That jasper I disarmed answers to the name of

Hyde. The bartender says he used to be a cavalryman, stationed right here at Griffin. He's been out of the military about a year, but just keeps hanging around. Killed a drunk right here in the saloon earlier this year, but he had enough army buddies for witnesses to get a self-defense ruling. If I ever catch him out in the open, I'll try to find out why he thought your back was so broad." Red poured a drink for himself, then added, "By the way, that fellow you knocked out goes by the name of Barney Hill."

Several minutes had passed since Hill had regained his senses and walked back to his chair, and the action and noise had resumed. In towns such as this, violence, at least to some degree, was something that happened every day, and was quickly forgotten. Hill sat at his table now, appearing to be at peace with the world. Sam poured another drink.

"How'd you find me, Red?" he asked.

"You're easy to find, Judge; you talk to an awful lot of people when you're traveling."

"I'll have to be more careful."

"Won't do you any good, you ain't gonna get information out of anybody." Red scratched his beard on both sides, then took a sip of whiskey. "You've got a problem, Judge, and that problem is this: you look like a gunslinger. If you took off that Peacemaker and hid it somewhere, you'd still look like a damn gunslinger."

"Maybe so."

"You need some help digging, Judge, and I've decided to volunteer. I—" The room had grown quiet again. Jordon pointed toward the center of the saloon with his thumb, and Sam turned to see Hill standing there staring at him.

"You want to go at it again?" Hill asked. Sam unbuckled his gunbelt and got to his feet.

"Can't really say that I do," he said, "but I guess I won't deny you a chance to redeem yourself." They met in the center of the room. While blocking and dodging three punches thrown by Hill, Curtin had thrown several of his own, and Hill was once again lying at Sam's feet. Sam now bent over the unconscious man for the second time. He cupped his hands around his mouth as if calling to someone far away.

"The name is Smith!" he yelled loudly. The uproar in the background was almost deafening. It seemed that every man present was laughing and applauding. The bartender approached Sam with a bottle of whiskey in his hand.

"Here, take this," he said, "you're the best damned entertainer we've ever had in here."

Sam accepted the whiskey and returned to Red's table. Uncorking the new bottle, Red began to laugh, saying, "That fellow might be strong, and he might be tough, but he damn sure ain't no good at reading sign." A few tables away some men could be heard discussing the fight.

"It's them shoulders," one man was saying. "Anytime you see a man with real wide shoulders like Smith's got, you're lookin' at punchin' power."

Jordon accompanied Sam to his hotel room for the night, and this time it was Red who slept on the floor. Sam had raised the window before going to bed, and he slept well in the cool room despite Red's loud snoring.

The first thing he saw when he opened his eyes next morning was the sparrow sitting on the windowsill. Sam remained very still as he watched the beautiful creature flit back and forth. He remembered that there was a time in his young life when he would have shot the tiny bird for target practice. Hamp had given him a small bore rifle when he was ten years old, and Sam had spent most of the daylight hours tramping the woods, shooting anything that moved. His favorite game had been sneaking up on birds and shooting off their beaks. As he got better with the rifle, he had even managed to hit a few birds on the fly.

It had been Lula who shamed him out of this practice, and insisted that he immediately begin attending church with her every Sunday. Sam had attended church services and listened to the preacher's sermons, many of which he remembered to this day. He had, however, never been much for turning the other cheek. "Fight evil people who would harm you with spiritual faith," the preacher had said, "pray for them. Pray that they may be healed." Sam had early on preferred a more down-to-earth method. He learned to fight with his hands, and usually kept some sort of weapon close by.

Jordon was getting to his feet, and the bird quickly flew away.

"Good morning, Judge," Jordon said, beginning to wash his face and eyes in the pan of water provided by the hotel. "I'm going up to the fort this morning. If Captain Henley is still there I can eat for nothing. I took an Indian off his ass a few years ago. I'll talk to a few people, and it could be that I'll hear something you need to know."

"Very good, Red," Sam said, thinking that Jordon probably knew somebody in every town in Texas, "I'll just stay in town and see what I run into."

Sam had breakfast in the hotel dining room, seeing no one he had seen the night before. Later, as he sat relaxing on a bench in front of the hotel, he was joined by a young man in his late teens who was very talkative, and obviously off-center. His blond hair was dirty and unkempt, and his teeth stained and yellow. He giggled as much as he talked.

"My name is Rick," he said for the third time.

"Hello, Rick." Sam saw no reason to divulge his own name.

"You got any chewing tobacco?" the kid asked.

"No, Rick, but I'll sure buy some." He handed the boy a quarter, adding, "You go get us a plug, then we'll sit right here and have us a chewing good time."

"Don't cost no quarter," the kid said, turning the coin from side to side.

"That's all right, keep the change for next time."

Rick left at a trot, and soon returned with the plug. Chewing tobacco was not one of Sam's bad habits. Nevertheless, he put a small piece in his jaw and watched as Rick packed his own mouth full. Deciding not to rush the conversation, Sam spat a couple times and leaned back on the bench. He wanted to listen to the youngster talk, hoping to learn something. Rick opened up right away.

"I sure do thank you for letting me keep the rest of that money. Did you know that'll buy four more plugs?"

"Sure I do. But a good man like you needs a whole lot of chewing."

"Yeah, ha ha, that's right."

With a small amount of prodding, Rick said that he had never known his father, and his mother had been dead for many years. He had been on his own since age twelve, doing odd jobs around town whenever he could.

"Mr. Spencer lets me clean stalls down at the livery stable, gives me beans and biscuits. And sometimes some meat. And sometimes a plug. Sometimes Miss Anna gives me money to buy me something to eat. She won't give me no plug. She says a plug is not a good thing." After listening to the young man talk for more than an hour, Sam decided that Rick probably knew more about what went on in the area than any man in town.

"Have you eaten today, Rick?"

"Not today; et twice yesterday, though."

"Follow me," Sam said, heading for the dining room, "let's get something to eat."

Rick hesitated, saying, "I don't think I can go in there, the cook ran me out one time."

"We'll see, come along," Sam said, opening the door to the restaurant. No customers were inside, and he saw no waitress. The sound of the closing door brought the cook from the kitchen.

"Too late for breakfast and too early for dinner," he said. "We start serving dinner at eleven."

"Special order," Sam said, burning the cook's eyes with a steely stare. "Give the boy a good steak and anything else he wants. I'll have coffee." The cook's chest swelled and his face flushed with a look of defiance, but he soon wilted under Curtin's steady gaze. He shrugged his shoulders and nodded, then returned to the kitchen.

The steak was soon on the table, accompanied by a large slice of blackberry pie. Rick sharked the food quickly, and the two retired once again to the hotel bench. No word was spoken between them for quite some time. Rick seemed to be pondering something beyond his understanding. Then he spoke.

"I don't like ugly people!" Sam said nothing, and Rick added, "You ain't ugly. Miss Anna ain't ugly neither, she's purty." Sam agreed with the kid, then changed the subject.

"Do you like horses, Rick?"

"Yeah, sure do, I look at horses all the time. Why I bet I could tell you who rides every horse in this country." Then, getting to his feet, Rick added, "I gotta go now, Mr. Spencer might need me at the stable." With that, he was gone. Rick's running off to the stable had upset Sam's plans, for he had intended to quiz the boy about Jess Badger.

Foot traffic was heavy in front of the hotel, and many people had passed while Sam was talking with Rick. Several had taken a second look, as if wondering what on earth the two could possibly have in common. He had politely said good morning to them all. He knew he was sitting in one of the town's popular loitering places, and was doing so purposely. The newest arrival to the bench was an aging farmer who introduced himself as Mark Sweather. After some initial conversation, Sam asked, "Do they buy produce from you up at the fort?"

"Yeah, they buy some. Steal a lot more than they buy, though. I don't mean that the army steals from me, but the soldiers do. They wander through my fields all the time, grazing on whatever's ripe."

Curtin sympathized with the farmer, but could offer no solution. He brought the conversation to an end, for he could see that Jordon had returned from the fort, and was now approaching the livery stable. Saying goodbye to Sweather, Sam headed for his hotel room.

Five

I didn't ask any direct questions about Badger," Red reported, "but I did make sure his name came up a few times. The general consensus around the fort is that he hangs out in the Arbuckle Mountains, up in Indian Territory. Chickasaw country, Judge; safe haven from all Texas lawmen."

"Anybody at the fort seen him lately?"

"Nope. Didn't meet anybody who wants to, either."

"Well, I do. If I have to go to Indian Territory to make that happen, so be it."

"The Arbuckles are a week's ride north and east of here. When you cross the Red River you're in Indian Territory. The Red is the boundary, all the way across the Territory."

Jordon, who seemed to get nervous sitting around, was soon out the door and gone about town. Sam lay on his bed relaxing, and thinking about the area north of

Texas that would eventually become the state of Oklahoma. In fact, some of the inhabitants of the western part were already calling it by that name. The word "Oklahoma" derived from two Choctaw Indian words: "okla," meaning people, and "humma," meaning red. An apt name indeed. Officially, the area was still known as Indian Territory, and with good reason: it had become a dumping ground for Indian tribes displaced by the white man's ever-increasing hunger for land. More than fifty tribes had been forced to join the local ones. Among the Territory's current inhabitants were the so-called five civilized tribes: the Choctaw, Cherokee, Chickasaw, Creek and Seminole. Some were sedentary, peaceful farmers, while others were migratory and belligerent. Still others were downright mean, and even barbaric. Sam suspected that Badger would find friends among the latter.

Curtin dozed off, and awoke some time later ravenously hungry. He headed for the restaurant, hoping he would not be too late for dinner. As he entered, he held the door open for Anna, who was just leaving the establishment. Once again, she turned on the charm.

"Hi Sam," she said softly, "the stew's excellent today."

"Thanks, I'll have a go at it." He was not used to shaking hands with women, but when she offered her right hand, he grasped it. Now, she stood holding his hand between both her own, smiling and fluttering her eyelashes.

"Will you come to see me, Sam?"

"Sure, next time I need something I'll come by."

"I wasn't talking about that," she said, releasing his hand and walking away as if spurned by a suitor.

After ordering his stew, he walked to a table. He was soon enjoying the tasty dish while trying to puzzle through his latest exchange with Anna. No doubt about it this time, the lady wanted to see more of him. Why? She had only seen him twice, and the town must be full of men that she had known for many years. He had always gotten along quite well with the opposite sex, but never had a woman been so quick to invite him anywhere. Especially a woman like Anna.

Sam turned his room at the Occidental Hotel over to Jordon the following morning, saying he would ride around the area for a few days to familiarize himself with the country. A short time later he guided the chestnut down the street to the Clear Fork, where he crossed easily on the river's natural rock bottom. Turning east, he spent the remainder of the morning riding over the level grasslands. Excellent cattle country, he decided. He ate his noon meal back in town, then rode halfway up Government Hill, where he sat under a mesquite tree, looking down at the busy town of Griffin.

Officially, both the fort and the town were named Griffin, though locally the fort was simply called Government Hill. The fort had been built on the highest point in the area, and could be protected against any anticipated number of aggressors with relative ease. A cool breeze, welcome in summer and unwelcome in winter, usually blew across the hill. Any enemy hoping to surprise the men at the fort would have found it very difficult, for the cavalrymen had a bird's-eye view of the area below, where all trails crossed.

The town, located only a short distance from the fort, had been known by many names: Griffin, Griffin-under-the-Hill, Hidetown and a few others. But the one name most commonly used by both locals and outsiders was the obvious one: between the hill on which the fort was located and the Clear Fork River to the north, there was a stretch of land half a mile wide that was almost as level as the water surface of the lake. It was on this plot that the town had sprung up in 1867, and was quickly dubbed "the Flat." Locals seldom spoke of the town by any other name.

West of the Flat was Collins Creek, whose banks supported many tall trees, mostly pecan. More than one man had met his maker at the end of a rope attached to one of the sturdy limbs. The town was bounded on the north by the Clear Fork.

To either side of the Flat's one street, buildings of many shapes and sizes cluttered the entire area in no particular order. Dozens of small trails leading in all directions passed traffic from one establishment to another. Ladies of the evening displayed and sold their wares all along the paths. Some plied their trade in large buildings supervised by a madam, while others operated independently in smaller places.

The Flat had quickly gained a reputation for violence and lawlessness that rivaled Dodge City and Tombstone. Countless saloons lined both sides of the street, all teeming with characters whose temperaments depended entirely upon how much whiskey they had drunk. Gunmen of much notoriety had been known to come calling. Wyatt Earp, Pat Garrett and Doc Holliday had all visited the Flat.

The town boasted a thousand permanent residents, with twice as many transients, few of them law abiding. Rustlers, murderers, gamblers, prostitutes and small-time thieves were abundant. Major W. H. Wood, commander of Fort Griffin, had once chased the criminal element out of town, declaring the Flat to be under martial law. The outlaws had merely eased out of town and bided their time.

With the organization of Shackelford County, of

which the Flat was a part, the troops relinquished control of the town. The news spread quickly, and soon the unsavory characters were back twofold, their pockets jingling with money from cattle drovers, buffalo hunters and the military.

On any given day a literal wagon train loaded with buffalo hides could be seen coming to the Flat. Business partners Frank Conrad and Charley Rath were only too willing to take the hides off the hunters' hands for two dollars each. After tanning the hides, the partners freighted them to the town of Weatherford for a handsome profit. Several acres of land around their store were usually covered with ricks of hides.

Many of the hunters stayed in the Flat till they had spent their entire earnings from a recent hunt. Then, Frank Conrad, who operated a banking business out of his store, could easily be talked into advancing them money for another hunt—at ridiculous, self-serving interest rates, of course. Of the millions of hides that eventually passed through the Flat, most were handled by Conrad and Rath.

By 1875, the main cattle trail to Kansas had shifted from Fort Worth to Griffin. Each spring and summer, dozens of herds from South Texas passed through on their northern drive to Fort Dodge, with most drovers stopping in the Flat for relaxation. They mixed readily with the soldiers, gamblers, con men and prostitutes in the saloons and gambling dives.

Gangs of cutthroats and killers roamed the area at will, sometimes killing at random. Aside from the many men who died in gunfights, it was a common occurrence when someone discovered a dead body outside the town. Though a vigilante group existed, and the town had law enforcement officers, no effort was ever made to bring the outlaws to justice.

William Gilson was town marshal, and a U. S. marshal named John William Poe was there. Shackelford County's sheriff was a man named William Cruger, who had ascended to that position in an unusual manner. He had been a deputy under John Larn, the previous sheriff. When Deputy Cruger killed an outlaw named Billy Bland, the sheriff's friend and accomplice in many illegal activities, Larn had resigned his office in a fit of anger. The county commissioners' court quickly appointed Cruger to succeed Larn as sheriff. Ex-sheriff Larn then went on a crime spree that eventually led to his being arrested for attempted murder. The warrant was served by none other than his former deputy, Sheriff William Cruger.

John Larn was held without bail in the temporary county jail at Albany. On June 24, 1878, a group of nine men stormed the jail and shot the shackled former sheriff to death. It was believed by most that John Larn was himself a member of the very same vigilante group that executed him. Whether he was killed for punishment or out of fear that he would reveal vigilante names is anybody's guess. The case was closed after the coroner ruled that John Larn died from gunshot wounds inflicted by parties unknown. His days as sheriff and vigilante chief, and nights as cattle and horse thief, had come to an end.

Curtin rode around the area for two days, camping the second night on Stone Ranch. He admired from a distance the beautiful stone buildings and corrals that had been built by stonemasons whose skill was obviously of the highest quality. The end result left little doubt as to the work and imagination that had been involved. The ranch house itself was a solid stone fortress.

On the third day he was back at his hotel room, after having passed the time of day with Sheriff Cruger and Marshal Poe, both of whom he had met on the street. Cruger gave Sam no more than a passing glance as the two exchanged greetings, but Poe had looked him over as one would a buggy bearing a FOR SALE sign.

He entered the room to find Jordon sitting on the bed, cleaning a rifle. Declining the drink of whiskey he was offered, Sam washed his face and hands, then sat in the chair beside the bed. Raising the rifle and sighting down its long barrel, Jordon began to speak.

"Been wanting one of these things for a long time. I ran into a hunter that was down on his luck; traded him the Sharps and ten dollars for this Spencer, along with three tubes of ammunition. My gun was beginning to shoot off-target, the rifles were worn out in the barrel. I tried this baby before I traded; shoots right on the money." Continuing to wipe the rifle with the oil-soaked cloth, he added, "It's a fifty-six caliber, you know."

"I've shot 'em, Red. They'll knock a buffalo down half a mile away."

"Guess it would if a fellow could hit him. I can't see that damn far these days, Judge." Changing the subject, Jordon continued to talk.

"I ran into a man I think you should talk with when you find the time; he's an Indian the white men call Choctaw Charley. He says Badger ain't in the Arbuckles at all, says he hangs out with some renegade Comanches in the Wichita Mountain area. They raid south into Texas anytime they feel like it, stealing cattle, horses and anything else that ain't nailed down, then run back across the Red into Indian Territory.

"Charley's got a decent rifle for shooting game, but he ain't got nothing else; says for a horse and some new clothes he'll track Badger down for you. I don't know how you're fixed, but if you need money I can lend you a little."

"No problem buying a horse, but how do I know I can trust the Indian?"

"Indians ain't known for breaking their word, Judge, or lying either. He says he can find Badger, and I believe him. Besides, he's got good reasons of his own for wanting the man put out of business. Badger beat him up and took a horse away from him last year. He's got some deep scars on his face from Badger's bootheels."

"All right, I want to talk with him. When can I do it?"

"I didn't have any idea when you'd be back, so I told him to be up on the Clear Fork every evening at sunset; that we'd meet him there when you returned. I'm sure he'll be there this evening."

Choctaw Charley had been sitting near the top of a large pecan tree when the two men crossed the river. Recognizing Jordon, he lowered himself from limb to limb and dropped to the ground. Communication was no problem, for Charley spoke passable English. Jordon introduced Curtin as "the Judge," and promised that the horse and clothing would be delivered at this same time tomorrow. The Indian began to smile and nod his head, then spoke.

"You judge—you kill Badger?" Laughing, Charley put one fist behind his head as if holding something, then began to kick his legs and stick out his tongue, as if he were strangling at the end of a rope. He was clearly happy thinking that he might contribute something to Jess Badger's demise. Looking at the purple scars on the face of the Indian, Sam decided that if and when he met Badger, the man would get no more than a fighting chance. Jordon answered Charley's question.

"Yes, kill." Overjoyed, Charley listened to his instructions. He was to seek out Badger, speak to no one and stay in the area only long enough to ascertain if the man would be there for a while. Then he was to beat it back to the Flat. Sam would bring the horse and clothing to this same tree tomorrow, along with enough food for several days. Charley continued to smile and nod, then disappeared into the thick stand of mesquite trees. As he stood looking after the Indian, Sam commented, "He's taller than most Choctaws, Red."

"Probably ain't even a Choctaw. White men hang any name they want to on an Indian."

"I didn't see a rifle, either."

"Hid it somewhere. He's afraid somebody will take it away from him."

The following evening, Curtin sat under the pecan tree, holding a strong gray gelding bearing a cheap saddle. Charley emerged from the trees in short order, carrying a Winchester that was at least as good as Curtin's own. No telling where he stole it, Sam was thinking, after all, stealing was a way of life among Indians. Charley's hand went first to the warm, fleece-lined coat, for the evening was already beginning to chill. Then, patting the blanket and clothing that were tied behind the saddle, he mounted the gray. Knowing that Charley fully understood his mission, Sam backed away, saying, "I'm counting on you, Charley, don't let me down. If you meet any white men who doubt your ownership of the horse, show them that piece of paper in the saddlebag."

"Charley not let you down," he said, beating himself

on the chest. "Charley word good. You see." He turned the gray north and galloped over the hill.

Sam found Jordon at the hotel bar, having a glass of whiskey. Ordering a beer for himself, he sat down beside Red.

"Charley headed north lickety-split," he said.

"He'll get the job done, Judge."

"Unless Badger sees him first, and shoots him."

"Charley knows Badger's a threat to him, and usually when an Indian don't want to be seen, he don't get seen."

"Aw, you're right, Red; it wouldn't be the first time I lost a hundred dollars, anyway." The bartender had served Sam's beer, and Jordon sat staring at the mug.

"How long you been drinking that stuff, Judge?"

"Several years. Why do you ask?"

"Just wondering, it gives me a headache. I spent a week in Denver last year drinking Coors. Now there's a beer for you; it'll turn a man against this horse piss they serve in Texas."

"I've never been there," Sam said, finishing off his beer. "If I'm ever up that way I'll give it a try."

After Jordon volunteered to pay the additional rental charges, Sam ordered a second bed erected in his hotel room. Perhaps with a good bed under him Red would not snore so much. They retired before ten, lying awake in the darkness and talking softly.

"I'm just wondering how I can separate Badger from his Indian friends," Sam was saying.

"You probably can't, but I doubt that you'll have to. He won't have more than three or four around. Comanches like to watch a good fight, and they'll usually let the winner walk free. Even when they've got you outnumbered and know they can take you in the long run, they also know that the first man who moves is gonna get it. In that regard they're about like white men, each one a little bit reluctant to sacrifice his own ass in order to get the action started. Anyway, I intend to be there with a cocked Spencer."

"I'd be happy to have a man like you around, Red." Sam turned over only once before going to sleep.

He awoke at sunup to find that Jordon was already up and gone. Nothing unusual about that, Red was frequently out prowling at the first hint of dawn. "A man can learn more about an area in the first half hour of daylight than at any other time of day," Red had once said to him. As Sam sat on his bed, he was thinking that Jordon was truly one-of-a-kind. Sometimes he talked like a college professor; at other times, like the mountaineer that he was. At all times, he was loaded with common sense and logic.

Sam had learned little about Jordon's early life in Virginia, Red only talked about his life on the frontier. He had worked as a scout for the army on several occasions, and joined them in battle whenever necessary. But by and large, he had lived his life as a loner, surviving by his keen wits when he could, fighting his own battles when he had to.

Sam had known no man who understood the thinking of an Indian as well as Jordon. Perhaps he understood the thinking of whites just as well, Curtin thought. Yesterday, he had seen Red checking the load in a forty-four caliber Dragoon pistol that he carried in his saddlebag. Sam had fired one of these a few years ago, and had some firsthand knowledge of its shooting power. Though its extremely heavy recoil made follow-up shots difficult, the big gun's reputation as a powerhouse remained unchallenged by any handheld weapon.

To simply say that Jordon rode around the country

armed would have been an understatement. In addition to the Spencer and Dragoon, he carried a forty-four Remington Army in his other saddlebag, a thirty-six caliber Colt in his pocket and a razor-sharp folding knife. Sam had the feeling that Red would use any of them at the slightest provocation.

Six

It was now the first week in October, and each evening of late Sam had spent the hour between sunset and dark on the Clear Fork, hoping for the return of Choctaw Charley. Today, he was sitting under one of the large pecan trees. He had shelled and eaten several of the delicious nuts and was about to return to the Flat, when he heard someone call out to "the judge." Recognizing the voice, he responded to his newly acquired nickname and led his horse into the mesquite trees to join the Indian. Charley stood in the dense thicket, holding the gray by its bridle, a broad smile on his face.

"Find Badger," he said, going through a series of gestures signifying the motion of someone dealing out poker hands from a deck of cards, "Wichita Mountains."

"Very good, Charley. Can you lead me to him?"

Charley held up four fingers. "Four days."

"We leave at sunup, then."

The Indian laughed loudly, nodded his head several times and disappeared into the trees.

Three days later, three horsemen crossed the Red River into the area west of recognized Indian Territory, which was already becoming known to its inhabitants as Oklahoma Territory.

They rode single file, with Choctaw Charley in the lead. Red Jordon followed close behind, his big Spencer always ready for action. Curtin brought up the rear, leading his black mare. The animal's back was loaded with blankets, cooking utensils and food, and it was the only pack horse the men had brought.

The treeless plain stretched north as far as the eye could see, and the wind was blowing very hard into their faces. Their horses were showing little inclination to continue walking into the strong, chilly gusts that threatened to stop them in their tracks. Horses, by nature, want to turn their rumps to the wind, and the pack mare had already begun to fight her lead rope. Leaning forward and yelling into the wind, Sam called Charley to a halt.

"Let's find a gully that runs east to west and get out of this wind." They were soon camped in an arroyo where the air was still, and Charley had built a fire for coffee. Their horses were picketed on the lush, short grass that only a few years ago had supported millions of buffalo. When he stood up, Curtin lost his hat to the wind and had to chase it more than a hundred yards. Almost being blown off his feet, Sam staggered back to the arroyo.

"That thick grass," he said, pointing to the swaying vegetation, "is the only thing keeping this wind from blowing all the topsoil to another continent."

"If the farmers come in and plow it up, that's exactly what will happen, Judge." Red had raised his voice as he spoke, sounding angry at the very thought. Charley, busily preparing the ingredients for a pot of stew, nodded in agreement.

"All blow away," he said, waving his arm toward the distant horizon. Turning his attention to the stew, Charley stirred it several times, then informed the pair that the wind would continue to blow throughout the afternoon, but would abate shortly after sundown. Sam supposed that the prediction would be accurate; after all, the man lived outdoors. Charley said he would have no problem guiding them north in the darkness of night.

At dusk the following evening, the three men lay on a hillside overlooking the log cabin in which Badger had been seen by Charley. At that time, Badger had been accompanied by one white man and three Comanches. The five had been involved in a poker game, the Indians no doubt losing their share of loot to the bearded outlaw. The building consisted of one large room, with no door or window on its backside, according to Charley, who had circled the cabin and peeked through its front window.

Lying on the hill, with a good view of the cabin's frontside, Charley explained the layout inside: the location of bunks, stove, table and chairs. Knowing that a man usually sits in the same chair, Sam had Charley describe the seating arrangements around the table. He had no intention of letting Badger get the upper hand, for he had been told by many men who would surely know, that the man was not only very fast with a gun, he was deadly accurate.

A small shed stood in front, and slightly to the right

of the cabin. A pole corral had been erected around the shed, and Sam counted six horses.

"Badger in there," Charley said, "ride that big pinto." Smoke was soon drifting upward from the chimney, and someone had lighted a lamp inside the house. Though it would seem that men such as these would have curtained windows, the cabin's lone window was bare. Sam could see more than one person moving around inside, even from a distance of several hundred yards.

An hour later, after securely tying the horses, Curtin added a sixth shell to his Peacemaker. Jacking a shell into the chamber of his Winchester, he announced that it was time to go. They crept down the hill slowly, making no sound as they felt their way through the darkness. After half an hour they were under the shed, behind some bales of hay. The horses quickly became excited over the presence of the unwelcome strangers and began to shuffle around. When one of them whinnied, the cabin door opened and a Comanche Indian came through. As he passed the first haystack he realized too late that he had company, for Curtin brought the barrel of the rifle down hard upon his head.

Charley quickly tied the Indian's hands and feet with rawhide, stuffing a dirty sock into his mouth. Moments later, the cabin door opened again. Jess Badger peeked through the doorway, his bass voice ringing loudly into the night.

"What's going on out there?"

Choctaw Charley, demonstrating a superb example of quick thinking, answered Badger, using the universal Indian word for cow, "Wohaw!"

"Well, get a rope on it, then get your ass back in here. We'll butcher the cow in the morning." The door closed, but Sam knew by the amount of light shining along its edge that it had not been latched. Badger had failed to lock the door because he was expecting the Indian back at any moment, and would not be surprised when the door opened. Curtin tapped Jordon on the arm.

"This is it," he whispered. Leaving his rifle in the shed, Sam hurried across the yard, approaching the cabin door with the cocked Peacemaker in his hand. Taking a deep breath, he kicked the door open, jumping inside with the same motion. His eyes took in the entire room instantly. Two Comanches stood beside the stove, their hands held out enjoying its warmth. Jess Badger and a one-eyed white man stood at the table, laughing. Perhaps they had been congratulating themselves for fleecing the gullible Indians, who loved to gamble, but were known to be lousy poker players. The smiles on their faces were quick to disappear, as Curtin waved his Peacemaker for all to see.

"Hands up! Everybody! Hands up!" he yelled. Both the Indians pushed their arms high over their heads. Not so with the white men. Both Badger and his friend died reaching for their guns. Two shots rang out almost in unison. Both had been fired by Curtin. The first shot took out Badger's right eye, and the second went through his friend's heart. Neither of the Indians had moved a muscle, for their rifles were leaning in the corner of the room several steps away. After tying their hands, Jordon spoke to Charley.

"See if you can rouse that sonofabitch in the shed. We'll take them all as far as the river."

Sam agreed, saying, "You're reading my mind, Red. I never intended to leave them on our back trail." Charley arrived soon, pushing the revived Comanche before him. The Indians were herded into a corner and told to sit. A conversation quickly erupted between Charley and the Comanches that was understood by neither white man.

"What's all the talk about, Charley?" Curtin asked.

"They say you ver' good, want to join your gang. I say you judge. No gang."

"Yeah . . . well, thanks." Curtin turned the body of the one-eyed man over. Her stared at the face of the blond-haired gunman for some time, then said, "I believe I have a dodger on him in my saddlebag; he's wanted in both Tarrant and Dallas Counties for murder. His name is Curtis Wheeler, and the rewards total a thousand dollars. As you might guess, his nickname is Bad Eye."

"You beat me to the trigger, Judge. I was about to put his other eye out with this Spencer." Jordon scratched his beard on both sides, then continued to talk. "What I just can't understand is them being dumb enough to reach for their guns with you holding a cocked Peacemaker right in their faces."

"I was expecting it. They probably talked it over a long time ago and decided that if they both drew at the same time, maybe at least one of them would survive. Any jury in Texas would have hung them both, and they knew it. They had nothing to lose, Red."

"Well . . . I guess by god you explained that!" Jordon said, sounding somewhat like a child who had been corrected after saying something stupid.

They wrapped the bodies in blankets and tied them on horses. As he helped with the work, Charley held a handful of Badger's hair for a long while, his eyes moving to the knife at his own belt. Then he raised his head to face Curtin, a question in his eyes. Looking into the scarred face of the Indian, Sam could read his thoughts very well.

"No, Charley," he said.

A short while later, Curtin stood close to the lamp, reading the dodger he had dug out of his saddlebag: CURTIS WHEELER, AGE 30. SIX FEET TALL, BLOND HAIR. HARELIP—RIGHT CORNER. THREE FINGERS MISSING ON LEFT HAND. LEFT EYE SIGHTLESS. Sam had read the description aloud, prompting Jordon to say, "Well, that's damn sure Wheeler on that horse out there; you can't miss the bad eye and harelip, and he ain't got nothing on his left hand but a thumb and forefinger."

"All right, we've identified him. Let's get these Indians mounted and start putting this country behind us." Charley had already brought their own mounts from the hillside, and was now in the corral catching horses for the Indians to ride. Within the hour the small caravan rode out of the valley. Charley rode in the lead once again. Behind him, tied nose-to-tail, were the horses bearing the three Comanches, whose feet were tied beneath the horses' bellies. Jordon led the pack mare and Sam rode behind, leading the horses carrying the dead men.

They rode south by the same route they had used coming north, making good time and seldom stopping. By traveling at night, they escaped the swift winds that blew incessantly during the afternoon, and arrived at the river at midday. Jordon cut the Comanches loose and flogged their horses north.

"Do you think they'll head back to the cabin?" Sam asked, after they had crossed the river and gone about preparing food.

"Of course they will. Didn't you see all that canned food stacked in the corner? They ain't about to take a chance on their so-called friends getting it." Jordon opened his saddlebag and extracted the two small cans he had lifted from the cabin. Tossing them to Sam, he added, "They won't be having these for supper. Put 'em in that pot there, a proper stew has got to have tomatoes." Sam did as he had been told, then leaned back against his saddle.

"We've got to rest the horses and give them a few hours on this good grass," he said. "The weather's been cold so far, but it'll warm up farther south. I want to go all the way to Fort Worth when we start again." As he talked, Sam had been pouring water out of his boot and wringing out a sock. Chuckling, Red seized the opportunity.

"When a man rides across a river he ought to hold his feet up out of the water, Judge, they'll get wet."

"No shit?"

Choctaw Charley let it be known that he was as close to Fort Worth as he intended to be, and was about to head for West Texas. Sam gave the Indian fifty dollars and promised to hire him again sometime, if the need ever arose. Charley answered with his usual smile, and nodded several times. He then mounted the gray and rode southwest at a canter.

"Do you think he'll go all the way to Griffin before he rests that horse?" Sam asked.

"Might. Indians think nothing of pushing a horse two hundred miles. They'll travel that far on foot, for that matter."

"He must have wanted to get home mighty bad," Sam said. "Can't imagine him not even staying around for dinner, though." He stoked the fire and stirred the stew, then added, "We'll rest right here till about midnight; by then the horses will be ready to travel. We'll have to set a fast pace and keep going till we get to Tarrant County."

"Even at that," Jordon said, pointing to the bodies,

"those bastards are gonna be getting mighty ripe by the time we get to Fort Worth."

Tarrant County's sheriff, Frank Bain, recognized the outlaws on sight. He quickly identified them and took charge of the bodies, saying it might be as long as a week before the bounties could be paid. He asked both men to stay in the immediate area; there were questions to be asked and papers to file, he said. A newspaper editor, after being refused by Curtin, sought out Red Jordon, who obliged him with an interview. Red detailed the entire manhunt and showdown.

As Sam sat in a hotel room, reading the resultant newspaper article, Jordon sat in a chair beside him, sipping from a glass of corn whiskey. Seemingly unaware of the potential problems that could be brought on by the publicity, Red had rushed the newspaper to Sam.

"They really wrote you up good, Judge," he said. Sam read the article quickly. Jordon had been right: they had written him up good. Nowhere in the article had he been referred to as Curtin, or Sam Curtin. The opening line called him "Judge Curtin," thereafter he had simply been referred to as "the Judge." In one paragraph Red was quoted as saying that no man in the world was as fast as the Judge with a six-gun.

Sam was certainly aware of the fact that half the people in Texas read the Fort Worth newspaper, and that someone would likely show up to dispute Red's claim. He also knew that damned nickname was here to stay. The article stated that he had outdrawn and killed both Badger and Wheeler, which was not the case at all. He had gone through the doorway gun-in-hand, while the outlaws had had holstered weapons. Folding the newspaper, he handed it back to Jordon.

"Damn, Red! I've never wanted to be known as a gunfighter, but you took care of that, old buddy."

"Now, I didn't say all of that stuff in there; he didn't write it just like I told it."

"They never do, Red. I learned something about newspapers when I was working with the trade show. Of the dozens of writers who interviewed me in those days, not a single one quoted me correctly. Not one, Mr. Jordon! I turned the editor down, I didn't think about him getting to you."

"That stuff about you being the fastest gun in the world—I didn't say anything about the world, I just said that you were the fastest man I'd ever seen."

"I believe you, Red. You'll do well not to talk to those people at all." Sam took a leather bag from the small closet and laid it on the bed, saying, "I've got a lot of money here and some of it's yours."

"That money is your own, Judge. You're the one who put those bastards down."

"Bullshit, Red. You laid your ass on the line in that cabin knowing damn well that if they got me you wouldn't stand up long."

"Well . . . guess I did at that. A couple hundred would help me get through the winter." Sam gave him a thousand.

"This should get you through the winter in style."

"I'll be going down around the border. The weather is mild, and money goes a lot farther." He had been busy counting the money, then added, "Never had this much in one wad before."

"Neither have I," Sam said.

The following morning the friends parted with a handshake. Red had promised to visit Sam in the spring if his health remained good. Curtin rode to Dallas, where he paid passage for himself and his horses and boarded the train to Calvert.

As the train's engine labored south with its heavy burden of loaded cars, Sam sat looking through the window at the cotton fields. On both sides of the track, men, women and children worked at what appeared to be a second picking as they dragged their long sacks behind them. He knew that Texas cotton farmers were having a banner year, and was happy for them. Though cattle production was rapidly becoming big business, cotton remained the number one contributor to the economy of the Calvert area.

As he watched the workers, some bending over, others on their knees, he recalled that he had done the same thing the year he was twelve. He had picked cotton every day for a month, then taken the money he earned to Lula. Though times were hard, and young Sam knew she needed the money, she had refused to accept it, telling him to buy himself some new boots and a warm coat. She had always been that way; always putting the needs of others above her own, especially those of young Sam. Once a beautiful woman, she had worked outdoors beside her husband till the wind and hot Texas sun had taken their toll. Now, like Hamp, she was beginning to look older than her calendar years. Sam had some money, now, and he intended to lighten the lady's load. He would start by buying her some pretty clothing when he got to Calvert.

Although he had been sitting in his seat for hours, he still wore his long coat, for it was chilly inside the car. The coat also served another purpose: it hid the Peacemaker on his hip. It seemed that ordinary people just had a natural tendency to shy away from men wearing tied-down quick-draw holsters.

He had spoken to no one since boarding the train,

and leaning back in his seat, he drifted off to sleep. He was soon awakened by a gray-haired woman who had obviously just boarded the train. He must have slept soundly, for he had not even been aware of the train stopping.

"May I sit?" she asked, pointing to the seat where his hat and saddlebags lay.

"Of course," he said, putting the hat on his head and the bags across his lap. He was soon comfortable again, and preparing to resume his nap.

"Going far?" the lady asked.

"No, just to Calvert." He closed his eyes again.

"Hear about the Badger gang?"

"No, didn't hear anything about a gang."

"Oh, yes. Some fellow named Curtin shot it out with the whole bunch up in the Territory. Brought all five of them in dead. This fellow Curtin must be something else, they say he's a judge somewhere. Seems to me that it's getting mighty bad when a judge has to leave his office and go out and show the elected lawmen how it's done." Oh, shit, Sam thought, if a woman is talking like this, what the hell are the men saying? Damn that Red Jordon! He excused himself and walked to the back of the train, where a man offered him a drink of whiskey. He accepted with gratitude.

"How much farther to Calvert?" he asked the man.

"Not far, an hour at the most." The man said nothing more, and very soon Sam began to recognize the terrain. As a youngster he had hunted game all through the woods he was now passing. Within the hour, the iron monster screeched to a halt at the Calvert depot. As was his custom when he happened to be in town, Sheriff Pate stood on the platform. He was quick to spot Curtin unloading his horses and strolled over.

"Welcome back, Sam," he said. "No need to ask what you've been doing, the news beat you home."

"You been reading the Fort Worth paper?"

"Yep."

"I brought Badger and Wheeler in, Wally, but most of what you read in that paper is bullshit."

"I don't doubt it, I've had a few write-ups in my time, but the fact that you brought them in speaks for itself." Pate instructed his deputy to care for Sam's horses, then invited Curtin to his office for a drink. And a talk. The sheriff produced a bottle and poured generous amounts of whiskey into tin cups. After some prodding, Sam related the most important details of the manhunt to Pate, downplaying the actual shooting.

"Nothing wrong with being modest, Sam, but let me tell you a few things that I know: Jess Badger was a fighter, and a damn good one. I also know that the sonofabitch put up a fight when you found him. Whatever you did, you did it exactly right, my friend, or you wouldn't be sitting here." Sam said nothing to that. He sat sipping his whiskey, knowing that truer words were never spoken. They talked of other things for a while, then the sheriff broke into laughter as he stood up from his chair and began to walk around the room.

"I was just thinking about that fellow named Pelt that you shot in front of the saloon a few years ago. He was too stupid to realize that you were just rattling his brain with that tale about his sister being a whore—he bought it hook, line and sinker." Pate walked around the room again, then continued, "If he had been a fish he'd be mounted on your wall right now." Sam could understand how this might be funny to the sheriff, but he himself did not laugh. He was on his feet now, for he had decided it was time to be on his way. Pate followed him to the door. The deputy had tied Sam's horses at the hitching rail, and as Curtin mounted, the sheriff had some parting words.

"You did an honorable service for the people of Texas, Sam, and don't you ever start thinking otherwise. You're a hero to a lot of people in this town. I think I would be foolish to run against you if you ever decide you want my job."

"That, sir," Sam said, "is highly unlikely." Smiling, he turned his horses toward the center of town. He had some shopping to do.

Seven

Lula had been sweeping the porch when she saw Sam riding up the hill, his pack mare loaded with packages. Dropping the broom, she ran into the yard and stood at his stirrup, waiting for him to dismount. Throwing her arms around his neck, she said, "It's real good to have you home, Sam. We read about you in the paper."

"Well, you probably shouldn't believe everything you read," he said, then asked in the same breath, "Where's Hamp?"

Bud, who had hurried up the hill from the barn, answered, "Pa had his foot cut off. He's down at the barn right now making himself a peg leg."

"The doctor amputated it at the calf, Sam," Lula told him. "It healed real good, too."

"I'm glad to hear that, Lu." Sam walked to the mare. "Here, I brought a few things from town." Handing a box to Bud, he said, "New coats for you and Hamp. Take them to the barn and see how they fit." He put the remaining boxes on the porch, adding, "These are yours, Lu. I don't know much about women's clothing, but the lady in town helped me. I sure hope they fit."

"I can make them fit, Sam, you know that."

"Yeah, I guess I do. Anyway, Miz Pitkin has seen you at church a few times; she thinks they're the right size." Lula kissed his cheek and picked up the boxes. As she walked into the house, she spoke again from just inside the door.

"Lord, I can't think of no place I ever go to be needing three boxes of new clothes." Even so, Sam knew by the sparkle in her eyes that the lady was well pleased. So was he.

When Sam arrived at the barn, the first words Hamp spoke were, "Come over here and let me hug you, brother." Hamp had not hugged him since Sam's boyhood days, and having the strong arms that had raised him around his shoulders once again was a good feeling indeed.

Hamp sat on a nail keg, with his crutches lying beside him. He had made his peg from a piece of hardwood that had originally been cut for the fireplace. Cutting it to the desired length, and hewing and sanding it into a circular form, he had then polished it to a high gloss. The leather harness he had made to strap the peg around himself was another piece of handiwork that Sam now held admiringly in his hands. Hamp had somehow made the leather as flexible as cotton cloth. Neat! Sam thought. Everything his brother did was neat. Hamp was now screwing a flat piece of iron he cut from the rim of a wagon wheel to the bottom of the peg. The iron would prevent any wearing down of the wood, making the peg too short.

"We've all been mighty worried about you," Hamp

said, "somebody told me that the fellow you went after was probably just as good as you are. I didn't get much sleep after that. I was sure relieved when Bud brought the newspaper from town."

"Well, that's over and done with," Sam said, feeling sorry for bringing so much worry to the family. "We've got a lot of things to do, Hamp. I'm gonna buy some more land and cattle, and we're gonna get you into the saddlemaking business. I want to build a big shop for you right beside the old cabin. We can cut the logs down by the creek and snake them up to the meadow. We'll put a new roof on the cabin so you can use it for a storehouse."

"Well, now, you might want to do a little more thinking on that when you see how much it'll cost. I don't even have the proper tools—I do everything the hard way." Hamp spat a stream of tobacco juice, then added, "Why, I bet they've got tools on the market that I've never even heard of."

"Maybe they do. I want you to ride the train to Dallas with me tomorrow; we'll find out how many time-saving gadgets are on the market."

Hamp noded, saying, "Well, it sounds like you're calling the shots, and I reckon you've got the money."

Christmas had come and gone, and today was the last day of 1878. Sam had bought two sections of land adjoining Hamp's ranch and two hundred head of cattle, all of which now wore his own brand. He had hired two good helpers, and the workshop had gone up quickly. Hamp had done much of the work himself, though all at ground level. Climbing a ladder was a difficult process for him. Sam and Bud were nailing the last section of roofing into place when Sam spoke to his nephew.

"Are you giving any thought to what you're gonna do for the rest of your life, Bud?"

"I'm gonna work with Pa and learn how to make things."

"Good. Boots and saddles are here to stay, and you sure won't find a better teacher."

"It ain't just boots and saddles, Uncle Sam, Pa can make anything. He made me a pair of gloves out of that deerskin you shot that are ten times better'n the ones I got from the catalog."

"Stay close to him, Bud, nothing would please him more. He needs your help, and he'll teach you things that will make life easier for you in the future." They had finished the roof and climbed down the ladder, when Sam said, "I saw that big buck again yesterday, I think I know where he's bedding. Do you think we should try to jump him this afternoon?"

"Yeah, but you better do the shooting; I can't hit nothing."

"We'll see."

Two hours before sundown, they approached the deer's suspected bedding place on foot. Sam pointed out a brushy area partially covering one end of a dead log. He thought the buck would be behind the log, and under the brush. He had cautioned Bud earlier, "I believe a deer is at least as smart as a dog, Bud; he knows his area like you know the back of your hand. Before he decides on a hiding place, he already knows which way he's gonna go if he has to run. He will always take the shortest route out of your sight. When you think you're about to jump him, look around you to see which route that is. The advantage shifts to you, then, because you already know which way he's going."

They continued to walk toward the mound of brush. Sam waved the barrel of his rifle toward the top of the hill, indicating that the deer would run in that direction. Then, rifles at the ready, they took another step forward. The huge buck suddenly burst from the brush with astonishing speed. He jumped the log and headed up the hill, taking the exact same path Sam had pointed out with his rifle. Sam held his fire, giving his nephew two shots at the running target. Bud missed both, and Sam dropped the animal at the top of the hill with a well-placed shot to the neck.

Sam was busy dressing out the deer when his nephew brought the horses up the hill. Bud sat on a log watching, as his uncle expertly quartered the venison.

"I guess he's about as big as they get, Bud, probably seven or eight years old."

"Biggest one I ever saw; you sure popped him pretty, Uncle Sam." Bud was now busy tying the venison onto the back of the pack horse. Sounding as if he were disgusted with himself, he added, "I told you I couldn't hit nothing!" Sam spoke in a soft voice, hoping to minimize the damage to the youngster's self-confidence.

"Aw, you just need a little practice with the rifle, Bud. You shot too quick the first time. You'll do better if you wait for the deer to select his running pattern. Follow him with your sights and don't rush it. He's not gonna give you all day to shoot, but one shot is all you need. Be sure he's in your sights when you squeeze the trigger. Otherwise, you'll have to eat something other than him for supper while he's out raiding your cornfield."

They had unloaded the venison and ridden to the barn, when Sam asked about Bud's six-gun.

"You don't practice with the forty-four anymore?"

"Naw, can't hit nothing with it either. The last time I used it I shot at a gallon bucket five times before I hit it." Bud unsaddled the horses and curried them, then continued to talk about his poor marksmanship with the pistol. "I keep remembering the time I saw you shooting the heads off of nails from thirty feet away, Uncle Sam. I guess the quickness runs in the family, but I sure didn't get your eye. I think I'm gonna trade the gun for something else when I get a chance." They returned to the house to find that Lula was already preparing venison steaks for supper.

"We're gonna have supper early," she said, "then I want you two to help me thrash them peas; the wind's blowing just right outside." After supper she led them to the front yard, where several bushel sacks of dry field peas were stacked. The peas had been allowed to dry in the hull for thrashing, a process much easier than shelling each individual pea by hand.

Lula began to beat the sacks with a stick, while Bud used the back side of a shovel, occasionally turning and shaking the sacks. The force of the blows easily cracked and shattered the dry, brittle hulls, thereby releasing the peas. The sacks were then emptied into a bed sheet. Holding the sheet by its four corners, Sam and Bud, on a count of three, would toss its contents high into the air, letting the strong wind complete the job. After a few tosses, the hulls and chaff would all be blown away, leaving the peas to settle back onto the sheet. They would now be stored for winter.

Sam had worked six days a week throughout the winter, and had accomplished much. His helpers, the Halley twins, were thirty-five years old. Named Mack and Jack, neither man had a family. They had agreed to work for standard ranch wages, and had built a four-man bunkhouse on the hill behind the barn. Sam had bought a stove for them so they could do their own cooking. He had no intention of putting more work on Lula.

Above the bunkhouse, and a hundred yards across the hill from Hamp's place, Sam now stood on the porch of his own new log home. He and the Halleys had worked for more than three months on the house, and the result was a well-constructed building that he thought would last much longer than he would be around to need it. Consisting of five rooms, the home was well insulated, with two fireplaces and beautiful hardwood floors.

This was the first week in May, and spring was bursting out in every direction. Knowing that the curtain was about to rise for the annual showing of the colorful bluebonnets, he sat on the rock doorstep, enjoying his excellent view from the hillside. Watching the cattle below, he could see that they had come through the winter in top shape, and were now busy stuffing themselves with the new green grass. He had moved his things into the new house only yesterday, and had sat on the porch last night till the late hours, intoxicated by nothing more than the crisp spring air in his lungs.

Hamp spent most of the daylight hours in his workshop now, and true to his word, Bud was usually at his father's side. Since getting his eyeglasses, it seemed that the youngster couldn't find enough work to do. Sam had become suspicious of Bud's eyesight the day he missed two broadside shots at the deer. When Hamp said he had noticed that Bud always avoided any type of work having small detail, Sam had taken the kid to Dallas, where doctors prescribed and fitted him with corrective lenses. Upon his return, Sam had said to Hamp, "One of the doctors said that for all practical purposes, Bud was damn near blind."

"I sort of expected that," Hamp said. "I ain't gonna be forgetting what you did."

"Sure you're gonna forget it, and I want you to start right now." Bud had been standing nearby, polishing the lenses.

"I didn't have no idea how much I was missing, Pa," he said, pointing down to the meadow, "looks like a whole new world down there." Father and son had then headed for the shop, Hamp showing only a slight limp as he walked on his peg leg.

Still sitting on the doorstep, Sam was having his third cup of coffee when Mack Halley walked into the yard. Both he and his twin were tall men, and both wore black mustaches. Both had brown eyes and were similar in appearance, but not identical. Mack was the most talkative, always seeming to speak for both men.

"You want me and Jack to put new poles on that old corral?" he asked, accepting the cup of coffee he was offered.

"I think so, Mack. Haul the poles from the other side of the hill; I don't want to cut anything else along the creek bed."

"Won't take more'n three or four loads; we'll take the bed off the big wagon and use it." He handed his empty cup to Sam and headed down the hill.

Sam had just raided the chickenhouse for a hatful of eggs, when Sheriff Pate rode up the hill.

"Hello, Wally," Sam said, walking along beside the lawman's horse, "had breakfast yet?"

"Nope. I was hoping you'd be kind enough to offer." A short while later they were enjoying biscuits, bacon and eggs, washing it down with strong coffee. Pate was quick to compliment Sam on the construction of the house. Walking around inspecting the corners, and the overall workmanship, he said, "By god you fellows put this building together to stay. If the wind ever takes it I believe it'll all go in one piece."

Sitting back at the table, Pate became unusually quiet. Sam suspected that the sheriff had more on his mind than he had discussed so far. Finally, pouring another cup of coffee for his visitor, he asked, "Something bothering you, Wally?"

"Well, Sam," Pate said, twisting around in his chair, "this probably don't amount to anything, but there's a fellow staying at the hotel in town that I don't like the looks of; he's been there three days. He won't talk to me much, but I understand that he's been asking a whole lot of questions about you. I looked at the hotel register. His handwriting is bad, but it looks like he signed the name Harlan Hyde to the book. Like I say, it might not mean anything. I just thought I'd ride out and pass the word to you." In his mind, Sam identified the man as soon as he heard the name.

"Red Jordon disarmed a man in Fort Griffin," he said, "didn't like the way the fellow was looking at my back. I'd say he was about six feet and a couple hundred pounds. He had black hair, and his name was Hyde."

"You just described the man in town—wears a Peacemaker in a tied-down holster."

Sam sat staring through the window. He had known all along that the Fort Worth newspaper article would be read by the people of Fort Griffin, for the paper was delivered to the Flat with regularity. He had bought several copies himself during his short stay there. The editorial had also been picked up by many other newspapers across Texas and beyond. Even so, Sam thought this fellow Hyde would be the ex-cavalryman from Fort Griffin.

Many questions began to run through Sam's mind: Why had Hyde come to Calvert? Had he been sent by Anna Newton? If he had come to avenge his embarrassment in the saloon it would seem that his wrath should be directed at Jordon, for Sam had neither touched nor spoken to the man. Sam did not believe that Hyde had intended to shoot him in the back, for no notoriety as a gunfighter could be gained in that fashion. He most likely had planned to wait, gun in hand, till Sam turned to face him. Had Hyde been practicing all these many months, and now wanted to try Sam because of all the recent publicity? Sam saw that as the most likely answer. He intended to ask Hyde these same questions very soon.

"I've got things to do in town tomorrow, Wally," Sam said. "If Hyde's still around I'll find out what's on his mind. If he's come here to confront me, then so be it. I think he wanted to shoot me in Fort Griffin, but when Red gave him a chance at an even draw, he turned tail. I doubt that he'll do that this time."

"I tell you it don't look right, Sam. He's got a big black gelding that he saddles every morning and ties to the hitching rail at the saloon. The horse stands there all day; fine animal, with white stockings. I'll keep my eye on the man, but I can't lock him up unless he does something."

"I know, Wally. Do me a favor and don't mention this to Hamp." Pate nodded. Returning to the yard, he mounted and rode down the hill. He stopped at the shop to talk with Hamp for a while, then took the road to Calvert.

The following morning, Sam rode down Calvert's main street. He had been able to see from a distance that Hyde's gelding was tied to the saloon's hitching rail. He dismounted, tying his chestnut to the same rail. Marshal Pond had been standing outside the saloon. He walked to Sam's side quickly.

"Been expecting you, Sam. No shooting unless it's absolutely necessary, all right?" Sam faced the marshal, a serious expression in his eyes.

"Did you ever know me to shoot when it wasn't necessary, Leo?"

"No," Pond said, looking toward the saloon, "can't say that I have."

Sam entered the building quickly, his eyes sweeping the room. Perhaps a dozen men were present, and he recognized all of them. Sheriff Pate stood by the stove, and Marshal Pond had followed Sam through the door, moving off to his right. Hyde sat at the end of the bar, a glass of whiskey in his hand. He laughed loudly as Sam entered.

"Well, if it ain't the big bad Judge. Where's that smart-ass old man with the buffalo gun?" Sam answered with a question of his own.

"What do you want, Hyde?"

"Oh, well, you should know what I want, you being a judge and all. Judges are supposed to know everything, ain't they?"

"Who sent you to Calvert?"

"Sent me? Nobody sent me, I'm a big boy now." Hyde began to laugh again, adding, "Guess you might just say that I come down here on my own, wanting to see if you'd growed any bigger."

Sam now knew what he had to do. He began, "You're an ugly sonofabitch, Hyde, ugliest bastard I ever had to shoot." Sheriff Pate's lips parted in a slight smile, for he knew Sam was up to his old tricks. Sam continued, "I'll bet your whole damn family ran away from home when you were born. Did any of your neighbors own any apes that could have gotten to your mother? I'll bet a dollar she—"

"Hit that street out there, Curtin!" Hyde was on his feet now.

Sam, standing calmly, with his feet spread apart and his upper body leaning slightly forward, continued to harass Hyde. Pointing to the bartender, he said, "Oh, Les don't mind if I shoot in here, he knows I'm not gonna miss something as big as you. Make your play, you—" Hyde made his play! He had no more than cleared his holster when a shot from Sam's Peacemaker took him in the nose. The heavy caliber knocked Hyde completely off his feet, and his body now lay under a nearby table.

Yout, the attorney, had been sitting at one of the tables. He was on his feet quickly, pointing to Sam and yelling at Sheriff Pate.

"What are you going to do, Sheriff? You heard him goad that poor man into—" Sam had one hand around the dwarfish lawyer's throat, cutting off all sound. His other hand held Yout by the seat of his pants. He stood holding the small man in midair for a few moments, looking around the room as if trying to decide what to do with him. Then, nodding, he walked to the end of the bar, where, amid much laughter from the barroom's patrons, he stuffed Yout headfirst into the garbage can.

Eight

During the month of June, Sam had caught two men in the act of driving six head of cattle off the Curtin spread, and had take them at gunpoint to Sheriff Pate. Upon learning that Sam had been the one to bring the prisoners in, Yout had taken their cases free of charge. During the trial, the men claimed that they had simply been riding across Curtin property, and the cattle had been wandering along before them. Sam testified that both men had been riding cutting horses, animals trained for the single purpose of keeping cattle moving in a rider's desired direction. He was a horse trainer himself, he stated, and knew that instances in which men rode cutting horses merely for transportation were rare indeed. He closed his testimony by saying that he had personally seen the men whipping the cattle along.

Yout had put on a courtroom show that did his profession proud, depicting Sam as no less than a vicious, overbearing gunslinger who was happy only when he could find some helpless soul to bully. The jury had failed to buy his ranting attack on Sam's credibility. After only twenty minutes of deliberation they had returned a verdict of guilty, and both men had been sentenced to prison terms.

"Your statement that men do not ride cutting horses for transportation was a cheap lie, Mr. Curtin," Yout had said after the trial, "half the men in this town ride horses that know how to work cattle. A man usually can't afford but one horse, and that animal has to know it all. Of course, those cotton farmers on the jury didn't know that."

"It was your job to tell them, Yout," Sam had said. "The simple fact is, the bastards were stealing my cattle and got caught."

The trial had taken place two months ago. This morning, Sam was headed west on horseback once again. He had just forded the Brazos and now sat in the shade, giving his horses a chance to blow. His destination was San Angelo, five days west.

He had been contacted last week by Sheriff Bain: another fugitive from Tarrant County was on the run. The county was offering a reward of one thousand dollars for the capture of Dan Brewster, who was wanted for the murder of a hardware store owner in Fort Worth. A local schoolteacher had also been shot down simply because she had seen Brewster's face. She had gone into the store to buy some nails, and stood watching helplessly as Brewster gunned down the merchant then turned the gun on her. The lady had recovered, and had no problem identifying her assailant, for she had known Brewster personally. Bain had assigned round-the-clock protection for the teacher, fearing that the fugitive might return to eliminate the only witness.

Sam sat cross-legged on the chestnut, closely studying the wanted poster he had been given: Brewster was a man of medium height and build, with brown hair and eyes. Now thirty years old, he had been arrested several times during his teenage years for petty crimes. He had worked for most of the nearby ranches at one time or another, and was known to be good with both cattle and horses. He had sometimes performed odd jobs around town, including building a picket fence for the schoolmarm. No question about it, she would have recognized him for sure, Sam was thinking.

Sheriff Bain had said the weapon used had been of no more than medium bore, probably thirty-six caliber. Something to remember, Sam thought; most men carried weapons with more shooting power. Bain said Brewster had worked around San Angelo in the past, and was probably hiding out in that area now.

Sam had long ago decided that he would go after no man unless he was personally convinced of that man's guilt. Juries had made mistakes before, and probably would again. He would deliver no man who might be innocent to an overzealous prosecutor trying to make a political name for himself. There could be little doubt in Brewster's case, for immediately after regaining consciousness the lady had not only described him, she had called him by name. Brewster's second charge, that of robbery, had been downgraded to attempted robbery, for it could not be determined that anything had been taken. The cashbox, sitting in plain view on the counter and containing money, had not been touched.

Nevertheless, it was believed by all concerned that robbery had been the motive; that Brewster had simply been afraid to linger after shooting the storekeeper and witness. He had been pursued by several men on horseback, and the fact that he had gotten away alive could be attributed only to the swiftness and stamina of the big strawberry roan he rode.

The community of San Angelo had grown up around Fort Concho, which had been established in 1867 at the junction of the north and middle branches of the Concho River. The troops were there to protect stagecoaches and wagon trains, and to escort the U.S. mail. Other duties included exploring and mapping new territory, and, at times, clashing with Indians.

Across the river from the fort was Concho Street, which hosted off-duty soldiers, drifters, cowboys and ranchers. The holiday spirit prevailed throughout the year along Concho, with the most famous structure being "Miss Hattie's." There, a man could buy a stiff drink at a reasonable price. There was never a shortage of "ladies of the evening," for the girls were also ladies of the morning, noon or any other time a man might get lonesome.

Today was Saturday, and Curtin had been in town for two days. He now sat at the end of the bar in Miss Hattie's, drinking a beer and watching the customers come and go. He had decided to keep an eye on this place, for Bain had said that the wanted man had a weakness for whiskey and loose women. Sam thought that most of the men in the area would eventually pass through these doors. He liked the way the place was run: the girls were not pushy; if a man preferred sitting quietly at the bar, he was left alone.

Sam had talked with several men since his arrival, some of them at length. He had learned the locations of the outlying ranches, and the names of their owners and foremen. In addition to cattle, many sheep were produced in the area. None of the sheep ranches kept a full crew year-round, for two or three well-trained collies could control a flock better than half a dozen men on horseback. Sam thought Brewster would more likely be working on one of the cattle spreads. Or, if he had money, he might simply be loafing in town. Multitudes of men from all walks of life moved shoulder-to-shoulder along Concho and other streets in town, and it would be easy enough for a man like Brewster to blend in with the crowd.

To every man he had talked with, Sam had introduced himself as Sam Kettle. Knowing that his own name might be recognized, he had simply borrowed the surname of one of his neighbors back home. He had taken lodging at a boardinghouse well off the beaten path, where, according to the other men who lived there, the food was excellent. So far, he had eaten all of his meals elsewhere, hoping to see a face that matched the poster in his saddlebag. Tonight, he intended to eat where he lived.

During the evening meal, Mrs. Simms, owner of the boardinghouse, was slicing the apple pie when she spoke to her husband, who was sitting at the end of the table.

"Do you think I ought to go ahead and rent that room upstairs, Herb? That feller's been gone more'n a week, now."

"Give him a couple more days. Did he say anything when he left?"

"Didn't say nothing. His rent was paid up till yesterday, but I don't never expect to see him again. I looked in that bag he left behind, and there sure ain't nothing in it that a man would ride too far to git: some soap and a razor, and wore-out britches." Sam was listening closely. When the conversation died, he spoke up quickly.

"I just rode in from the east, could be that I ran into him along the way. What does he look like?"

"Just an ordinary looking feller," Mrs. Simms said. "I never did see his horse, but one of the men said he rode a high-stepping roan." A high-stepping roan! Sam swallowed hard.

"What name does he go by?" he asked.

"Bynum," Herb said. "Dave Bynum." Sam quickly remembered the Texas Ranger telling him that for some unknown reason, men wanted by the law frequently selected aliases having the same initials as their own names.

"Well, maybe Mr. Bynum will turn up," he said, making a mental note to go through the bag upstairs. He finished his meal, then sat on the porch, talking with other boarders. After an hour of meaningless conversation, he began to yawn, saying, "I think I'll turn in, see if I can get a good night's sleep for a change." The yawn had its seemingly contagious effect, and soon everyone had yawned and retired for the night.

Sometime after midnight, Sam stood in his room, examining the contents of Bynum's bag by lamplight. He turned the pants pockets inside out, searching for anything indicating that Bynum was in fact Brewster. Nothing! Mrs. Simms had been right: the bag held nothing of value. He returned it to the empty room stealthily, then slept till sunup.

After a big breakfast in the dining room, he saddled the chestnut and crossed the river. Skirting the fort, he rode north to visit a ranch he had been told about. The boarder had said that the Cromwell spread hired more men than any place in the area, and usually kept at least half of them year-round. Bill Cromwell was the man to see, Sam had been told, but since the rancher was highly religious it was doubtful that he would talk business on Sunday. Very good, Sam thought. He did not want a job anyway, he merely needed an excuse for showing up at the ranch.

Deciding to refuse any job offer he might get by complaining that the wages were too low, he guided his horse through the Cromwell gate and down the road to the ranch house. A man of large stature, appearing to be at least seventy years old, stood on the porch, a cup of coffee in his hand. His head was hatless, and almost hairless. The small amount that grew along the sides of his head was milky white. Sam stopped his horse a few feet away, saying, "Good morning, sir. My name is Sam Kettle; are you Mr. Cromwell?"

"Yes, I am," the man answered, his voice somewhat shaky. He took a long sip of his coffee, then added, "What can I do for you?"

"I'm an out-of-work horse trainer," Sam said, then added with a straight face, "but, me being a religious man, I never talk business on Sunday. I'm really just riding around to get the feel of the country, trying to figure my chances of finding work in the area." Cromwell finished his coffee. He handed the empty cup to someone inside the door and stepped into the yard.

"I've got some green horses," he said, "but I don't need any help. I hired a man just last week who says he'll work with them this winter, when everything else slows down. Says he'll do it for regular wages, too. He must be mighty good, that big roan he rides can do about everything but talk." That big roan! Sam's mind hung onto the words. He had the feeling that the old man wanted him to be somewhere else, for he had not even been invited to dismount. He decided to go fishing for the name of the newly hired hand.

"I'm acquainted with a lot of men who break horses for a living," he ventured, "could be that I know this fellow."

"Could be," Cromwell said, volunteering no name. Sam tried again.

"Might be a friend of mine; care to give me his name?"

"Nope."

Knowing he had all the information he was going to get out of Cromwell, Sam said good-bye and cantered off the ranch. He felt reasonably sure that he had located his man; that the new hired hand was Bynum, who was, in fact, Dan Brewster. He thought he would find out tomorrow. He intended to carry the bag from the boardinghouse out to the ranch and ask that he be allowed to deliver it to Dave Bynum personally. Yep, that was the way to handle the situation, he decided.

He arrived at the house just as dinner was being served. A dozen men sat at the long table, and Sam took a seat near the end. After accepting food from the many plates and platters being passed around, he said to Mr. Simms, "I found out where that fellow Bynum is working, Herb. If you don't mind, I'll take his bag to him tomorrow. I'm gonna be riding that way on business."

"Aw, he came by and picked it up this morning, paid his back rent, too. He said he had signed on with the Cromwell spread. I'm mighty proud for him; Cromwell's a good man." Damn! Sam thought, his only excuse for getting back onto the ranch shot to hell. Dan Brewster had walked right into this house while he himself had been out on a wild-goose chase. Sam finished his meal in silence. Then, with renewed determination, he spoke to Herb again.

"They say Bynum's a good man with horses. I'd like to talk with him, maybe pick up some pointers. Did he say anything about when he might be back in town?"

"Naw, I think the fellers who work out there stick

pretty close to home." Sam climbed the stairs to his room.

He lay on his bed for the next hour, trying to figure a way to bring himself face-to-face with Bynum, for he was convinced that Bynum and Brewster were one and the same man. Bain had said that Brewster was indeed a carouser; that he liked to drink alcohol in any form, and had been known to spend his entire paycheck for a month's work on a single evening with loose women. A man who would do that would surely find it difficult to stay out on the range for long periods of time. Miss Hattie's, dammit! Sam thought. Brewster would eventually show up where the action was. When he did, Sam expected to be there, for he had decided to be in the lounge every evening shortly after sunset.

Sam had always liked a drink now and then, but had never been one to hang out in saloons. After a period of time, the nonsensical conversations of heavy drinkers would get on a man's nerves. It was possible to sit in a barroom all night without hearing a single intelligent statement from anyone. Miss Hattie's was no exception. His nightly vigil at the fun parlor had now stretched into two weeks, with no sign of Dan Brewster. The end of the month, when ranch hands were usually paid, and the men did their partying, had come and gone. Each night, he had sat at the far end of the bar, where he had a good view of the front door. He had asked no questions of anyone concerning Brewster, but tonight he decided to change his strategy. He spoke to the fat bartender.

"Oscar, did you ever run into a man named Dan Brewster?"

"No, not by that name, anyway." Sam had expected that answer, for along the frontier, some men changed their names more often than their clothing. Sam got to his feet and hurried out the door, for he had made a decision. The hell with it, he thought. He would no longer sit at the bar six hours a night waiting for Brewster to come to him. He would get a good night's sleep, then ride to Cromwell's spread in the morning. He would allow no one to give him the runaround; when he left the ranch, he would have Dan Brewster in tow.

When Sam rode into the ranch house yard two hours after sunup, a young man appearing to be about twelve years old was busy drawing water from the well, filling several buckets that sat beside him. Sam rode to the youngster and spoke.

"Hello, is Mr. Cromwell around?"

"He's gone to town; you should have met him on the road somewhere."

"I didn't come that way, rode across the country. I don't really need to talk to him anyway, the man I came to see is Dave Bynum; I have a message for him." The kid continued to pour the water and Sam's chestnut stepped forward, attempting to drink from one of the buckets.

"You can water your horse over at the trough, mister," the boy said. "Grandma sees him messin' with that bucket she'll be all over you." Sam did as he was told, then rode back to the well. The youngster spoke again.

"I guess you'll have to come back in a few days. Mr. Bynum ain't here."

"Do you know where he is?"

"He's up at the line shack, been there more'n a week."

"Any reason why I can't talk to him up there?"

"Don't guess there is, 'less some of the men spot you and chase you off. They don't like people wanderin' around up there."

"I'll chance that, son. Which way to the shack?"

"Just keep riding north about six miles, you'll see it."

Sam thanked the young man and hurried out of the yard to avoid having to explain things to Grandma. When he was over the hill, he took to the trees, not wishing to be seen by any of the hired help. He rode along quietly, doing nothing to attract attention. Nevertheless, he had traveled no more than a mile when he met three men riding south. They stopped their horses a few yards away. Though all were armed, none had made a move toward a weapon. A tall, skinny man, who was probably the foreman, was the first to speak.

"You look like a nice enough fellow, so I'll have to assume that you're lost."

"I hope not, I'm headed up to the line shack to see Dave," Sam said, his words implying that he was a friend.

A blond man, who appeared to be the youngest of the group, asked, "Whatcha wanna see 'im about?" Sam ignored the question.

The foreman, speaking directly to the young man, said, "It ain't none of your business what he wants to talk about, Sandy, you don't like Bynum nohow. Maybe this fellow wants to do you a favor and give him a job somewhere else." Then, speaking to Sam, the foreman added, "Mr. Cromwell know you're up here?"

"I've talked to him; he's gone to town right now. The folks at the house know I'm here."

The foreman nodded, saying, "Well, just keep riding north a few miles. I doubt that you're gonna find him around the cabin at this time of day, though."

An hour later, Sam was on the hill overlooking the line shack. Standing in his stirrups and leaning forward, he had an excellent view of the cabin and surrounding area. He could see a horse in the small corral, but no human activity. The cabin stood several hundred yards down the hill, on a large plot of cleared land. It was nearing the noon hour, and though no smoke was coming from the section of stovepipe that jutted from the roof, Sam felt that would change shortly. He thought Brewster would be coming home to cook his noon meal and change horses. He tied his chestnut on the other side of the hill and settled down to wait.

His wait was not a long one. Within the hour, a rider appeared in the clearing. The big roan that had been on Sam's mind for more than two months was now in plain view, drinking at the spring. Though the distance was too great to distinguish facial features, Sam was confident that he was now looking down the hill at Mr. Dan Brewster. Sam watched as the man unsaddled the roan and turned it into the corral, then caught the fresh horse and transferred the saddle to its back. He then turned his attention to the horse he had been riding all morning. He brought a feedbag from the shack and curried the animal as it ate the grain. He returned to the cabin, and soon smoke was pouring from the flue. He's cooking his dinner, Sam thought, time for me to move.

Getting to his feet, he moved his gun up and down a few times to make sure it was riding loose in its holster, then walked quickly to the corner of the cabin, easing along the side of the building to the open doorway. Peeking inside, he saw that the man was busy stirring something on the stove, his back to the door. With his hand close to his weapon, Sam stepped inside the cabin. Hearing the footfall behind him, the man whirled and stood frozen, a large spoon in his hand. Sam knew instantly that he had blundered badly. Hell, this ain't Dan Brewster, he said to himself. The man bore no resemblance whatsoever; he was at least ten years older, sandy-haired and twenty pounds lighter. Though bewildered and embarrassed, Sam recovered quickly and spoke to the man.

"I feel like a damn fool, fellow. Let me start by saying that I'm sorry I barged in on you like this. Truth is, I was expecting a gunfight, but you're not the man I'm looking for." Putting the spoon back into the pot, the man chuckled good-naturedly.

"Well, from the looks of you I'm sure glad I ain't." He walked forward, offering a handshake. "My name's Dave Bynum," he continued, "from Arizona Territory. First time I've had a good scare in God knows when."

Taking the outstretched hand, Sam introduced himself, then added, "Like I said, I'm sure sorry. I've been trailing a killer who rides a big roan, and that horse of yours led me to you."

"That's twice you've apologized, and once ought to be enough for any man," Bynum said. Pointing toward the stove, he continued, "That stew's hot and I got more than enough for the two of us. What do you say?" The smell had already reminded Sam that he was hungry.

"I say let's eat."

They were soon seated at the table, eating the rabbit stew and washing it down with cold spring water. Between mouthfuls, Sam described Brewster and his big strawberry roan.

"Well, it sure ain't my horse you've been trailing," Bynum was saying, "he ain't been nowhere lately."

"I haven't been trailing a horse, just talking to people."

They finished their meal, and walked into the yard. Seeing no strange horse Bynum asked, "Where'd you hide your animal?"

"He's on the other side of the hill," Sam said.

Bynum cut himself a chew of tobacco with his pocketknife and poked it into his mouth. Then, speaking more softly, he said, "Well, since you ain't no lawman, and since that feller you're after is such a bad egg, I believe I can tell you where to find him."

"The hell you do!"

"I met a man that looks exactly like the one you described, met him on the road about six weeks ago. He was headed into Big Spring, and asked me how far it was. He rides a roan a little bigger'n mine, with three stockings and a blaze."

"Sounds like Brewster," Sam said. He thanked Bynum, and was about to walk away, when the same three men he had met this morning rode into the clearing. They were soon in the yard, sitting their horses and staring down at Sam. The slim man spoke.

"Best I remember, you led me to believe that the boss knew you were up here. Well, he didn't, and he wants you gone." Sam pointed toward the hill.

"My horse is over there, and I was just leaving." The blond man who had gotten on Sam's nerves this morning spoke.

"I think he needs to be taught a lesson, Slim." Sam turned to face the younger man, making direct eye contact and speaking loudly.

"You figure to do the teaching, punk?"

"Well, now, me and Blackie, here—"

"I wasn't talking to Blackie," Sam interrupted, "you're the one who mentioned teaching. Do you think you know something I don't?"

"There ain't gonna be no trouble!" Slim said, speaking directly to Sandy, and raising his voice almost to a shout. He lowered the volume and turned to Sam, adding, "Just get your horse and ride west, you'll be off Cromwell property in less than a mile."

"Thank you, Slim," Sam said. He pointed to Sandy.

"I hope you'll keep that big old mean man from shooting me as I walk away." He climbed the hill, mounted his chestnut and rode west. As soon as he could gather his things from the boardinghouse and his pack horse from the livery stable, he would be on his way to Big Spring.

Nine

The town of Big Spring was much like dozens of other small towns along the frontier, its one distinctive feature being the huge natural spring on Sulphur Draw. Comanche and Shawnee Indians, as well as wild mustangs, antelope and buffalo, had early on used the spring as a watering hole. The first white men arrived on the site about 1849. After establishing the town around the spring, they scattered about the countryside, each to pursue his own interest. Most turned to cattle, for the typical West Texas terrain and lack of precipitation made the land unsuitable for farming.

Curtin sat in his saddle beside the blacksmith shop. He felt that his visit to Big Spring would be a short one, for, looking down the street, he could see that a big roan with three stockings stood at the saloon's hitching rail. He attracted little attention as he rode to the saloon and tied his own horses. The street was almost deserted, the midday sun having chased most people inside. He stood beside the building for more than an hour, and had almost decided to go inside, when Dan Brewster came through the doorway and walked to the hitching rail. He wore no gunbelt, and was apparently unarmed, for his clothing fitted too tightly to conceal a weapon. Sam stepped forward.

"Hold it right there, Dan Brewster!" In what seemed to be a single motion Brewster jumped the rail, untied the roan and kicked the animal down the street and out of town. Sam had no desire to shoot the man, especially in the back. He mounted the chestnut and took up the chase. He knew that he could stop Brewster by taking out the roan with his Winchester, but he was also reluctant to shoot the beautiful animal. Knowing that the roan's stamina had already been tested by the posse in Fort Worth, Sam set a comfortable pace that he knew his own horse could maintain for hours, content to just remain in sight of Brewster for the time being.

The fleeing man was a good rider astride a good mount, and after a few miles the same distance of several hundred yards still separated the horses. Like Sam, Brewster was saving his mount for the hard run. As he approached a stand of trees on his left, Brewster turned right, onto a plain that was at least five miles across. One thing is for sure, Sam was thinking, he's got confidence in that damn horse. Nevertheless, Sam thought the plain would be Brewster's undoing. Being the horseman that he was, Sam had looked the roan over good back at the hitching rail. He had decided that the horse had been on a steady diet of grass, and seriously doubted that it could fight off a hard charge by his own grain-fed chestnut.

When they were two miles out onto the plain, Sam decided that the race had gone far enough. He would charge the roan; if that failed, he would shoot the animal, for he had no intention of running his own horse to death. Bending over the chestnut's neck, he clucked into its ear and loosened his hold on the reins, sending the signal the horse had been waiting for. The animal pinned back its ears and stretched out, overtaking the roan in less than a mile. Riding alongside Brewster with his gun drawn, Sam commanded him to stop.

"What are you chasing me for?" Brewster asked, after he had brought the lathered roan to a halt.

"For the same reason you're running." Ordering Brewster to dismount, Sam searched him for a weapon, then went through both his saddlebags. Extracting a thirty-six caliber Colt, he held it in his hand, asking, "Is this the gun you used on the storekeeper?"

"I don't know nothing about no storekeeper, ain't never even been in no hardware store." Damn! Sam thought, smiling, this fellow's gonna be a tough nut for the prosecuting attorney to crack; he's sharp. Sam had mentioned nothing of a hardware store.

After tying Brewster's hands to the saddle horn and his feet beneath the roan's belly, Sam insisted that they ride side by side, attracting as little attention as possible. A short while later he retrieved his pack mare from the saloon's hitching rail and headed east.

They rode only a few miles, then camped at a spring. Both the saddle horses had had a hard run, and needed rest. Leaving his prisoner lying on the ground with hands and feet tied securely, Sam watered the horses, rubbed them down and picketed them on good grass. Afterward, he put together an inadequate meal from his dwindling supplies.

Brewster refused the three-day-old biscuits, and Sam ate them all. He would try to shoot some game early in the morning. It would be dark soon, and the day was already beginning to feel like a cool night lay ahead. Sam had three blankets, enough to keep both men warm, but so far he had not been able to figure out what to do with Brewster for the night. He knew the man would kill, and he had already proved that he would run if given the chance. Finally, Sam settled on the only solution he could think of:

A tree with a diameter of at least two feet stood no more than twenty feet from the fire, and Sam decided that was about the right size. He began to smooth out the area around the tree, brushing away all rocks and sticks. That done, he made a bed of leaves and grass beside the tree. Untying Brewster's feet, Sam ordered him to lie on the bed and wrap his legs around the tree, one leg on each side. When Brewster's crotch was against the tree and his legs around it, Sam tied his feet together with rawhide. He then covered the man with two blankets, one around his legs, the other over his body.

"You should be almost comfortable," Sam said. "Of course, you'll have to sleep on your back all night, but that's the best I can do."

"You mean you're gonna leave me like this all night?"

"Sure. If I can't find a tree tomorrow night, I'll think of something else."

"Well, you ought to at least untie my hands so I can roll a smoke."

"I'll roll it for you." Taking the Durham from his prisoner's vest pocket, Sam fashioned a cigarette and lighted it with a burning stick. Handing it to Brewster, he said, "I'll put this thing out myself when you're through with it. These woods are mighty dry." Checking the knots around the man's wrists, he added, "If I see you trying to untie these knots, I'll tie your arms around the tree."

When he had put out Brewster's cigarette, Sam made a bed for himself a dozen yards away. He extinguished the campfire just before dark, wanting his eyes to adjust to the night as it came on. He knew that a man would be half-blind after staring at a campfire for a while.

He rolled into his blanket at dark, his head resting on his saddlebags. He lay awake for what seemed like hours, and after a while began to think about Red Jordon. He had been worried about Red for some time, and wondered why the man had not visited him in the spring, as he had promised. Perhaps his health was failing, or maybe he had gotten into some kind of trouble. Sam had no way of knowing, and no way of finding out.

He also wondered about Anna Newton. Had she had anything to do with Hyde's coming to Calvert to seek him out? He wanted to think not, for Hyde had not even been a good gunman. Living in a hell-raising town like the Flat, she would surely know someone who was handier with a weapon. Was she the type to hire a gunfighter? He did not know her well enough to even make a guess. She was easily the most beautiful woman he had known, but beautiful women had been known to topple empires. Anna always looked so small and helpless walking around town, but it could be that she was about as helpless as a damn rattlesnake. Reaching no conclusion, he pushed her out of his mind, checked his sleeping prisoner and went to sleep.

He was awake at dawn, but made no effort to build a fire. Instead, he sat motionless with the Winchester in his hand, waiting to see what kind of game might come to drink from the spring. A strong breeze blew directly into his face as he looked out across the meadow. He could barely make out the figures of the horses in the dim light of dawn, but it looked as if something else was out there—something smaller. He would have to wait for more light.

As dawn progressed into daylight, he could see a half-grown deer bravely grazing beside the horses. With the wind blowing toward the camp, the young doe had been unable to pick up the human scent. When he jacked a shell into his rifle's chamber, she raised her head quickly, staring in the direction from which the sound had come. Sam sat very still, and after a few moments the deer lowered her head and continued her grazing. As the report of the rifle broke the early morning silence, Brewster sat up quickly, a startled expression on his face.

"What the hell are you trying to do?" he yelled. "You scared me half to death!"

"You like to eat, don't you?" Sam walked to the meadow and dragged the carcass into camp. Soon, both men were enjoying the tender venison. Sam had untied Brewster's hands so he could help roast the meat, but the rawhide still held his feet together. Sam had no intention of allowing Brewster the freedom of having his hands and feet untied at the same time. He did not want to shoot the man, and certainly didn't feel like chasing him again.

Speaking around a mouthful of venison, Brewster said, "Never did get around to asking your name; you that fellow they call the Judge?"

Sam took his time about answering. He was busy roasting large chunks of meat for the trail. Positioning another steak over the hot coals, he said, "My name is Sam Curtin."

Nodding, Brewster began to roll a smoke, saying, "Yep, you're the Judge, all right. People say you're the best there is with a six-shooter; ain't nobody else even come close, is what they're saying." Sam dashed the remainder of his coffee into the fire.

"It's a long ride to Fort Worth," he said, "we'd better get moving."

Today was the fifth day, and they were two hours out of Fort Worth. Brewster had spoken very few words this morning, understandably dreading his no-win situation in town. At times, Sam had felt himself developing a certain amount of compassion for Brewster, but each time, he had forced himself to think of the innocent victims in the hardware store. His own job was almost completed, and though he had little doubt that a jury would hang the man, he himself must remain detached. They were coming into town, when Brewster said, "Do you think they'll hang me?"

"I don't know what they'll do, I won't be on the jury."

"Well," Brewster said, his eyes focused between the ears of his horse, "I'm gonna be needing a lawyer, and I ain't gonna need this roan. You want to buy him?" Looking straight ahead, Sam continued to ride toward town. He was beginning to feel bad again. Brewster continued, "I know he ain't as good as yours, 'cause you ran me down, but he'd sure make you a good spare."

"I don't think any man who knows horses would call him a spare, Brewster. He's just as good as mine, probably better. Your mistake was dodging the trees and heading out across the wide-open plain on a grass-fed animal. If a man put that roan on oats for a couple months, he'd probably chase down a damn antelope." Brewster was silent for a moment, then spoke softly.

"Well, I guess I'm going where there ain't no oats. Would you pay a hundred dollars for him?"

"Most definitely," Sam said. "You tell Sheriff Bain and get him to witness a bill of sale, I'll see that you get the hundred."

Half an hour later, Dan Brewster had been lodged in the Tarrant County jail. Sheriff Bain seemed relieved, for public opinion had begun to let itself be known. People were demanding action in the case of the hardware store shooting. Bain was smiling as he said to Sam, "You've delivered the goods, Judge. I'll have your reward money within the hour." Damn! Sam thought. Even the sheriff is using that nickname. Thanks a lot, Red Jordon!

"Thank you, Sheriff," Sam said. "Did Brewster say anything about me buying his horse?"

"Sure did. Have him write a bill of sale and I'll sign it."

"Should I give the money directly to him?"

"No, no, leave it here at the desk. I'll give you a receipt to pass on to him." Then, chuckling, the sheriff added, "These deputies don't get paid very much."

Standing in front of Brewster's cell, Sam learned that the prisoner could neither read nor write.

"All right, Dan," Sam said, pushing the receipt between the bars, "this paper says that I have deposited one hundred dollars with Sheriff Bain, and the money is yours. You can use it for whatever reason you might have. I'll write the bill of sale and you can sign it."

"I can write my name, all right." Brewster scrawled his name at the bottom of the paper, leaving room for the sheriff's signature.

"What about the saddle, Dan?" Sam asked.

"Best one I ever owned, worked nearly half a year to pay for it. It's the only saddle the roan's ever had on his back. I'd hate for him to have to break in a new one, so I'll just give it to you." Sam knew the saddle was a good one. In fact, it was good enough that even a man like Hamp would appreciate it, critical though he might be. "Whoever made that saddle took his time about it," Sam could almost hear his brother saying, which was as close as Hamp ever came to complimenting another saddlemaker. Sam took the receipt back to the sheriff.

"Make it out for fifty dollars more," he said, "I'm buying his saddle."

When informed that he now had a hundred fifty dollars, Brewster said, "That ought to buy me a good lawyer."

"It certainly should." Sam felt the lump in his throat again. He turned to walk down the hall, then said over his shoulder, "Good luck, Dan Brewster." And he meant it.

Ten

Today was the first day of 1880, and Sam sat on the porch of his home, surveying the valley below. He had bought yet another section of land, and shipped in two prize-winning bulls from Dallas. His intent now was to continuously upgrade his herd. A local farmer had agreed to supply him with hay, but so far, he had needed none. The weather had been unusually warm throughout the winter, and the grass was still green in most places. He would hire some farmers during the coming growing season, and next winter he would have his own supply of hay.

Seventy-nine had been a good year for the Curtin spread, and Sam was expecting a good calf crop in the spring. Some of the worry lines had disappeared from the faces of both Hamp and Lula, and Bud was showing more interest in learning his busy pa's craft. Hamp's business had taken an upturn shortly after Sam scattered signs throughout the Calvert area advertising the shop. At this very moment, Hamp had four customers awaiting their new custom-made saddles.

Sam had also been lucky in acquiring the Halley twins, for they were good workers and needed no supervision. He had given them generous Christmas bonuses, and promised them year-round work. Neither man seemed to have any interests other than the ranch, and each time Sam decided to do something himself he would find that it had already been done by one of the Halleys. Upon his return from West Texas, he found that they had done any number of things during his absence to increase the value of his holdings. Unlike most cowboys, neither of the twins seemed to be humiliated by tasks that could not be performed from the back of a horse. If something needed doing, they simply hopped to it: mending fences and corrals, digging ditches and cutting wood. Without being asked, they had placed a full winter's supply of firewood within easy reach of every building on the hill. Both men had dispositions that were easy to digest, and Sam intended to provide employment for them as long as they cared to remain.

A Fort Worth judge had sentenced Dan Brewster to hang, and the sentence had been carried out last month. The newspaper article stated that he had died bravely, making no apologies to anyone. When Sam first brought Brewster's roan to the ranch he felt a twinge of guilt every time he saddled the animal. That feeling had eventually been put to rest by Hamp. "For some reason, Brewster wanted you to have that horse," Hamp had said. "He's one of the best horses I've ever seen. Brewster could have sold him to anybody, but he wanted you to have him. Besides, you didn't kill the man; he killed himself when he shot down that merchant and the schoolmarm." Nowadays, Sam's mind was at ease.

The roan had turned slick and sassy now, having been fed a bucket of oats morning and night for the past several weeks. Only last week he had run a five-mile neck and neck race with the chestnut. Bud, who had been astride the roan, had proclaimed him the better horse, giving no account to the fact that the chestnut had been carrying a heavier load. Sam outweighed his skinny nephew by seventy-five pounds. Since both horses were big, strong animals, Sam also doubted that the difference in weights had been of much consequence in the outcome of the race. Two days later, they had switched mounts and run the same race again, with the same result. No doubt about it, the chestnut had met his match.

Red Jordon had come by early in December and spent several days with Sam. He had been in Mexico for the past year, where he had been living with a young Mexican woman who spent most of her time drinking, cursing and fighting. Each time Red had tried to leave, she had threatened to kill herself, saying she could not live without the handsome, lovable Red Jordon. When she began to sneak around with a man thirty years younger, Red decided he would not be missed, and headed north.

Jordon had left for Fort Griffin two weeks ago. He wanted to do some snooping and listening, he said, for he believed that Hyde had indeed been sent to Calvert by Anna Newton. Red thought that she had at least coaxed Hyde, perhaps teasing him into thinking he could gain her favor by doing away with Sam.

"Women can sometimes be meaner than any man who ever walked, Judge," Jordon had said. "When they're sweet on a man, they'll do anything in the world for him. When they fall out of love, they'll do anything in the world *to* him. I think Anna Newton knew who you were all along, that's why she played up to you. No telling what kind of surprises she had in mind for you. She's a looker, for sure, but I'll bet you it don't bother her a damn bit that she sent Hyde to the graveyard."

"I've thought about that many times, Red. It could be that you've hit the nail right on the head. How'd you learn so much about women?"

"You see these gray hairs?" Jordon asked, pointing to his head, "I've been around a while. Maybe I don't look like it now, but when I was your age I got around plenty, and not without learning a thing or two."

Red had then loaded his pack horse with grain from Sam's bin and headed west, saying he would hang around the Flat till he learned which way the wind was blowing. He had a strong feeling for Sam Curtin, and was concerned that the man might fall victim to a hired killer. Though he had never met a man whom he thought could take Sam in a face-to-face showdown, he knew that many gunmen did not operate that way. Some might ambush, or fire from concealment, while others preferred to creep in the dead of night. Sam's quickness with a six-gun was well known throughout Texas and beyond, and Jordon thought it highly unlikely that a hired gunman, though he himself might be very fast, would care to run the risk of facing Sam head-on. Only novices, fools bolstered by liquor or men desperate for cash would even attempt such a thing knowing the price for failure would be certain death. Upon his departure, Jordon had cautioned Sam to be watchful of his back trail, and to always know who was behind him.

Now, sitting on the porch daydreaming, Sam had not even known Lula was on the premises until she spoke.

"Ain't seen you up close in more'n a week," she said. "I came over to cook you a decent meal."

"Oh, I've been getting along all right, Lu."

"No, you ain't. You're just like every other man I ever saw—fill up on whatever's easiest to fix. Go down to the shop and talk to Hamp for a couple hours, then come back and eat." Sam was off the porch and down the hill quickly.

At a long table nearest the front door, Bud was busy putting together a harness.

"Double harness for Mr. Horn's buggy team," he said.

"Looks good, Bud."

"Mr. Horn thinks Pa's doing the work his own self, but Pa says this is just as good."

"Of course it is. Anyway, if you make a mistake, Hamp will spot it."

"Aw, Pa won't let nothing go out that door till it's been done right."

"No," Sam said, smiling, "I guess not." He walked to a rear table where Hamp sat working on a saddle. Another saddle, elegantly tooled and apparently finished, hung across a sawhorse, ready for delivery.

"Things are looking mighty good down here, Hamp. Have you got plenty of work lined up?"

"As much as we can do in the near future. Bud's coming along good since he got his eyeglasses. He can see what he's doing now, and it's made all the difference in the world in him."

"It does me good to hear that, Hamp." Then, changing the subject, Sam added, "Lu chased me off the hill; she's up there now cooking a meal for me."

"Lu thinks she's your mother, Sam, she worries about you just like she always has. If you'll start eating your meals at her table so she can see it, she'll leave you alone the rest of the time."

"All right, Hamp," Sam said, laughing, "tell her to ring the bell at mealtime and I'll walk over."

Two hours later, Sam was enjoying the delicious food Lula had prepared. She sat across the table as he topped off his meal with a large slice of the cake she had baked last night. She was refilling his cup with coffee, when she said, "You need a woman in this house, Sam, and some kids running around. Have you done any thinking about that?"

"Nope. Besides, I don't know any women that I'd care to bring home with me."

"You've been looking in the wrong places. You ain't gonna find a decent wife in a saloon."

"I haven't been looking anywhere, Lu. It never crosses my mind." Just as if she had not heard, Lula continued to talk.

"You take that Henderson girl, she ain't got no man; close to twenty years old, too. Prettiest thing you ever laid eyes on."

"I wouldn't be interested, Lu."

"She beat out more'n forty women to win that sewing bee last spring."

"Well, I'll just knock along like I've been doing, Lu. I'm happy enough."

"And as if the sewing bee wasn't enough, she entered that cook-off in Calvert last fall and won that too." Sam began to laugh.

"Lu, I'm not ready yet. If and when I decide that I need a wife, I'll probably look up Miss Henderson." Lula headed for the door.

"Don't wait too long," she said, "somebody will be done snapped her up."

A large dog of mixed breed had adopted Sam a month ago. The animal had simply trotted up the road from the direction of Calvert and staked out one end of

Sam's porch. The dog had learned quickly that by lying quietly and staying out of Sam's way, he could gain a meal each evening. Sam had named the big dog Spot, and considered him to be worthless, for since his arrival, the animal had never barked once. Sam decided to see if the dog would hunt. Taking his shotgun from the wall, he whistled up Hamp's hounds; he would shoot some rabbits for Lula to put in tomorrow's stew.

The sight of Sam standing in the yard with the gun in his hand was all it took to send Hamp's hounds toward the creek, for they were born hunters. Spot walked halfway down the hill with Sam, then tiredly trotted back to his resting place on the porch. Chuckling to himself, Sam followed the hounds to the undergrowth along the creek.

As he stood listening for the dogs to strike a trail, he thought of the Henderson girl Lula had spoken of. He had not seen her since she was maybe ten years old, but she had been a very pretty girl even then. If his memory served him right, her given name was Mary. Lu had made her sound like someone special, all right, but he needed no wife. He was never home long enough or often enough to keep a woman happy. What Lu did not know was that anytime Sam needed physical contact with a woman he had no problem finding a willing partner, though pedigreed she might not be. For the present, his life was running smoothly and uncomplicated, just the way he wanted it.

At sundown, he dropped off two rabbits for the Halley brothers, then dressed out two more for Lula. He ate supper with the family, then crossed the hill to his own place.

Red Jordon returned from Fort Griffin the following day, saying he had just spent ten days watching the town die. The southern herd of Texas buffalo had been exterminated, and the hunters had all moved on. The Texas Central Railroad was building west from Weatherford and would pass through Albany, several miles south of the Flat. Raids by marauding Indians, which had brought the fort to being, had now ceased, and the army felt that military presence was no longer needed in the area. With the advancement of population along the frontier, many military posts would soon be closed. There was much talk that soon the flag would be lowered for the last time at Fort Griffin. With all contributors to its economy gone, the Flat would have no reason to exist, and would surely die.

"I tell you, Judge, there's a long line of wagons leaving the Flat everyday," Jordon said, "and they ain't hauling buffalo hides. Most folks have everything they own piled onto them."

Jordon said it appeared that most of the cutthroats and gunmen had pulled stakes for greener pastures, and that he had seen a FOR SALE sign on Anna Newton's dry goods store. He expressed doubt that she would be able to sell the land at any price, since most folks were at least fair hands at reading signs. Perhaps she could freight her merchandise to another town and set up shop, or wholesale it to another merchant. In Jordon's opinion, the town of Griffin would very soon pass into history.

"Did you find anything to indicate that Anna sent Hyde?"

"Nope, and there ain't nobody there now that she could send. All of the rowdy bunch scattered to God knows where. The bars have all cut their prices in half, and they still don't have any business. A cavalryman got beat up in one of the saloons and the camp commander set the Flat off-limits to all military personnel till further notice. That further notice may never come, Judge. The only thing left for the Flat is its burial."

"All boomtowns die when their economy does, Red. The same thing would happen right here if the bottom fell out of beef and cotton."

"That's true, but it ain't gonna happen. Cotton cloth will probably be around forever, and people will keep eating beef because it's better food; and it's cheap."

Jordon felt that Anna Newton was no immediate threat, but he emphatically believed that she had been the instigator behind Hyde's feeble attempt to end the life of one Sam Curtin. He also predicted that she would continue her efforts to avenge the death of her brother.

"You be careful, Judge, you ain't seen the last of her."

"It just seems unbelievable that a delicate little thing like her could be that way."

"Aw, shit, Judge, wake up and face reality. Otherwise, that bitch will bury you!" Jordon walked outside and mounted his horse, adding, "I'm going down to the shop and order a new saddle from your brother."

Bud, who had seen it before, asked Red to put his horse through the dancing routine. Jordon obliged.

"Is he as fast as he looks, Mr. Jordon?"

"Sure is, son, best horse I ever owned."

"One of these days I'm gonna have me a horse like him."

"Sure you will. If somebody shoots me you can have this one."

"Ain't nobody gonna shoot you, Mr. Jordon. A fellow would more likely get shot hisself, messing around with you."

"Yeah . . . well, I hope you're right." Jordon walked to the rear of the shop. Hamp measured both man and horse with a tapeline, saying it would be several weeks before he could start on the saddle. He promised to have it done by late spring or early summer.

Joshua Jordon was full of stories, some adventurous, some humorous. After settling into Sam's house for the night, he told one that he recalled from the year of 1859. Sam had made him comfortable with a warm fire and a stiff drink, and after sampling the whiskey, Red began the story:

He had ridden into a small community in the hills of Arkansas on a cold, wet afternoon. It had been raining day and night for almost a week, and all of the lower elevations were under water. He had crossed a swollen creek on horseback to get to the town's only saloon. He quickly warmed his insides with whiskey, then stood beside the wood-burning stove till his clothing was dry. He learned that there was no hotel in town, but that the saloon stayed open all night. Some men just spread their blankets along the wall and slept right there, he was told. He had just ordered his third drink, when a man came through the back door with an armload of wood for the stove.

"Old Dudley's got that whole shed stunk up sump'm awful," the man said. "Rain or no rain, we jist gon' hafta do sump'm about 'im, an' that's a damn fact."

"Please, Bert, jist one more day, please!" a feminine voice could be heard begging. "That grave's half full of water anyway."

"Now, Colleen," Bert said, "the Lord called old Dudley an' we got to give 'im up. The onliest way we can give 'im back to the Lord is to put 'im in the ground. We can dip the water out of the grave mighty easy."

"Leave it in there!" someone at the bar yelled. "Be the first bath old Dudley ever had."

"Wouldn't be no sitchy thang," Colleen said. "Dudley was clean, I bathed 'im myself now and again."

Colleen was sitting at a table, concentrating on a glass of whiskey someone had handed to her. In bygone days she had been a beautiful woman, and one of the busiest and most prosperous whores in Arkansas. As her beauty faded, her business had done likewise, and she had eventually become addicted to strong drink. She had moved into a shack at the edge of town, where she and Dudley shared a single room. Their world had shrunk to the size of their daily need for alcohol, and they did most of their drinking alone.

Colleen had retired from prostitution through no fault of her own. Once her youthful figure had deserted her, there were simply no takers. In the good old days she had had plenty of money, and had been a soft touch for any man who was down on his luck. It was common knowledge around town that she had given away more money than most men earned in a lifetime. For the past year she had been content to play her guitar and sing songs in the saloon to earn drinks for herself and Dudley.

"Old Dudley jist sat down in a chair over there by the stove and died," a man had said to Jordon, "been drunk for over a month. Couldn't nobody git 'im to eat nothin', not even Colleen."

A local cotton farmer had volunteered two slaves to dig the grave, but the Negroes had begged off on the actual burying, wanting nothing to do with a dead body. After finishing her drink, Colleen stood up from the table and resumed her begging that Dudley's body be left in the dry shed for one more day.

"Dammit, Colleen, he's got to go in the ground today, and that's final," Bert said. "I pulled that sack off his head and looked 'im over. The rats ain't got to his face yet, but they've damn sure been nibblin' on the rest of 'im. Besides, ever'body knows that if you don't bury a dead man before the fifth day the devil steals his soul, and he won't never give it back."

"Old Dudley didn't have no soul!" a man yelled from the bar.

Colleen obviously knew the speaker, for she answered, "He did so have a soul. He was a good man, a damn sight better lover even when he was drunk than you ever was on your soberest and strongest day." Nothing else was heard from the man.

While Bert called a conference of the burial detail in the corner, Shorty the Midget, who stood little more than three feet tall, sat beside Colleen attempting to console her. Shorty had long held a hankering for Colleen's body, and only the two of them knew if he had ever succeeded. Though midget in size, his body was well proportioned, and more than one man who had seen him without clothing had said he was not small all over. In his squeaky, childlike voice he was saying to Colleen, "Bert is right, honey, old Dudley has to be buried." As if he had heard, Bert announced loudly that the burial would take place shortly. But first, they must each have a drink to ward off any attempt the devil might make to seize old Dudley's soul. Jordon had joined them in their drinking, for the whiskey was on the house. Soon, Colleen was standing beside his table.

"Maybe you can help me talk 'em into waitin', mister," she said. "I want to play sump'm nice at the grave, and the secont strang's broke on my gittar. I could find a new one tomorrow."

"Why not play something without that string? I've seen guitar players do it lots of times."

"Dudley liked his music in the key of D, and I cain't play no proper D chord without that strang."

"Well, go over and tell that to Bert, maybe he'll change his mind." Bert did not change his mind. He sent four men for the coffin, telling them to nail a makeshift lid onto it. They arrived soon with the pine box resting on two long poles, one man at each of the four corners.

"The rain's let up fer the time bein'," Bert said, "let's git on with it."

"Git on with whatever you're gonna do," the bartender said, "git that damn smell outta here." More than a dozen men walked out the front door, led by the four pallbearers. One man held the coffin on each side to keep it from slipping off the poles. They were unsuccessful. After the coffin had slid off twice, it became so slippery with mud that the chore became impossible, at which time the poles were discarded. Everyone in the party had slid down at least once, when the men decided to climb the steep hillside on their knees, pushing the coffin along before them. Colleen climbed the hill upright, clutching her guitar under her arm.

In attempting to lower the coffin into the grave, two men lost their footing, and the box tumbled into the hole upside down. A loud protest from Colleen prompted Bert to say, "It don't matter a damn bit which way old Dudley's facin', Colleen, that damn box is gon' stay right where it is. We couldn't turn it over if we wanted to. You sang 'im a song, now, then git on back down to the bar. We'll finish up here."

Colleen began to wail an old Irish song about the green hills and pastures, pausing after each line to say, "This is fer you, Dudley, this is fer you, baby." She stopped her singing abruptly after only two verses—the midget had somehow managed to slide into the grave headfirst, hitting his head on the pine box and breaking his neck. Colleen fainted dead away, and two men carried her back to the saloon. When Shorty was handed up from the grave, all agreed that his neck was broken.

"He's still breathin'," Bert said, "but he shore ain't gon' be alive tomorrow. If he'd hurry up and git it over with, we could use this same hole to bury 'im."

"Hell, Bert," one of the men said, "it looks to me like he's jist a-layin' there a-sufferin', why don't ya jist shoot 'im an' git 'im outta his misery?"

"Colleen would hear the shot. Besides, powder an' lead cost money, an' it's hard to find." Bert stood looking toward the saloon for a while, as if making sure that the woman was out of earshot. Then, raising it high into the air, he brought the backside of the shovel down onto the midget's head so hard that the handle broke. The tiny man twitched once, then lay still. With his foot, Bert rolled the small body into the hole.

"He wouldn't have lived till mornin' nohow," Bert said. "That damn rain is about to start again and I don't reckin none of us feels like diggin' another hole." Picking up another shovel, he began to push mud into the hole, adding, "I better not never hear that any of you fellers told Colleen about me gittin' Shorty outta his misery. That's what I done, all right, an' I done it as a special favor to Shorty. Got the pore little feller outta his misery."

Colleen was told that Shorty had died of a broken neck, and had been buried with old Dudley.

"That would have pleased him and Dudley both," she said, "they was the best of friends."

Jordon had stayed in the saloon till the rain stopped two days later, then rode on to Texas.

When Red had finished telling the story, Sam handed him another glass of whiskey.

"Is that a true story, Red?" he asked.

"As sure as I live and breathe. Every damn word." He drank the whiskey in one gulp, then headed for the bedroom.

Eleven

The town of Franklin had been made the Robertson County seat, and the courthouse had been moved there in March. Plans were already being made for a new stone building in which to hold court. Located ten miles northeast of Calvert, the town was directly in the geographical center of the county, which was the main reason for its being selected as the seat. Established in 1871, when the International–Great Northern Railroad surveyed its route across the county, the community had first been named Morgan, in honor of one of the railroad officials. When they applied for a post office the name had to be changed, for there was already a town in Texas named Morgan. The inhabitants had simply renamed their town Franklin, in honor of the original county seat.

It was to the town of Franklin that Anna Newton had moved her dry goods business. She had rented a building in the center of town and set up shop last week. Bud, who had been in town putting up posters advertising the shop, had brought the news to Sam.

"She's sure got plenty of stuff in there, Uncle Sam; three wagons parked outside with men unloading more. I looked at a lot of things; didn't buy nothing, though."

"Maybe you should have bought some new clothing."

"She offered me a good price on some overalls and pants. She's got shirts too, but don't none of 'em look as tough as the ones Momma makes for me. Momma's got store-bought stuff beat all to hell."

"She certainly does, Bud," Sam said, remembering that Lula had made dozens of shirts for him over the years. "She certainly does," he repeated, then added, "you could have used a new hat, though." Taking his hat in his hands, Bud spun it around a few times, looking it over inside and out.

"This hat's all right," he said. "Anyway, I'm saving my money. One of these days I'm gonna have me a horse like Mr. Jordon's."

"Did you ever ride his horse?"

"Nope. Mr. Jordon ain't never offered. I tried to race him on your roan last week. The roan couldn't do nothing with him."

"Did you kick him all-out?"

"I got all he had, it just wasn't enough. We raced for three miles or more, but the farther we went, the farther I was behind. Couldn't do nothing but eat that big black's dust." Bud was thoughtful for a moment, then added, "That chestnut wouldn't be able to handle him neither, Uncle Sam."

"No," Sam said, chuckling, "I suppose not."

Bud headed for the shop, while Sam sat down to think: Anna Newton had set up shop only ten miles away. Why had she come to Franklin? Why would she pass up Waco, Fort Worth and Dallas, all larger and richer towns and closer to Fort Griffin than was Franklin? The move made no sense whatsoever businesswise, for Robertson County was known to be poor country for the peddling of manufactured goods. Most folks made their own clothing, or bartered with someone who could sew a better seam. Red Jordon would be back from town before nightfall, and Sam would get his view of the matter.

"Hell, yes," Jordon said, upon being apprised of the situation, "she's here because you are. It's just like I told you from the start, she intends to see you in the ground. Bad trouble is coming your way, Judge, and I'd say it won't be long."

Jordon's prediction turned into reality one week later. Sam had been down at the barn feeding and watering the horses when suddenly he felt something tug at the sleeve of his coat. A split second later he heard the report of a heavy-caliber rifle, and knew that someone was firing on him from the hillside. Diving behind the water trough, he lay flat on his stomach. He could see that the bullet had left a hole in his coat, narrowly missing his body.

Red Jordon, who had been inside Sam's house working on a quart of whiskey, had also heard the shot. He had no problem identifying the sound of the rifle: a fifty-caliber Sharps. He raced to the window and saw a puff of smoke as another shot came from the hillside. He could see that Sam was pinned down behind the trough, and knew immediately what the shooter had in mind. He intended to shoot enough holes in the trough to drain the water, then the rifle could easily penetrate the wood and kill Sam. Another shot! Another puff of smoke! Red had the shooter located, now.

He grabbed his Spencer and dropped to the ground from a window on the backside of the house, crawling halfway up the hill on his belly. He could see Lula standing on the porch, trying to see what all the commotion was about. He motioned her back inside the house and she disappeared quickly. When he made it to cover, Red began to run full speed across the hill. He was above and to the left of the shooter now.

Behind the trough, Sam had had the same thoughts as Jordon. He knew that the water in the trough was the only reason he was still alive. The would-be killer had just put two new holes in the side, and the water was draining fast. He had seen Hamp in the doorway of the shop with a rifle in his hands, but had waved him back inside. The shooter was out of range for Hamp's rifle, but could easily pick Hamp off with the big Sharps. Sam had no idea how much Jordon knew of the situation, for he had been into the whiskey all day. He decided that when the water drained low enough to equal the thickness of his body he would make a quick dash for the barn, for the rifle could not penetrate the heavy logs. The water was low now, and Sam had just gathered his feet under his body for the dash, when he heard the report of Red's cannon. No doubt about it, he thought, that was the Spencer!

All was quiet now, and soon Jordon could be seen standing on the hill, waving his hat. All of the Curtins were up the hill quickly. Standing on her tiptoes, Lula threw her arms around Jordon's neck and kissed his bearded cheek.

"You surely saved Sam, Mr. Jordon, and we ain't gonna be forgetting it." Red said nothing, just pointed to a man lying nearby with much of his neck shot away. The man was still alive; but fading fast.

Sam stared into the face of the brown-haired man, who appeared to be forty years old. When all had taken a good look, he asked, "Any of you ever seen him before?" No one answered. The man began to move slightly, and spoke softly through frothy lips.

"Water. I need . . . water." Sam knelt beside him, speaking loudly.

"Tell me who sent you and I'll give you water!" Getting no reaction, he began to speak softer. "Come on, tell me." The result was the same. Thinking he might not be able to hear, Sam grabbed one of the man's boots, giving the leg a hard shake.

"Tell me who sent you, dammit!" he yelled at the top of his lungs. "Tell me; I've got water!"

The man attempted to turn his body over, but was unsuccessful. He opened a glassy eye, then said, "Miss Anna. She . . . she promised—" He exhaled with an audible sound, and both his eyes opened wide. He was dead.

"Well, at least you won't have to go get water," Red said.

Sam searched the man's pockets for identification. He found none. Speaking to his nephew, he said, "Saddle a horse, Bud. I want you to ride to Franklin and get Sheriff Pate." Bud was already headed for the barn.

"Take my horse, son," Jordon shouted after the kid.

Within two hours, the sheriff was on the scene, saying Bud would be along later. The kid had wanted to walk Jordon's speedy black home, for the animal had made a hard run to Franklin. When Pate had counted the dead man's money, he said, "I sure never saw him before, but he was mighty well-heeled for a drifter; more than four hundred dollars here."

"I have no doubt that it came from the dry goods lady, Sheriff," Jordon said.

"Neither do I, but I can't arrest her. It would come down to her word against his, and a high-priced lawyer would laugh me out of the courtroom. Even you would have to testify that he stopped short of saying that Mrs. Newton had actually hired him to do the shooting. What I know and what I can prove are two different things."

The body was loaded onto one of Hamp's horses, and the sheriff carried along the Sharps for evidence—if it was ever needed. He stopped at the barn and examined the water trough. Standing in the mud that had been created by the draining water, he poked his finger into the holes, saying, "Seven holes. He just about had you, Sam. A few minutes more and your protection would have all drained away."

"He was in no hurry, Sheriff," Jordon said, "he thought he had all day. He must have somehow known that the Halleys were gone to Dallas, and he had the Curtins pinned down. He had no way of knowing I was on the premises, and I imagine that he might have been lying there laughing while he waited for the water to drain."

"Could be," Pate said, turning his horse toward town.

"There ain't gonna be no more to it, Sheriff?" Hamp asked. "I mean, is this the end of it?"

"All except me delivering this corpse to Mrs. Newton," Pate said, turning his horse once again. "Oh, by the way," he added, taking a bill from the dead man's roll, "we can't let this fellow leave without paying for that water trough." He dropped the money beside the trough and rode away.

Two hours later, Pate tied the horse bearing the

corpse to the hitching rail in front of Anna Newton's store. Inside, he stood around looking over the merchandise till the store's lone customer departed.

"May I help you, Sheriff?" Anna asked, flirtatiously.

"You might help yourself," Pate said, offering the roll of money to her. "That back-shooting bastard you sent after Curtin wasn't good enough. Here's the remainder of your money; he spent twenty dollars on a new water trough." Anna backed away from the counter, looking as if she might faint.

"What . . . what on earth are you talking about, Sheriff?" She made no attempt to accept the money. Pate took her arm and forcefully led her through the doorway and out to the hitching rail, where he pulled the blanket from the dead man's face.

"Take a good look, Mrs. Newton," he said, "his damned head's nearly shot off. This is what happens to amateurs who go after Sam Curtin." Anna gasped, then ran back into the store. The sheriff was close behind. He laid the money on the counter and continued to speak.

"That corpse is gonna stay right where it is until you bury it, Mrs. Newton. Tell whoever handles the job to bring the horse by my office. I will be waiting."

Later in the afternoon, a man tied the horse to the rail in front of Pate's office. The sheriff led the animal to the edge of town, pointed it toward the Curtin ranch and gave it a hard whack across the rump.

The Halley twins had frowned on Sam's offer to hire hay farmers. By mid-April, they had plowed and sown more than fifty acres themselves, saying no additional help was needed at "Curtin Hill," as the ranch was now being called. They were both daylight-to-dark workers, and many nights Sam had seen a light at the barn, where the men were helping the cows with their calving. Sam was convinced that no better help could be had at any price. He had never discussed it with either of the men, but it appeared that one or both of them liked a drink now and then.

Several months ago, Sam had left a quart of whiskey on a table in the bunkhouse. When he checked the following week, he found that the whiskey was being appreciated. Each weekend since, he had replaced the near-empty bottle with a full one. Lula, also appreciative of the Halleys, served them at least two woman-cooked meals every week. They were aware of the shooting that had taken place on the Hill recently, and had begun to carry rifles on their saddles. Sam felt that neither man would hesitate to defend the ranch.

On the twentieth day of May, Lula stated at breakfast that she had things to do in Calvert, and asked Bud to drive her there. She had been unusually quiet for more than a week, keeping to herself most of the time. The family knew and understood her great concern about the hired rifleman's visit to the ranch. She had mentioned it only yesterday when she and Sam were drinking coffee alone.

"Something's got to be done about that Newton woman. I don't know what, but something's got to be done."

"Well, Wally says he can't arrest her," Sam said, "and I sure don't know anything I can do. I certainly don't intend to get lynched for beating up a woman." Lula had dropped the subject, and Sam returned to his own home.

Today was the coldest spring day in recent memory, and both Bud and his mother bundled up in heavy coats before leaving the ranch. When the buggy reached the crossroads, out of view of the ranch, Lula spoke to her son.

"Take the road to Franklin, Bud. I just said I was going to Calvert for Hamp's benefit. I'm gonna talk to Mrs. Newton."

No customers were in the store when Lula arrived, and Anna stood beside a clothing display, rearranging dresses that hung from the rack.

"Good morning," she said, smiling, "may I help you?"

"My name is Lula Curtin, and I want you to stop making trouble for Sam."

"Oh, that," Anna said with a smirk. "It would seem that Sam Curtin makes enough trouble for himself, without any help from me. What are you asking me to do?"

"I'm not asking, I'm telling. Sam is a good man, and I know for a fact that you've been sending men after him; two that I know of myself." Anna threw her head back, laughing.

"And just where did you learn so much? Out slopping the pigs?"

"From the lips of a dying man; heard it with my own ears." With a stern expression on her face, Anna spoke through clenched teeth.

"Sam Curtin's day is coming, and anything I can do to speed matters up will be done." She shoved Lula backward a full step, adding, "What do you propose to do about that, pig woman?"

"This!" Lula said, pulling Bud's forty-four from inside her coat. The first shot went between Anna's breasts, knocking her into the clothing rack. Lula fired again. The second shot hit Anna just below her nose, turning her beautiful face into an unsightly mess. Bud, who had been waiting in the buggy, was inside the store immediately, his eyes reading the scene at a single glance. Lula stood staring at the wall, as if in a trance.

"It had to be done," she said, tears falling on her cheeks. Bud grabbed his mother and headed for the buggy, leaving the gun lying on the floor where she had dropped it. As he whipped the horse out of town at top speed, he could see that many people were hurrying toward the dry goods store, brought out by the sound of gunfire. Lula spoke only once during the frantic ride home, repeating, "It had to be done." On any but a cold day such as this, the run to the ranch would have killed the horse, for Bud whipped the animal relentlessly, constantly looking over his shoulder for the pursuit that did not come.

Sam was at the barn when he saw the buggy cross the creek and start up the hill, the horse running at a tired, stumbling gait. He ran to the road and grabbed the lathered, heaving animal by its bridle, stopping the buggy.

"You've probably killed this horse, Bud," he said, "what's the problem?" Bud said nothing, just tied the reins and jumped to the ground.

"I shot the Newton woman," Lula said, as Sam helped her down.

"Oh, no!" His eyes grew wide. "Is she dead?" Lula nodded, and spoke softly.

"Think so. It had to be done, Sam." He carried her into the shop, where the fire in the stove kept the building warm. Sipping coffee from a tin cup, Lula related the story in a calm voice, ending the narration by saying once again that it had to be done. Jordon had also listened to the story, and for once in his life, had nothing to say. Sam walked around the room in circles, shaking his head in disbelief. Hamp spat out his tobacco, washed his mouth out with water and spoke to his son.

"Bring all of the guns and ammunition down from

the house, Bud; I expect we'll be having company before long."

"No need for that," Sam said. Bud had not waited to hear Sam's argument, he was out of the shop and up the hill. His father had spoken. Sam continued to speak, looking through the window toward the creek.

"No question that Wally will be here, but I expect him to come alone; I never knew him to organize a posse for anything. Nobody's taking Lu off this ranch, Hamp!"

Bud arrived shortly, carrying three rifles and a pillowcase containing ammunition. He laid the small arsenal on a cutting table, then went to care for the horse he had almost killed.

The Halley brothers were busy plowing fields more than two miles from the ranch house, completely unaware of developments on the Hill. That was as Sam wanted it, for he did not want them involved. All afternoon the Curtins waited, but no one came from Franklin. As darkness fell, food and bedding were brought into the shop and the Curtins, along with Red Jordon, spent the night there. Not knowing what to expect, they had prepared for the worst. The main house would not be good protection against rifles, as would the shop, with its construction of heavy logs.

"If it comes to it, I can keep people out of normal shooting range," Jordon had said. Then he added, "Of course that might only be temporary; this ain't the only Spencer in Texas."

It was past ten the next morning when Sheriff Pate rode up the road to the shop. Dreading the confrontation, Sam stepped out to meet him. Pate did not dismount.

"I'm sorry about what happened, Sam," he said. Neither man spoke for quite some time, each waiting for the other. Sam finally broke the silence.

"Well, I guess you know, Sheriff, that I won't stand by and see Lu carried off to jail."

Pate spoke quickly, looking Sam straight in the eye. "I didn't come out here doubting that you would defend your sister-in-law, Sam, and I guess we both know that I couldn't handle you in a fight. However, I had no intention of locking her up. The only reason I didn't come yesterday was because I wanted to see Judge Kasem this morning." The fact that Sam had called him "Sheriff" did not go unnoticed by Pate. He could never recall Sam using the title when referring to him; always it had been Wally. Just Wally. Sam motioned for the sheriff to dismount.

"What did the judge say, Wally?" Now, that sounded better, thought Pate. Smiling, he answered the question.

"He says he'll set her bail at two hundred dollars, but she does have to make an appearance. I have a warrant and a duty, and I'm asking you to put yourself in my shoes."

"Do you intend to take her back now?"

"No. You can bring her in tomorrow morning, sign her bail yourself and bring her home with you."

"I have your word on that, Wally?"

"You have my word." Pate remounted and turned his horse around. As he headed down the hill he waved to the Curtins, who had been watching through a window.

News of the incident spread quickly throughout the area, and Lula was visited almost daily by sympathetic well-wishers from the surrounding farms and ranches. Several church groups offered donations for legal assistance. Sam had already hired a well-known defense attorney from Waco who had never lost a case. The good-looking, blond-haired lawyer, who stood six-foot-seven, expressed the opinion that Lula's case would be no exception. Named Shannon Page, the attorney had defended a dozen capital cases in McLennan County in recent years, losing none. When informed that Yout had been appointed to prosecute the case, Page chuckled, saying his first move would be to block Yout's request for a change of venue, which he was sure the pint-sized lawyer would make. Page wanted Lula tried by a jury of her peers: friends and neighbors from Robertson County.

The trial opened in July, with the midday portions being held outside the courthouse under the trees. It was simply too hot inside the building except during early morning and late afternoon. Yout had indeed made a request for a change of venue, which was denied by Judge Kasem. The judge added that a change of venue was often granted at the request of defense attorneys, but that never in all of his years on the bench had he known a prosecutor to make such a motion. Motion denied.

For a day and a half, Yout paraded back and forth before an obviously bored jury. Most of the men did not know Lula Curtin personally, but their wives did, and knew her to be a woman of impeccable quality. Sam suspected that at least some of the men had had their instructions before leaving home.

The prosecution had no eyewitnesses, though Lula had never denied firing the shots that killed Anna Newton. On the second day, Yout began a prolonged declamatory censure against the entire Curtin family. Page jumped to his feet to object, then, thinking better of it, eased back into his chair, apparently willing to let Yout hang himself. After all, the Curtin family was not on trial here. Yout rested his case shortly before noon, and the jury made a hasty retreat from the courtroom.

In the afternoon, the jury was seated under the trees on the courthouse lawn. Page opened the defense by passing each of the jurors a cardboard fan, and demanding that they be given plenty of cold water. He then called witnesses from several religious organizations, all of whom testified to the good character of Lula Curtin: a decent, God-fearing woman. Realizing that some men believed that not much happened to a person in the so-called hereafter, Page refrained from calling many of Lula's churchgoing friends to the stand. His next witness was Sam Curtin, a man known to every member of the jury.

Page led Sam through a brief history of his relationship with Lula, how she had almost single-handedly raised him after the tragic deaths of his parents. When Page pulled the information out of Sam that Lula had once claimed she did not like cherry pie, so the youngster could have two pieces, Yout hit the floor. Judge Kasem went along with Yout's objection, and ordered Page to restrain himself.

Yout tore into Sam mercilessly during his cross-examination, painting him as a gunslinger and bounty hunter who would do anything for money, and suggesting that it had been Sam himself who had put Lula up to the shooting.

"Isn't it true, Mr. Curtin, that you are no more than a common ruffian?"

"I never roughed up anybody who wasn't overdue," Sam said, then added, above much laughter in the courtroom, "like you were the day I stuffed you into that garbage can." Yout sat down in a huff, saying he had no more questions for the witness.

Page called Bud Curtin, then Red Jordon. Both testified that they had heard the dying man's words, suggesting that he had been hired by Anna Newton.

Lula turned out to be her own best witness. Taking the stand wearing the plain, simple dress Page had instructed her to wear, she told the jury the entire story, with little prodding from her lawyer: Anna Newton had been vicious and unrelenting in her quest for revenge over the death of her outlaw brother. The unwritten code forbidding men fighting women had left Lula no choice, she said. She had had to protect her men, and her home. Yout made an attempt at cross-examination, but was unable to shake Lula. The defense wisely rested its case.

Judge Kasem allowed the prosecution and the defense ten minutes each to charge the jury, and defense chose to speak first.

"Thank you, Your Honor," Page said, "but I won't need that much time." Pacing back and forth in front of the jury, he was careful to make direct eye contact with each man.

"No, I won't take up ten minutes of your time telling you what you should believe; you're all intelligent men, and you've just heard the prosecution fail miserably in its attempt to depict this noble woman as a ruthless killer. You all know that Lula Curtin did no more than your own wives or mothers would do: she protected her men, and her home." Yout, who chose this inopportune time to remove himself from behind his desk, walked out beside Page, directly in front of the jury. Page, looking down on the top of Yout's head, which was six inches below Page's own shoulder, proceeded to paraphrase Abraham Lincoln during the Lincoln-Douglas debates: "That, gentlemen," he said, "is the long and the short of it." As Page returned to his seat, Judge Kasem was busy banging his gavel to quell the laughter throughout the courtroom.

Yout charged the jury for ten minutes, but was unable to regain their attention. One hour later, back inside the courthouse, the foreman announced a verdict of justifiable homicide. Yout had literally been laughed out of court, and nobody seemed happier about it than Red Jordon.

"Page made Yout look like an idiot," he said, "and showed all of us the difference between a man and a monkey."

Twelve

The town of Luling, which lay fifty rugged miles east and slightly north of San Antonio, had been established in 1874 as the terminus of a branch of the Southern Pacific Railroad. A thriving cattle center and shipping point at the end of the old freight trail from Chihuahua, Mexico, the crossroads settlement had quickly become known as "the toughest town in Texas." The county of Caldwell was only a few years older than the town, having been carved out of the existing counties of Gonzales and Bastrop in 1845 by the state legislature. The county's claim to fame was that the Comanche raid of 1840 was terminated in the battle of Plum Creek by Texas volunteers under the command of General Burleson, General Felix Huston and Captain Mathew "Old Paint" Caldwell, for whom the county had been named.

Sam Curtin stepped from the train into a hard-driving

rainstorm. This was the last week in November, and for the past month he had been on the trail of a killer named Sammy Singer, who on many occasions had demonstrated a complete disregard for all laws governing human behavior. Information Sam had gained from an informant in San Antonio had brought him to Luling. He stood on the platform watching the slicker-clad man from the livery stable unload Sam's horses from the train. Sam thought that the stable business must be highly competitive in Luling, for never in his life had he seen a liveryman soliciting at a train depot. Sam had happily turned his horses over to the man. With his own slicker buttoned tightly, he headed for the nearest saloon, hoping to glean information from some of its patrons. Winter was coming on, and he wanted Singer now.

Like most hardened criminals, Sammy Singer had become a problem for the law at an early age. He had been a confirmed thief by the age of twelve, and once when he was fourteen, and drunk on beer that he had brewed himself, had taken a badly aimed shot at a judge he thought had given him a raw deal.

Singer's current problem had begun two years ago on a farm a few miles outside Waco. George Merriman, owner of the farm, was the proud master of a hunting dog that was coveted by all hunters in the area. It was claimed by many that the dog would hunt down and bay any given species of game on command. All the hunter had to do was speak the name of the desired quarry to the dog before the hunt began.

Singer and a companion had gone to the farm, intent upon buying the dog from Merriman. When a deal could not be struck, Singer had gone berserk, shooting Merriman in the spine and paralyzing him. He had then gouged out both the dog's eyes with his pocketknife.

Both man and dog survived, but were doomed to a life of helplessness. During the senseless melee, Singer's companion, fearing for his own life, had run through the woods and notified McLennan County authorities. Deputy Sheriff Wade Harrelson had arrested Singer early next morning, but had not lived to deliver his prisoner to Waco. Harrelson's body had been found in a shallow ravine the next day. His throat had been cut and his eyes gouged out.

McLennan County had immediately posted a reward of one thousand dollars for Singer, dead or alive. A few brave souls had taken up the chase, but had given up when Singer fled to Indian Territory. The county had now doubled the reward, and during the past few months Sam had received three tips from as many different sources that Singer had spent the summer in the San Antonio area. Curtin had begun his search there. He had traced Singer's picture from the wanted poster, just as he had Curly Cook's a long time ago.

For three weeks he had prowled the streets of San Antonio and its outlying areas, showing the picture and asking questions of selected people. Two nights ago he had been feeding liquor to a man who was already drunk, when he struck pay dirt. Slurring his words with a thick tongue, the drunk claimed to have worked with Singer clearing railroad right-of-way only a few weeks ago. He said the wanted man had been using the name Joe Beam, that he had worked for a month and drawn his pay, complaining that the work was hard and the pay scant. The following morning, Sam found the man in the same saloon, about to begin his drinking day. Now sober, the man repeated his story, adding the same details.

"There ain't no doubt in my mind," he said, pointing to the picture, "that's Joe Beam. He told me two or three times that he was going to Luling." Curtin bought the man a bottle of whiskey and left town.

Now, sitting on a stool in Luling's leading watering hole, he was sipping a beer and sizing up the customers as they came and went. He had seen no one resembling Singer, a tall, thick-chested man with round shoulders, who weighed about two hundred pounds. He had dark hair and eyes, and a long, sunken jaw that could be described as lantern, making his face appear thinner than it actually was. Sam had talked to no one who could attest to Singer's skill with a six-gun, or lack of it, but none could remember ever seeing him walking about unarmed. He was also known to be left-handed.

Sam stayed in the saloon all afternoon and early evening, then took a room at a nearby hotel. He had engaged in small talk with the bartender and a few others, but had asked no questions concerning Singer. The rain had continued all day, as it had the day before, and was still falling when Sam left the saloon. He had talked with an old man who believed that the entire area south of town was about to be under water. The San Marcos River had jumped its banks many times in the past, flooding all of the surrounding lowlands.

"I've seen watermarks more'n six feet high on that old pecan tree south of town," the old man had said, "that's the oldest tree in Texas you know." Sam nodded and said nothing. With most of Texas being unmapped and uncharted, he was quietly wondering how anyone could point to any single tree and proclaim it Texas' oldest. He climbed into his bed early, for he was very tired. The sound of the pounding rain outside put him to sleep quickly.

He awoke thinking of Curtin Hill, and Red Jordon. When informed that Sam was taking up the trail of Sammy Singer, Red had said, "That sonofabitch is guilty, all right. If he bats an eyelash you better gun him down quick. I can maybe understand him shooting Merriman during an argument, and the deputy may have damn well needed killing, but cutting that dog's eyes out calls for the death penalty. Besides, from what everybody says, it was a good dog."

Jordon had become a somewhat permanent visitor at the ranch, to the delight of all the Curtins. Lately, he had complained of stiffness and soreness in his joints and muscles, and seldom took to the saddle, saying the jostling motion sometimes caused him great pain. He bought a month's supply of liquor at a time, and usually had Bud drive him to town in the spring wagon. The fancy saddle Hamp had built for him hung on a peg inside the barn except at those times when Bud used it to exercise Red's gelding. Bud ran the animal at least twice a week, and Sam thought that someday Red would probably give the horse to the youngster. When Lula expressed the opinion that perhaps Red used his aches and pains as an excuse for consuming large quantities of liquor, Sam offered his own view of the matter.

"Red needs no excuse for anything he does, and he's definitely not the type to offer one. I doubt that he ever apologized for anything in his life." Drunk or sober, Sam felt that Jordon was good protection for the Hill, and had extended an invitation to Red to stay as long as he wished.

Sam had brought both the chestnut and the roan to Luling, and had decided to keep one of them saddled and waiting at one of the many hitching rails around town; no telling when he might need a horse in a hurry. The rain had stopped before noon, and the chestnut was now tied in front of the hotel. Sam spent the afternoon walking about the town familiarizing himself with the business establishments, always on the lookout for

Singer. The twenty-six-year-old killer was known to frequent bars and poolrooms, and any place else where loose women might be found.

The following night, Sam heard something that convinced him he was in the right town. At a billiard hall across the tracks from the hotel, two men were engaged in a game of pool. Sam sat having a beer at a table within easy earshot of the players. When one of the men was about to attempt a very difficult shot, his opponent laughed, saying, "I'll bet a dollar you miss it; Joe Beam's the only man I ever saw make that shot." Sam perked up quickly. The shooter refused to cover the bet, and he did miss the shot. When the game was over, one man departed the building, while the player who had mentioned Joe Beam sat down at the bar, ordering a drink. Sam sauntered over, offering to pay for the man's drink. He now had something to talk about without seeming to be on a manhunt.

"Have that drink on me, mister," he said, "I enjoyed watching you fellows play the game. Didn't I hear you say that you know a man who can make that shot your friend missed?"

"Aw, I don't know 'im all that good," the man said, "but I've damn shore seen 'im make that shot."

"He must be mighty good; does he play around here?"

"Used to, won't nobody play 'im no more. I hear tell he's moved on down to Gonzales; probably down there right now cleaning fish." When Sam failed to laugh, the man slapped him on the back.

"Git it? cleaning fish?" Sam got it, and knew that he would be in Gonzales tomorrow.

Gonzales lay a dozen miles south of Luling, and was the site from which the first shot for Texas' independence had been fired from the "Come And Take It" cannon on October 2, 1835.

The cannon had been loaned to the Gonzaleans in 1831 by the Mexican government for protection against the Tawakoni Indians. In late September, 1835, Santa Anna ordered Colonel Ugartechea, commandant at San Antonio, to return the cannon to the Mexican army, sending Lieutenant Castaneda and a hundred fifty men to pick it up. The request was refused by eighteen local men on the east bank of the Guadalupe, the spokesman being Joseph Clements, who said: "I cannot, nor do I desire to deliver up the cannon, and only through force will we yield!"

The cannon was dug up from its hiding place in the peach orchard of George W. Davis and mounted on the axle of Eli Mitchell's cotton wagon. Sarah Seely and Eveline DeWitt took a wedding dress and stitched it into a white flag bearing a black star, the likeness of a cannon and the words "Come And Take It."

On the evening of October 1, one hundred sixty Texans, under the command of Colonel John H. Moore, crossed the muddy Guadalupe. Next morning, in a dense fog, they encountered the Mexican forces on Ezekiel Williams' ranch. Here, the cannon fired a charge of pieces of chain and scraps of metal, scattering the Mexicans in retreat to San Antonio. The Texas Revolution had begun.

Sam made the short ride south the following morning, his horses wading water deeper than their fetlocks in many places. The old-timer had been right, the San Marcos River had flooded the area.

Shortly after dark he had entered a busy Gonzales saloon and now sat at a table enjoying a plate of Mexican food. There were perhaps forty men in the room, and several card games were in progress. Directly behind

Sam, on a low platform built of raw lumber, a scrawny, long-legged man sat at a piano, displaying his limited knowledge of the instrument. Scarcely able to believe his ears, Sam dropped his fork noisily when a man from the audience yelled to the musician, "Hey, Slim, how 'bout sangin' 'at song 'bout Judge Curtin!" In a raspy, nasal voice that was piercing to the ear, Slim began to sing the badly worded lyrics of a song written to a monotonous melody:

"Judge Curtin they say is a dandy
Who makes all the outlaws pay
If you don't do right he'll find you some night
And haul your carcass away . . ."

Slim halted his rendition long enough to inhale the drink someone had just handed him, then continued,

"You renegades better take warning
If the Judge rides into your town
He'll get on your trail and put you in jail
Or six feet under the ground . . ."

Sam listened as the man sang at least a dozen verses, some of them naming men who had fought Sam and lost. Though Curtin disliked both the singer and the song, several men applauded when Slim finished. Standing beside the piano stool and bowing graciously, Slim announced that he would break for a few minutes. Sam invited the man to his table for a drink.

"Where'd you get that song about Judge Curtin?" he asked, when Slim had seated himself.

"Wrote it myself a few months back."

"How come you know so much about the man?"

"Well . . . I really don't know much, just read about him in the newspaper a few times. Why do you ask?"

"Because I'm Judge Curtin," Sam said, keeping his voice down almost to a whisper. Visibly shaken, Slim sat his glass down heavily. Beginning to stutter slightly, he spoke again.

"Well . . . I . . . I ain't never heard of you shootin' nobody for writin' a song. The only people you git after is killers, right?" Sam did not answer, and Slim continued, "I mean . . . I ain't done nothin' wrong; nothin' a-tall."

"No, I suppose not," Sam said. "But I want you to give me a straight answer, Slim. Do you know Sammy Singer or Joe Beam?" Slim answered quickly.

"Joe Beam *is* Sammy Singer. He just uses that Beam name so he can catch more suckers playin' pool." Slim took another drink of his whiskey, then began to shake his head. "I tell you . . . just to think that I wuz up there singin' about the Judge and him settin' right here a-lookin' at me. I tell you—"

"How often does Singer come in here?" Sam interrupted.

"About ever' night. Ain't been in tonight, yet." Sam leaned forward, speaking in low tones.

"My identity is a secret between you and me, Slim. I'm asking you to get back to the piano and do your regular show. You have a good view of the front door; when Singer comes in, I want you to break into the Judge Curtin song again. Will you do that?"

"I shore will," Slim said, finishing off his drink. He had no more than returned to the platform, when someone requested the ballad again. Slim begged off, saying the high notes were hard on his throat; that he would sing the song later in the night after he had warmed up on some songs with less vocal range. He could not sing the song at this time without sending a false signal to the Judge. The thought that the song might be the last one Singer ever heard bothered Slim not in the least, for he did not like the man. Singer had mistreated him on more than one occasion, and only last week had poured a glass of water into the piano when Slim had been singing the very same song.

Sam had been sitting at the table for more than an hour, when Slim suddenly stopped the song he was singing and eased into the now familiar "Ballad of Judge Curtin." Sam craned his neck so he could see around the bar. Singer stood in the center of the room, a few feet inside the door. Clean shaven and neatly dressed, he stood with his feet apart, a Peacemaker on his left hip, tied down with rawhide.

"Shut up, Slim!" he ordered. As Slim stopped singing and the room became quiet, Singer yelled loudly, "They say that so-called Judge is in here! Where is he?"

"I'm right here, Singer," Sam said, stepping out to meet him. "I—"

"I know exactly why you're here, Curtin," Singer said. "I can tell you right now, you ain't taking me nowhere. I can outdraw you on the best day you ever—" Curtin's bullet struck Singer on the chin, ricocheting upward through his mouth and taking off much of his face. Singer had not lived to fire his own weapon; he had been talking while Sam had been shooting.

Curtin had just holstered his gun, when a young man appearing to be in his early twenties bounded through the doorway.

"Who shot Joe?" he shouted. "Whoever done it's gonna answer to me!" An older man, who might have been the young man's father, stepped in front of him, pinning his arms and taking his gun from its holster.

"Let it go, boy, you can't beat him. That's the Judge

standing there and he'll cut you down quicker'n lightning."

Looking as if some of the blood had drained from his face, the young man began to stammer, looking directly at Sam.

"I'm . . . sorry, I . . . I didn't know who you wuz." Nodding curtly, Sam said nothing.

As talk resumed throughout the room, one man asked of another, "Did you see that draw, Caleb?"

"Nope. Singer didn't see it neither."

Two hours later, riding the roan and leading the chestnut, Sam headed east. No way was he going to spend the night in this town; he had already narrowly missed having to fight one of Singer's friends. In his pocket he carried a letter signed by the town marshal and a deputy, stating that one Sammy Singer would kill no more. Supposing that Slim would now be writing some more verses to the song, Sam rode off into the night.

Thirteen

A week passed before Curtin returned to Calvert, for he had spent two days in Waco waiting for a judge to authorize payment of the reward. Now, with the money deposited into his own bank account, he rode through town and headed toward the ranch. He passed very few people that he recognized, for much of the daily activity had moved to Franklin when it became the county seat. The chestnut, looking forward to being at home in his own barn, fought the bit all the way, insisting on carrying Sam to the Hill quickly.

When he dismounted at the shop, his nephew greeted him from the doorway.

"Bad news, Uncle Sam. Mr. Jordon's dead." Handing the reins to Bud, Sam entered the shop.

"What happened to Red, Hamp?"

"Don't know for sure; week ago last Tuesday he just didn't wake up. Bud took him to Dr. Barnes the week before that; Doc said he probably had some kind of blood disease that had spread to his bones. Of course, Doc ain't all that educated; might be able to diagnose a horse with a broke leg, but I wouldn't bet no bunch of money on that. Red told me a few days before he died that he thought he'd about played out his string."

"Damn," Sam said, pouring himself a cup of coffee from the ever-present pot that sat on the back of the stove. "Where did you bury him?"

"Off to the left of the barn, there. Didn't have no idea where you'd want to put him."

"We'll move him up on the hill. He picked out his own spot one day when we were sitting between those two big oaks. Red was sitting on the ground drinking whiskey when he said, 'This sure is a pretty view, I'd like to be buried right where I'm sitting.' "

Sam and Mack Halley buried the coffin between the trees the following day. As he patted the mound of earth into place with the back of his shovel, Mack began to talk.

"You sure had a friend in that man, Sam. I had taken to sitting up at your house, drinking with him every night after my chores were done. He was a mighty lonesome man, and he sure loved to talk. He told me a week before he died that he respected you more than any man he had ever known." Halley took a long drink from the water jug, then continued. "He knew he was dying, and told me so, but I just took it to be whiskey talk." Taking a leather pouch from his pocket, Mack handed it to Sam. "He told me to give you this," he added. "Call me nosey if you want, but I counted it. There's more'n six hundred dollars there." Sam accepted the money, saying nothing.

Lula had taken Jordon's death hard. She had carried

food across the hill to him daily, but her efforts were of no avail.

"I couldn't never get him to eat nothing," she said to Sam. "Far as I know he never took a bite of food the last two weeks he lived. I cooked everything I could think of, but he never touched it."

Later in the afternoon, Sam stood in the corral, checking the hooves of his horses. Bud stood close by, leaning against the top pole. Dropping the chestnut's foot back to the ground, Sam said, "I've got to get Hamp to shoe these horses when he has the time."

"I can do it, Uncle Sam."

"I'm sure you could, but the chestnut's mighty finicky about somebody messing with his feet; we better let Hamp do it."

"I guess Mr. Jordon's black belongs to you now," Bud said. "I know that's the way he would've wanted it." Sam sent the horse trotting across the corral with a slap on the rump, then turned to face Bud.

"I'm not so sure about that," he said. "Red certainly never said anything to me about it. Who's been taking care of the horse?"

"Well, I've been feeding and exercising him; Mr. Jordon couldn't get around no more. He was awful weak there at the last, Uncle Sam. He couldn't even—"

"Sounds to me like it's your horse." Sam smiled.

"You mean it? he's really mine?" Sam nodded, and Bud ran to catch the big gelding.

Sam spent the following week helping the Halleys with the last cutting of hay. They had fenced in a large plot of ground with poles, and worked from morning till night stacking hay into shocks inside the fence. Many cattle milled around the fence, for the weather had turned cold early in the season and the frost had killed off most of their grazing. At times, as many as a hundred head could be seen incessantly pacing back and forth, lowing impatiently for their daily handout.

Two days before Christmas, Sam was in Calvert to buy gifts for the Curtins and the Halley brothers. He had spent two hours in the saloon drinking with his friends, when he decided it was time to do his shopping and go home. As he neared the dry goods store, he spoke casually to a cotton farmer named Matt Henderson, who sat on the seat of a wagon nearby. The farmer had been a member of the jury that had acquitted Lula in the Newton shooting. Sam was about to strike up a conversation, when Henderson's daughter, Mary, appeared, her arms loaded with packages. Doffing his hat, Sam stepped aside quickly, saying, "Good afternoon, Miss Henderson, my name is Sam Curtin; I—"

"I know who you are, Mr. Curtin, but I don't have any time to waste talking to you." Her father helped her into the wagon and drove down the street, leaving Sam standing with his hat in his hand.

One of his longtime acquaintances, who had heard the exchange, said to Sam, "She's a purty one, all right, but I think you'd be wasting your time. I've heard it said that she likes other women, not men."

"Who says?"

"I dunno, people just say that. Sure as hell ain't nobody never seen her with a man." Sam had heard of such a thing before; in fact, it had happened to him once. He had been trying to close the gap with a woman in Dallas, when she straight out told him that she preferred other women.

"How long have you been hearing that, Ollie?" he asked.

"Oh, quite a while. Maybe three or four years." Damn, Sam was thinking, as he stared after the wagon that was fading from view. The girl was such a beauty, too. Unwilling to take Ollie's word for it, he headed for the saloon. By god, he knew someone who could give him an expert opinion. Stopping at the bar, he bought a bottle of whiskey and walked to a table. A saloon girl whom he had known for years stood close by, and he motioned her over. When he had poured a drink for her, he began to ask questions.

"Do you know Mary Henderson, Katie?"

"Sure."

"Do you know anything about her sexual preference?" She began to fidget about in her chair, her eyes glancing toward the ceiling.

"Well?" he said.

"Why don't you just look somewhere else, Sam?"

"Dammit, Katie, I need some answers. Does she like men, or not?"

"I doubt it."

"Then she likes other women, huh?"

"Umm-huh."

"Are you absolutely positive, Katie?"

"Umm-huh."

"How long have you known?"

"Since she was fourteen, fifteen." Sam finished his drink and pushed the bottle toward Katie.

"Have a drink," he said, heading for the door. Then, having second thoughts, he walked back to the table. "Do girls like that ever change?" he asked. "I mean, do they ever turn around?"

"Occasionally, for short periods of time. I doubt that they ever make a complete change in preference, though."

Back on the Hill, Sam laid his packages on the porch for Lula to put under the tree. He put up the buggy and stabled the horse, then walked up the hill to his house. He soon had a roaring fire going in the fireplace, for the evening was very cold. He had eaten his supper in town, and now sat by the fire drinking coffee and thinking of Red Jordon. He missed the man terribly, and wondered if the outcome would have been any different if he himself had been home. He would have carried Jordon to a good doctor in Dallas. Would that have bought Red any time? Sam would never know. He wondered what Jordon would have thought about Mary Henderson. "Don't surprise me a damn bit," he could almost hear Red saying, "I've seen it all in my time." Sam had been surprised when Hamp told him that Red was sixty-seven years old. Sam had never asked the man's age, but had always considered him to be at least a dozen years younger. He had moved about like a young man, and only in the past few months had he slowed down noticeably. Joshua Jordon had been a man for all seasons, and one Sam would remember respectfully.

Throughout the year, Sam had occasionally spent some time thinking about the kid named Rick in Fort Griffin, and he wondered if the boy was being fed and sheltered properly. Now that the Flat was dying, would anyone be concerned about the young man's welfare? The answer was probably no, he decided, as he stoked the fire. Shortly before bedtime he walked outside to relieve himself. The ground was frozen, and the night was getting colder by the minute with the wind whistling through the trees and down the hillside. Almost cold enough to freeze piss in midair, he thought. He began to wonder if Rick had a warm place to sleep tonight. By god, I'll go out there next week and see, he decided. He had three beds inside the house with nobody in them.

He rode into Fort Griffin on New Year's Eve. He had taken the train as far as Weatherford, then traveled west on horseback. He could see at a glance that the Flat was becoming a ghost town. No more ricks of drying buffalo hides; no more bustling activity along the street. Most of the businesses had closed and boarded up their windows. The gamblers, prostitutes and other assorted characters of ill repute had long since departed for greener pastures. Looking down the street, he could see only one wagon and two saddle horses. All were tied in front of what appeared to be the last remaining saloon. He rode there now, and stepped inside.

Two men, appearing to be cattlemen, sat at the far end of the bar, and Sam took the stool nearest the door. Only three tables remained standing, the rest stacked on top of each other waiting to be hauled off. The bartender offered a big smile, and Sam ordered a beer. The man had no beer.

"Ain't got nothing but bad whiskey," the barkeep said, "and I ain't got much of that left. Soon as I can sell what I've got on hand I'll be doing like ever'body else: gittin' the hell outta here." Sam smiled, and nodded, indicating that he had been known to drink bad whiskey. After one sip, he decided that the bartender had described the brown liquid accurately.

The cattlemen soon left the building and Sam ordered another drink, motioning the bartender to pour one for himself. The man served himself a stiff one, and pulled his stool to the end of the bar, opposite Sam.

"I remember you from two or three years ago," the bartender said, "remember the show you put on the night you wuz tryin' to convince Barney that your name wuz Smith. I hear talk now that your name ain't Smith, and that you've been a busy man since then."

"Maybe so," Sam said, then changed the subject. "Do you remember the kid named Rick, who used to work at the livery?"

"Oh, yeah. Ben Hatch took 'im to Albany last summer, said he was gonna use 'im at the livery down there. Hatch has got a lot of business, and with the railroad comin' through town, he's expanding into other things. That man's gonna git well." Sam was already on his feet.

"You think Rick is working at Hatch's place, then?"

"Far as I know. You can't miss Ben's layout, you'll run right into it as you ride into town."

Sam left the saloon and headed south. The town was a distance of less than twenty miles. After passing the fort, he switched his saddle from the chestnut to the roan, and three hours later sat on a hill overlooking the busy town of Albany. Since becoming the seat of Shackelford County, the town's economical fortunes had increased steadily. The railroad was already building west from Weatherford, and Albany was on its chosen route. The town fathers were quick to boast that Albany was about to become "the richest town west of Fort Worth." Sam could see Hatch's stable at the edge of town, and he rode to the hitching rail.

When he opened the office door, the first thing he saw was Rick. The boy was on his knees with a bucket of soapy water, scrubbing the rough plank floor with a wire brush. When Rick raised his head and smiled in recognition, Sam could see that he had a black eye, and his right cheek was swollen.

"Ain't seen you for a long, long time," Rick said, laughing childishly.

"Yes, it has been a long time, Rick." Sam handed the youth a plug of chewing tobacco.

"Don't know that I ought to chew none of this; that's why I'm having to scrub the floor. Mr. Hatch says some of my spit got on it."

"Who's been hitting you in the face, Rick?"

"Ain't supposed to tell."

"I'm your friend, Rick. You can tell me."

"It's my own fault. I forgot to close the gate and one of Mr. Hatch's best horses got out. Took us all day to catch him."

"He punched you in the face for that?"

"Not at first. He was gonna whup me again with that razor strop, but I run. I sure won't run from him no more; I'd rather be stropped than punched on." Sam sat on an upended wooden crate for several minutes explaining to the youngster that he did not have to live this way, that there was a home waiting for him at Curtin Hill.

"You can just do whatever you want around the ranch, Rick. You'll have your own horse and saddle, and plenty of good food and chewing tobacco."

"Bet you got something to eat besides beans, too."

"Sure do."

"Bet I'd have my own room, and my own bed."

"That's right, Rick." Using his foot, the kid pushed the bucket aside so hard that much of the water spilled on the floor. Throwing the brush into a corner, he took a pair of pants and a shirt from a box underneath the counter and rolled them into a ball.

"This is all the clothes I got, lost my coat somewhere last summer."

"Get on the chestnut, Rick; you'll have to ride bareback." Sam stopped at a dry goods store and took the kid inside. A matronly saleslady was at his side quickly.

"Fit Rick with a good coat and warm gloves," he said. "Give him a good hat, too." When they were back outside, Sam asked the boy which saloon Hatch did his drinking in. Rick pointed the way, and they led the horses down the street, tying them at the hitching rail.

"Come on inside with me, Rick," Sam said. Reluctantly, Rick followed. Stepping inside the doorway, Sam shouted, "I'm looking for Ben Hatch!" A dark-haired, overweight man of medium height stepped away from the bar.

"I'm Hatch, who are you?" Sam began to walk toward him.

"My name is Sam Curtin. Some folks call me the Judge." The room grew quiet instantly, for every man present had heard the name before.

"What do you want?" Hatch asked. Sam took one final step and hit Hatch in the jaw with his right hand, sending the man sprawling. Hatch raised his head, but made no attempt to get up, for Curtin was standing over him.

"I just wanted to make sure you wake up with a sore cheek in the morning, you sonofabitch. Like this kid you've been beating on. You'd better listen good, goddam you, 'cause I won't say this but one time: I'm taking Rick with me, and if you ever come near him again you're a dead ass." He kicked the man in his other cheek, adding, "On second thought, let's make that two sore cheeks." Motioning to Rick, he then left the building.

They rode east, following the railroad right-of-way, which had already been surveyed, cleared and staked. When they reached Weatherford, they boarded a train to Dallas. Another train would then carry them to Calvert.

Curtin had to caution Rick several times, for the kid was talkative to a fault. He was quick to point out to fellow passengers that the man seated beside him was the Judge. When they changed trains in Dallas, Sam seated Rick next to the window and took the aisle seat himself, thus making it harder for Rick to talk to people. Sam thought so, at least.

A fashionably dressed woman who appeared to be

about Sam's own age sat directly across from him, reading some type of published material. Occasionally, she would cast her eyes in his general direction, a faint smile on her face. With deep blue eyes and a pale complexion that Sam thought had not seen enough sunlight, she had raven-black hair rolled into a bun and pinned at the back of her head. A beautiful woman indeed, he thought. While Sam was searching his brain for a good way to start a conversation, Rick solved the problem.

"This here's the Judge," he said to the lady, pointing to Sam. "He ain't married, neither."

"Oh?" she said. Then, apparently sensing Rick's mental imbalance, she directed a question to him.

"Are you, yourself, married?"

"Lord, no," Rick said, hiding his face behind his callused hands. She then spoke to Sam, the smile remaining constant.

"You are a judge, then? Which is your district?"

"I'm not a judge, ma'am, that's just a nickname I've picked up along the way. My name is Sam Curtin; I'm a rancher at Calvert."

"Sounds like a wonderful way to live," she said. "My name is Anita Keeling. I teach school at Hillsboro." Their conversation flowed for many miles, with the lady speaking freely of her limited activities in Hillsboro, and of her original reason for being there. She moved to the town from Tennessee three years ago, intent upon marrying a surveyor who worked for the railroad. Before the wedding could take place, the young man had been killed by Indians in West Texas. Hill County had then hired her to teach school.

During the conversation, Sam asked if he might visit her sometime. Just before departing the train, she said yes to his offer of a buggy ride in the spring. As they said their good-byes, he knew that he would write letters to her, for he would take no chances that she might forget him before warm weather arrived.

A few hours later, Sam and Rick halted their horses at Hamp's shop. All of the Curtins knew that Sam had been to Fort Griffin, and why. Hamp and Bud now welcomed Rick to the Hill.

"Lu's been over at your house all day," Hamp said. "She must be doing something awful important. Me and Bud had to fix our own dinner."

"I guess I'll find out shortly," Sam said, heading for the barn. As they walked up the hill to his house, Sam told Rick, "You'll be living over here with me." Pointing to his brother's home, he added, "Hamp and his family live over there; you'll probably be eating some of your meals with them. Just don't try chewing your tobacco in the house; Hamp can't even get away with that."

Lula stood in Sam's front yard, a shovel and posthole digger lying at her side. She had transplanted a line of rosebushes that completely encircled the yard. After the introduction, she hugged Rick and welcomed him to the ranch.

"The roses are gonna look mighty nice in the spring," Sam said. "Don't guess I ever would have thought of it."

"A man ain't gonna plant nothing pretty," she said. "I don't suppose anybody expects 'em to. I keep hoping you'll bring a woman up the hill one of these days; I guess she'd appreciate the roses. You put some stakes beside 'em now, so they'll have something to run on."

"I will, Lu," he said, smacking his lips and blowing her a kiss, "and I do appreciate pretty things."

She picked up her tools and headed across the hill, saying, "You two must be half-starved. Come over to the house about sundown and I'll have a feed on."

Fourteen

In late February, Sam was riding home from Calvert when he heard gunfire. He knew the sound was coming from the Hill, and kicked his horse into a hard run. As he splashed across the creek, he could see Bud standing behind the shop, the forty-four buckled around his hip once again. The same wooden blocks he had used earlier were set up as targets. As Sam loosed his horse into the corral and walked over, Bud stood wiping his glasses.

"You doing any better, Bud?"

"Naw, I guess not. I did hit one of 'em, though." Sam had dreaded the day that the youngster might pick up the gun again, and had encouraged him to concentrate on being a saddlemaker, not a gunman. Sam suspected that some men, such as himself, were simply born with good hand-eye coordination, while others were gifted only with one or the other. Or in some cases, neither.

Though Bud was extremely quick with his hands, Sam had long ago decided that his nephew did not have the eye.

"Well, don't mind me," Sam said, "go on about your business." Bud whipped the gun from its holster and began to fire in one continuous motion. Fanning the hammer with his left hand, Bud got off four shots as rapidly as Sam had ever seen it done, but failed to hit any of the targets. Sam saw dirt kick up several feet from one of the blocks. Smiling, he walked into the shop.

"Bud's got that gun out again, Hamp."

"I can hear it. That seems to be what he wants to do and there ain't much I can do about it; he's grown, now. Guess there ain't much you can say about it either, you were already getting paid for trick shooting when you were younger'n him."

"Right you are, brother." Sam changed the subject. "Do you know where Rick is?"

"He's out working with the Halleys; moved his stuff into the bunkhouse this morning. I guess that makes him feel more like a man, like he's one of the regular hands. He sits a horse pretty well, and the twins seemed to be all for him moving down there."

"Wait till he keeps them up all night talking."

"Think that was part of the deal. Mack told him he'd have to shut up at nine o'clock every night. Them keeping him busy will be a big help to me; every time he comes in here he handles everything in sight, and I have to go behind him putting things back where they belong."

"I'll talk to him about that, Hamp." Sam headed for the door, saying over his shoulder, "If Rick don't start keeping his hands in his pockets when he comes around, I'll make him stay out of here." He climbed the hill to his house, wanting to be alone when he read the letter from Anita Keeling that was now in his pocket. He had heard from her a month ago in answer to a letter he had written. He had answered quickly, and had picked up her second letter in town this morning.

Miss Keeling wrote in such a beautiful, easy-to-read hand that Sam became self-conscious about his own scribbling. She apparently had no problem reading his writing, for she answered all of his questions. She wrote that she would have no leisure time until after the current school term expired, for in addition to her regular duties, she had volunteered to teach adult reading classes three nights a week. She already had ten students: five men and their wives. She wrote that she was looking forward to Sam's visit in the spring, and signed the letter "Affectionately yours." He folded the letter and put it in the shoebox under his bed. Affectionately yours, he repeated to himself. The words had a nice ring.

The following morning Sam was standing on his porch when he heard Hamp calling to him from the doorway of the shop, and motioning for him to come down. At the shop, Hamp handed him a letter he had received in today's mail. The letter was from a government agency inquiring as to how soon Hamp could turn out fifty saddles for the army.

"Can you handle an order that big?" Sam asked.

"Sure. I can build a saddle a day like the army rides on, but I sure as hell can't make one for twenty-five dollars that I'd put the Curtin name on. Besides, I've got seven customers waiting on custom-made saddles."

"Well, the letter says that twenty-five is all they'll pay."

"This business ain't mine, Sam," Hamp said, "it's ours. You built the shop and you bought the tools. I'm dumping the decision right in your lap. Bud could build the saddles if he'd get his mind off that gun for a couple months. If I cut him a simple, one-size-fits-all pattern, he could turn them out about as quick as I could."

"You want me to talk to him?"

"Yeah. We can make the saddles for less than twenty dollars apiece, and I sure don't know any place else that he can earn five or six dollars a day. I'd bet there ain't more'n a few men in this county who make that kind of money. Won't be no transportation problem; the army will pick them up right here at the shop."

"I'll talk to Bud, Hamp."

"You do that. The only tooling necessary will be the U.S. Army identification; nothing fancy. I'll figure out some other name for them; I sure as hell ain't gonna put my name on an army saddle."

Hamp was the most meticulous man Sam had ever known, extremely precise about even the smallest and most trivial detail. His work was rapidly becoming known as the very best that could be had, at any price, and Sam could well understand his brother being careful about what he put his name on. Before Sam left the shop, he learned that Hamp was currently building a saddle for a wealthy cotton farmer who lived at Bryan. The price to be paid was four hundred dollars, and the man had left a two-hundred-dollar deposit. Four hundred dollars! For one saddle? Sam left the shop shaking his head. Hamp sure don't need me, he was thinking. Knowing that some high-ranking army officer might have seen one of Hamp's saddles and thought the army would get the same thing for twenty-five dollars, Sam had mentioned that fact to Hamp.

"I know that," Hamp had said, "but I'll just make one saddle and let them approve it before I start cutting up all my leather. Anyway, I want a written contract." Sam called for Bud to meet him at the barn, and after a long discussion, Bud seemed eager. He did, however, have one problem.

"Pa orders me around so much that sometimes I don't know what to do. Talks to me like I was a little kid. I get nervous trying to work with him looking over my shoulder."

"I can understand that, Bud. Give me two days, and I'll fix it. I'll partition off one end of the shop and cut a door on the far side. You'll have your own working area, and you can come and go without disturbing Hamp. If you knuckle down and handle this right, you might end up getting your own contracts with the army. They use an awful lot of leatherwork and none of it is complicated."

"Pa's making all kinds of money, Uncle Sam."

"I believe you're right, and so will you when you have his experience. Nobody says you have to make saddles for the army all your life."

"Quick as Pa gets the first one approved I'll start copying it. If he'll leave me alone I can work faster than he can."

"That's the spirit, and I think he'll leave you alone. Bank your money, Bud, there are some more hills behind this one that could be bought." Bud smiled, heading for the shop.

An army lieutenant picked up the first saddle the following week, and on the first day of April, Hamp received a contract for the remaining forty-nine, along with orders and specifications for twenty bridles and harnesses. Bud was in business.

A few days later, Bud stopped working two hours before sundown and hurried up the hill to the house. After spending a few minutes in his room, he spoke to Lula, who was busy preparing the evening meal.

"Momma, you know where my gun is?"

"I sure do," she answered, "your Uncle Sam's got it."

Oh, hell, Bud thought, then skedaddled back down the hill. If he worked fast he could finish another bridle before dark.

In early May, Sam stood on the platform at the train depot in Calvert. Dressed in a new spring suit he had bought only yesterday, along with new hat and boots, he had been asked by some of his friends where he was preaching today. He laughed off their remarks good-naturedly. As he passed two men standing in front of the hotel, one said to the other, "Cain't hardly believe what I see. I shore ain't never seen Sam without that Peacemaker on his hip."

"He ain't that dumb," said the other. "You can bet your butt that he's got some kind of protection on him." The second man was correct. For a man with Sam's reputation and potential enemies to walk around unarmed would have been pure folly. Riding easy inside his coat, tucked behind his waistband, was Bud's forty-four. Saying good-bye to a man he had known since childhood, he exchanged greetings with the conductor and boarded the train. Today, he was headed for Hillsboro.

Being six hundred thirty-four feet above sea level, Hillsboro was only three hundred feet higher than Calvert, but the incline was neither constant nor gradual. At times, the steep grades pulled the lazy train down to little more than a walking pace. It was at such times that Sam usually walked to the rear platform, to avoid the feeling that the passenger car was sitting still. He did not enjoy train rides. In that regard he agreed with his chestnut, who fought every time he was being loaded into a stock car. Perhaps the horse knew that his own back offered a much smoother ride than any train.

When he arrived in Hillsboro he made arrangements to rent a horse and buggy in the morning, then registered at the hotel, for the day was almost gone. He slept soundly on the comfortable bed, and the sun was already shining through the window when he awoke. A beautiful day for a picnic with a beautiful woman. After shaving and bathing, he ate a hearty breakfast at the restaurant, then walked to the livery stable. Waiting for him in front of the establishment was what appeared to be a new buggy, to which was hitched a dapple-gray mare.

"Don't know for sure how long I'll need it," Sam said to the liveryman, "probably just today."

"Keep it as long as you want," the man said, untying the mare from the hitching rail, "that's how I make a living. Just don't forget to feed the mare if you keep her overnight."

"I wouldn't dream of it." Sam turned the buggy around and headed through the town. Miss Keeling had given him clear directions to her small cottage that was owned by the county. He passed the schoolhouse and turned right at the corner, then he could see her standing in the yard. She had been at the gate for quite some time, eagerly awaiting his arrival. She had not tried to hide her anticipation, as had some women in his past. All of the other women he had known would have stayed inside the house and made him knock several times before answering the door. Anita was far too intelligent to play such feminine games with a man. As she opened the gate he jumped to the ground, taking both her hands in his own. Squeezing his hands, she was first to speak.

"It's so good to see you, Sam. I've been looking forward to this all winter." He believed her, because her eyes were dancing with joy, not unlike those of a little girl.

"I wouldn't have missed it for the world," he said. "Any man I know would cross all of Texas to be with you."

She brought a picnic basket from the house and Sam helped her into the buggy. Climbing up beside her, he clucked to the mare and said jokingly, "School's out, teacher, it's time for you to see the world." He turned the buggy west, and two hours later they spread their blanket on the east bank of the Brazos River.

"This is the first time I've seen this part of the Brazos," she said when they had seated themselves on the blanket, "it looks like a long train coming around that curve up yonder." Sam said nothing; the sound of her voice almost had him hypnotized. He was happier right now than he had been in a long time. He had finally met a beautiful, untarnished woman he could respect, and knew that this would not be his last trip to Hill County.

They talked of many things for the next two hours, then she surprised him. Over a mouthful of chicken, she asked, "Why do people call you the Judge?"

Oh, shit! was his first thought. Though he knew that his reputation had spread far and wide, he was reluctant to talk about it. He stared at the river for a while, then said, "It's a long story." She refused to accept that answer.

"I have plenty of time," she told him. "It's as you said: school is out." Sam picked up a flat stone and attempted to skate it across the water, the way he had done many times as a young boy. The stone sank instantly. He felt as though his heart was about to do likewise. Nevertheless, this woman must be told the truth. He would pull no punches.

"Like I said, Anita, it's a long story. I really am a rancher, but I've also been involved in some gunfights. As you can see, I managed to win them all."

"I'm listening," she said.

Never before had Sam related his life story to another person. He began by speaking of the day the small fishing boat had capsized in rough water in the Mississippi Sound, drowning both his parents. Leaving out nothing of consequence, he talked for a long time. He told of the days when he had practiced with a six-shooter as a teenager, sometimes all day. About breaking horses for the army, and his days as a prize-fighter. He spoke of his involvement with the traveling trade shows, and the hucksters posing as doctors who peddled phony cure-alls. There had been nothing phony about his own part in the shows, for he had merely performed seemingly impossible tricks with his six-shooter. Still, he had always felt uncomfortable with the overall game of deceit.

He told her of Jack Pelt, the first man he ever shot. Of all the wanted men he had tracked down, and what he had done with the reward money. Though she did not say so, she seemed to enjoy some of the stories about Red Jordon. He finished his narration by telling her about Anna Newton, and that Lula had shot and killed the woman. Anita had listened quietly, and though at one time her eyes seemed to be moist, she remained attentive.

"You've heard the story firsthand," he added. "If you don't want me around, that train runs in both directions."

"Forget the train," she said. "Folks don't call you a bounty hunter, Sam. They say you are a protector of the people." She then puckered her lips prettily, adding, "I don't suppose I'd have to worry about someone beating me up as long as I'm with you. One of the men in my reading class told me that you were a salty son of a bitch. Those are his words, not mine." Sam said nothing for a while, then reached for her hand.

"Should I pay for another night's rent at the hotel, then?"

"Please do," she said, squeezing his hand. Just before dark he returned the rig to the liveryman, saying he would not need it any longer.

In the morning, he walked to Anita's cottage and spent the early part of the day sitting on her porch. She talked of her girlhood back in Tennessee, and what it had been like growing up as the only child of a minister who had insisted that she get a college education. Majoring in English and history, she had never intended to become a teacher. After the death of the young surveyor to whom she was engaged to be married, she had applied for the schoolteaching job and had been readily accepted, for she was the best-educated person in Hillsboro.

The county had treated her well, paying a good wage in addition to furnishing the neat cottage in which she lived. A man in her reading class had offered her a horse and buggy, for which she had no use. She had only to walk around the corner to her work. Though many had tried to give her money, she accepted no pay for the adult classes.

"To see a man who could not even read last year standing on the corner waiting to buy a newspaper is all the pay I need, Sam." Damn! he thought, what a woman. Sure hope she likes me. Hope she loves me. Dozens of people had passed in front of the cottage, some afoot, some on horseback. Some of them waved hello, others just stared.

"Do you always have this much traffic on your street?"

"Lord, no. Word travels fast in this town; they're all coming by to get a good look at the Judge." Laughingly, she added, "Come on into the house and I'll pull the curtain."

"You're not afraid people will talk?"

"I'll use a phrase you men seem to think fits almost any occasion: I don't give a damn."

When he kissed her good-bye in the afternoon, she clung to him tightly, and her kiss was wet.

"I'll be coming back soon," he said, as he held her in his arms.

"I'll be waiting, Sam, and I will have no suitor until you return." He kissed her again, then hurried down the street to the depot.

It was long after dark when he arrived in Calvert. He found that Arkansas was nowhere around the livery stable, and walked to the saloon. The liveryman was sitting in a chair beside a poker table, where a game was in progress.

"I need to get my horse, Arkansas," Sam said.

"Help yourself, the lantern's hangin' on a peg just inside the door; you can pay me next time you see me.

I'm waitin' on a seat to come open in this game, don't want to lose my place in line."

"All right, just don't lose your stable." Sam saddled the roan, and half an hour later he was home. From Hamp's yard, he called to the house without dismounting. The hounds never barked unless a man was a total stranger. Bud opened the door and walked onto the porch.

"I'm home," Sam said. "Just wanted you to know it's me moving around out here." Without speaking, Bud walked back inside the house and closed the door. Sam sat his horse quietly for some time, then yelled, "Bud, come back out here!" Bud opened the door again and walked down the steps to the horse.

"Here," Sam said, handing the kid's pistol to him.

"Thanks, Uncle Sam." Bud pocketed the weapon, then asked, "Did you have a good trip?"

"Very good," Sam said, heading for the barn.

Sleep was slow to come when he climbed into bed. He had enjoyed his visit to Hillsboro immensely, for Miss Keeling was by far the most interesting woman he had ever known. And she was beautiful; almost as beautiful as Anna Newton had been. He supposed that every unattached man in Hill County was after her, and had been pleased when she said she would see no one else.

His immediate concern was closer to home. Rick was wearing out three horses a day keeping the cattle out of the hay meadow. Although the kid enjoyed the work, and was successful during the daylight hours, the cattle helped themselves at night, eating and trampling the growing hay. The hay would grow out again, but the cattle must be kept out of the meadow day and night.

Last week he had looked at a thing that was new to

him known as barbed wire. The wire was marketed under the name "Baker's Perfect." It had a two-point barb made of flat wire that made one loop around one of the two-strand wires. And the barbs were very sharp. Running his hand along the wire, Sam was quickly convinced that it would discourage trespassing livestock. Tomorrow morning, he would send Mack to Dallas to pick up barbed wire, then mount a horse himself to help Rick with the cattle. When Mack returned, all hands would go to work fencing the hay meadow.

Fifteen

It was now the middle of July, and though the weather was almost unbearably hot, things were looking exceptionally good at Curtin Hill. Hamp had as much business as he could handle at the shop, and Bud had already received two hefty paychecks from the army. The spring calf crop had been excellent, and several mares had produced healthy foals. Sam sat on his porch reading a newspaper, occasionally glancing to the valley below. Heat waves danced crazily between himself and the cattle that were lying lazily throughout the valley floor, taking advantage of whatever shade they could find.

Most of the newspaper's front page had been devoted to the story of a shooting out in New Mexico Territory. On the fourteenth of July, William "Billy the Kid" Bonney had been gunned down by Sheriff Pat Garrett. The article, which vainly attempted to depict both men as heroes, stated that Garrett had outdrawn the young outlaw and killed him with a single shot. Doubting the accuracy of the story, Sam laid the paper aside, already feeling sympathetic toward Garrett. No doubt, gunfighters from all over would be hunting the man, eager to gain a reputation by shooting the man who shot Billy the Kid.

Sam had made two return visits to Hillsboro, and just last week had brought Miss Keeling to Curtin Hill, where she spent two days with Lula. She had endeared herself to all the Curtins, and had eagerly accepted Sam's proposal of marriage in the fall. Though she had been slow to let him know it, she had fallen in love with him on his first visit. He had been totally honest with her, and the way he laid out his life story like an open book had done the trick. The prospect of living on the Hill as Mrs. Sam Curtin seemed like a fairy tale come true, and she had already served notice to Hill County that she would not be teaching when the fall term began. Lula had been overjoyed at Sam's decision and had not been reluctant to say so.

"I know you're doing the best thing, Sam," she said. "Deep down, that young woman's just plain old country folks like us, just went off and got a lot of book learning; ain't nothing wrong with that. She's pretty, too; the two of you are gonna have some mighty handsome children."

"Maybe, if they take after their mother."

"Aw, Sam, you're the best-looking man in the county."

Now, sitting on the porch fanning himself with the folded newspaper, Sam was watching his nephew race up and down the road astride the gelding he had inherited from Red Jordon.

Bud had named the animal Charley Horse, and

treated him like one of the family, always measuring his feed carefully and exercising him daily. Charley Horse was in excellent physical condition. Last week Sam had used him for a trip to town and had come home knowing that Charley was the strongest horse he had ever ridden. Upon his return from Calvert he had said, "No use for you to go looking for a better horse, Bud. You won't find one."

"I know. Mr. Jordon said he could run all day. Said he was the toughest horse he had ever seen, and I know he saw plenty."

"Yep, he saw plenty," Sam said. Bud changed the subject.

"You gonna marry Miss Keeling?"

"Yes."

"She sure is nice," Bud said, continuing to work on the harness he was making. He punched a couple more holes in the leather, then asked, "Has she got a sister?"

"I'm afraid not," Sam said, chuckling, "she's an only child." Bud frowned, then went back to work.

Late in the afternoon, Sam decided to ride into Calvert. Les, owner of the saloon, was a good friend, and Sam would have a few drinks and talk with him a while. During the middle of the week business was slow, and Les would probably appreciate the company. Only three horses were present at the hitching rail. Sam tied the roan and stepped inside, taking a stool at the corner of the bar. It had long been his habit to sit where he could see everyone around him. With the wall on his left, and spinning his stool slightly to the right, he had a good view of the entire room. He exchanged greetings with Les and ordered a beer. Les served, then dragged his own stool down the bar opposite Sam.

"Well, I can see by the looks of you that Trent Sampson ain't found you yet," Les said.

"Who's he?"

"He's a brawler, Sam, and he's good at it. Says he's gonna whip your ass when he sees you."

"What's his problem?"

"He just likes to fight, laughs all the time he's doing it. Says he's tired of hearing people talk about how tough you are. When I told him he'd be better off to leave you alone he just laughed, and said, 'We'll see.' "

"A man who likes to fight has got something wrong with his mind," Sam said, "either that or he just ain't been hit hard enough." The three-handed poker game that had been in progress when Sam arrived had now broken up, with the participants arguing over a moot point. One man had seemingly settled the argument by buying drinks for the other two, then all three had departed the building.

Night soon settled in and Les had lighted all the lamps. Sam was sipping his third beer when three men walked through the doorway. Les identified the tallest one as Trent Sampson. He was a narrow-shouldered man who was an inch taller and perhaps a few pounds heavier than Sam, with close-cropped hair that looked as if it belonged on a brush. He wore no hat, and was apparently unarmed. The three men walked to the far end of the bar and ordered whiskey. Sam continued to sip his beer, ignoring the newcomers. After putting away two drinks, Sampson began to speak loudly, looking directly at Sam.

"Hey! Ain't you the feller they call the Judge? The so-called Judge that ain't got guts enough to fight a real man without using a six-gun?" Sam had known dozens of men like Sampson, and knew that he would be wasting his breath if he tried to reason with the man. He yelled back to Sampson, who had moved away from his stool.

"No, I'm not that Judge! I'm the Judge with guts enough to put your ass in line in short order." Sam handed his gun to Les, then continued to speak to Sampson. "Soon as I finish my beer I'll meet you in the middle of the floor, there." He took a small sip of the beer, wanting to give Sampson plenty of time to stew. The man walked to the center of the room and stood waiting.

"Come on," he said, "let's get on with it."

"I never saw a man in such a hurry to get his ass kicked," Sam said, mockingly. "I'll be there when I finish my beer; don't want it to get hot while I'm fighting."

"I'll buy you another beer," Sampson answered, laughing. "I'll buy you anything you want after I'm through mauling you."

"Oh, all right," Sam said, laying his hat on the bar and walking out to meet his antagonist. He struck Sampson's face with three quick jabs and the fight was on. Sam scored well with a fast flurry of punches that wiped the smile off the brawler's face, but he kept coming eagerly, hitting Sam with a hard right that cut his cheek and brought blood. Damn, Sam thought, I can't let that happen again; this fellow's got punching power. During the next few seconds both men scored with hard punches. Sam's lip was cut and his right eye swollen, but he continued to keep a string of viperish left jabs in his opponent's face, cutting it to pieces. Sampson's swarthy face was covered with blood. Raw, red gashes gaped above both his eyes. His lips were cut and bleeding freely, and his mouth was puffed out of shape. Sam continued to dance around him, searching for the opening that might end the fight. He landed two quick punches to the throat, then scored with a left hook to the jaw that sent Sampson to his knees. He was up quickly and kept coming doggedly, but the force had gone out of his punches. He was floundering and groggy.

Curtin, confident but cautious, moved in for the kill. He staggered Sampson with right-hand smashes to the heart and jabbed him incessantly, making his head bob back and forth as if it were on springs. Sam continued to land an occasional right hand as he danced away from Sampson's harmless blows. Worried and desperate, the brawler attempted to overpower Sam, and it cost him dearly. Stepping in to meet Sampson's mad rush, Sam landed the hardest punch of the fight. A right hand flush on the jaw sent Sampson down—and out! The fight was over.

"By god I guess you handled that all right," Les said, as Sam walked back to the bar. "Want another beer?"

"Give me a bottle of whiskey to carry with me," Sam said. Then pointing to the unconscious man, he added, "Charge it to Mr. Sampson, he said he'd buy me anything I wanted."

When he looked into the mirror next morning, Sam decided to have breakfast with Lula and get his tongue-lashing over with. His cheek was swollen badly, and his right eye had already turned black.

"I reckon you've been off fighting again," Lula said, as Sam seated himself at the breakfast table. "Seems like a sorry way for a man to act who's thinking about starting a family. Seems like—"

"Don't ride him, Lu," Hamp interrupted. "There comes a time when a man has to stand his ground." Turning to Sam, he asked in a soft voice, "Did you get him?"

"It took a while, but he finally got sleepy." Hamp nodded and began to sop his gravy with a biscuit.

When Sam returned to his own house, Mack Halley was sitting on the doorstep.

"There's a fellow down at the bunkhouse I'd like for you to meet," he said.

"Yeah?"

"Showed up right after you left for town yesterday. I told him to stay around till I talked to you. Truth is, he could help me and Jack an awful lot, and he's looking for work."

"What does he do?"

"Says he'll do anything that needs doing, but the main thing I wanted you to do is watch him work cattle. He rides a horse like a damn Comanche, and he beats all I've ever seen with a rope. He can rope a steer on any leg you name and any jump you call, and he can do it at a full gallop."

Sam walked to the bunkhouse and was soon shaking hands with Jeff Kirby, who had recently come to Texas from Arizona Territory. He was a man of medium height with thick chest and muscular arms, and Sam guessed him to be close to forty years old. His leathery face showed the usual signs of wear associated with men who spent most of their time in the sun and wind. Above his wrinkled brow, his dark hair was beginning to sprinkle with gray, giving his face a handsome, well-seasoned look. His green eyes held a youthful sparkle of intelligence, and Sam liked what he saw.

"You want him to saddle a horse and show you what he can do?" Mack asked.

"That won't be necessary," Sam said. "Sign him up."

Kirby walked forward with his right hand extended, saying, "I've been turned down a lot lately, and I certainly appreciate the job, Mr. Curtin."

"The name is Sam," he said, walking through the doorway.

He drank half a pot of coffee, then taking a hoe and shovel walked farther up the hill to clean out a spring that was clogged with leaves and other matter. Even as he worked, he could not rid himself of the thought that there was more to Jeff Kirby than met the eye. The man carried himself in a certain confident manner that suggested he knew how to do something other than rope cattle. Tonight, he would talk further with Kirby.

Shortly after dark, Kirby readily accepted Sam's invitation for a drink, and the two sat on his porch drinking whiskey and water. After an hour's conversation Sam began to press Kirby with hard questions. The man opened up right away.

"Of course I knew who you were before I came here," he said, "everybody who reads the papers does. But that's not how I first learned about you. Red Jordon told me about you and this ranch when he was living down on the border. I rode with him off an on a few years back. I probably would have been with him when he died, except that sometimes he took spells when he simply didn't want me around, and told me so.

"I was born in Virginia, in the same hills Red came from. He left there before I was born, but I've learned from at least a dozen sources that my mother worshipped the man. Half the people in Virginia Gap have told me that the two were almost constant companions less than a year before I was born. You see, Sam, I have every reason to believe that Joshua Jordon was my father."

"Well, I'll be damned!" Sam said, passing the bottle to Kirby. They talked till late in the night, with Sam mentioning the day Red had saved his life when Sam was pinned down behind the water trough.

"Did you ever tell Red that you thought you were his son?"

"Oh, yes. I believe that he knew he was my father. One night when he was drunk he introduced me to some folks as his son, then when I called him Pa next morning he told me to call him Red; said he was not my father."

"When were you born, Jeff?"

"December, 1851." Sam sat thinking. It all tied together very neatly, for Jordan had definitely told Sam that he had come west in '51. Jeff appeared to be several years older than he was claiming, but it could be that he had just ridden some tough roads. Sam offered him the last drink in the bottle, then spoke.

"It sounds to me like he was your pa, all right. I'll show you where we buried him in the morning. I already put up a headstone, but you might want to change it." Jeff left for the bunkhouse, and Sam went to bed. He lay awake for a long time thinking about the current situation. Jeff said that he had been raised by his maternal grandfather, whose name was Kirby. His mother had died when he was six years old, after accidentally falling onto a pitchfork that punctured some vital organs. Jeff had considered himself a man by the age of sixteen, and, convinced that Red Jordon was his father, had left home in search of the man. Jordon was not a hard man to trace, for he talked with people wherever he went. After a few months in the saddle Jeff had found him on the Platte River, where he had a trapline. The two had spent a hard winter running the traps and living in a small dugout. In early February, a rainstorm had ruined the last of their matches, and they had to take turns running the traps. One man had to remain near the dugout at all times to keep the fire going, for without it they could not survive. In the spring Red sold the furs and split the money with Jeff, then said good-bye. Two years passed before Jeff saw him again. Sam went to sleep thinking of the seemingly uncomplicated Red

Jordon. He had indeed been a curious and complicated man.

As he made his coffee next morning, Sam could see through the kitchen window that Jeff was standing on the hill beside his father's grave. One of the Halleys had obviously told him where to find it. Half an hour later Jeff walked down to the porch where Sam was sitting and accepted the cup of coffee he was offered. His face held an expression of pain and grief.

"Nothing wrong with Pa's headstone," he said, "and I appreciate you putting it up."

"It was the least I could do," Sam said. Jeff rolled and lighted a cigarette, inhaling deeply. With smoke billowing from his nostrils, he spoke again.

"Jeff Kirby just died up there on the hill. From now on my name is Jeff Jordon; I don't think Pa would mind."

"Neither do I," Sam said. "That Spencer hanging on the wall inside the house belonged to Red; you're welcome to take it."

"Naw, I don't need it; got a good Winchester."

"Well, I can't give you his horse; gave him to Bud."

"That's all right. The one I'm riding won't do for working cattle, though, he's more'n twenty years old."

"No problem. One of the things we're not short on is horses." Jeff nodded, and Sam changed the subject. "How are you fixed for money, Jeff?"

"Down to thirty cents, but that'll buy my smoking tobacco for a month."

Sam gave him twenty dollars, saying, "This is not a draw against your wages, consider it a bonus for signing on. When you've had breakfast you can throw a saddle on that roan in the corral; I'd like you to spend the day riding with me." For the first time, Jeff seemed to be staring at Sam's black eye.

"Got into a tussle in Calvert a couple nights ago," Sam said. Jeff nodded again, and walked down the hill.

They spent the day in the saddle, riding the boundaries of the entire ranch. Late in the afternoon, they spent an hour in a saloon in Franklin. Sam introduced Jeff to several of his friends, including Sheriff Pate, as the son of Red Jordon, which seemed to please Jeff immensely. Shortly after sundown they loosed the horses into the corral. The roan trotted off bucking, still full of energy.

"That horse has got it all," Jeff said.

"I believe he does," Sam agreed. "Use him for your work." Jeff headed for the bunkhouse and Sam was quickly gone up the hill. He picked a bunch of roses from his yard for Lula, then walked to her house for supper.

Sixteen

The following morning, Sam dropped a saddle beside Jeff's bunk.

"Hamp made this saddle for your pa, Jeff. It's paid for and it belongs to you, now." Jeff looked it over for quite some time, running his hands along the beautifully tooled leather.

"This thing is a masterpiece, Sam," he said, "and I'll surely accept it. After I work a while and get a good horse to put it on I'll be fixed for years to come."

"You're already fixed, Jeff; I'm giving you the roan." Jeff stared at the floor, looking as if someone had just slapped his face.

"Hell, Sam, you don't have to do that!" he said loudly. "I won't have no problem working out the price of the horse; just tell me what you want me to do."

"The horse is a gift, Jeff. Check with Mack; he's the

closest thing I have to a foreman, he'll tell you what to do."

Sam prepared his breakfast and sat at the table eating. Though his conscience was clear, he was beginning to have second and third thoughts about bounty hunting. He was thinking about the incident that had happened in Franklin yesterday: two small boys had trotted alongside his horse all the way through town, pointing to him and laughing, calling him a bounty hunter. Last night he had reached a decision: he would never hunt another man down for the sole purpose of collecting a monetary reward. He was a successful rancher now, and would soon be a married man.

In the afternoon, he was standing in his yard when he saw a rider splash across the creek and stop at Hamp's shop. In a short while he could hear Hamp calling from the doorway and motioning for him to come down. Sam walked down quickly.

"Sheriff Pate's dead," Hamp said, "and Bud's been shot all to hell." Clyde Wink, who had brought the news, stood by nodding as Hamp spoke.

"What happened, Clyde?" Sam asked.

"I don't know the whole story; it happened in the saloon, and I wasn't in there. The way I heard it, Sheriff Pate was shot dead when he tried to put down some trouble. Your nephew tried to help the sheriff and took two slugs himself. Doc Vine told me to tell you that Bud's gonna live, but he's lost a lot of blood. One slug passed through his left side without doing any permanent damage, but the other shattered his right elbow. Damn near took his arm off is what the doc said."

"Where is Bud now?" Sam asked.

"Lying on a cot in the doc's office."

"Is he conscious?"

"Was when I left, but they were feeding him an awful lot of liquor—for the pain, of course."

Asking his brother to go to the house and break the news to Lula, Sam headed for the barn to saddle the chestnut. Less than an hour later, he tied the animal in front of Doc Vine's office. Several men stood around outside, and one of them said to another, "There's the Judge, knew damn well he'd be along. Them fellers that done the shootin' are gonna rue this day." When Sam entered the office Bud was sitting on a cot with his back leaning against the wall. He said he was feeling no pain at the moment. He was also drunk.

"I had him beat on the draw, Uncle Sam," he said with a thick tongue, "but I missed him." Sam smiled, and headed for the saloon. The bartender related the story:

Bill Chance and two of his cousins, the Streep brothers, Clem and Cooter, had spent much of the afternoon in the saloon trying to goad a local man into a gunfight. The bartender had sent for the sheriff, and the gunmen had surprised the unsuspecting Pate with gunfire. Pate had been hit twice before he drew his own gun, and his only shot had gone through the floor as another bullet tore into him. Each of the gunmen had shot Pate at least once. When Bud, who had been sitting at the bar having a beer, decided to assist the sheriff, he made a draw that the bartender described as lightning, but missed his shot when he fired. It had been Bill Chance himself who put two shots into the youngster. All three men had then mounted fast horses and headed west.

"Was Bud drunk?" Sam asked.

"Nope. Just bought that one beer, and most of it was still sitting in front of him."

"What time did the shooting take place?"

"About five hours ago. Wally's deputy, Frank Lister,

ain't no more than two hours behind them; took a posse of a dozen men with him. He's good, Sam, and I expect him to come dragging them back here."

"Yeah. Well, let's hope so."

The doctor insisted on keeping Bud in the back room of his office for the time being, fearing that the jostling ride home might reopen his wounds and start them bleeding again. Sam agreed, and, after talking with another eyewitness to the shooting, headed home. He put the chestnut to a slow canter and gave the animal its head, for darkness had closed in. The horse probably knew the way home better than its rider, anyway.

He arrived home to find Hamp and Lula sitting on the porch, where they had been all evening. Sam spoke hurriedly, saying, "He's gonna be fine. Well, maybe not fine, but he'll get along all right. Doc says one shot went through his side clean as a whistle, and should heal quickly. Says he can't even guess how well Bud will be able to use his right arm; the elbow's shot up pretty bad." The bartender had picked Bud's gun up from the floor after the shooting, and had given it to Sam. He handed it to Lula, now, saying, "Maybe you'd better hide this again. I guess Bud was telling me the truth when he said he couldn't hit anything."

"He ain't got no business with a gun nohow," she said, taking the pistol inside the house. With Lula out of earshot, Sam told Hamp the story of the shooting as it had been told to him, adding, "Bud fired mighty quick, according to the witnesses. If he hadn't missed his target the whole thing might have turned out differently."

"It's like Bud himself has said a hundred times, Sam. He's fast, but he just don't have your eye. I don't know that I'm not glad he took some lead, might teach him something."

"Maybe. The doc says he'll never draw another gun with his right hand."

"You think the deputy'll catch the killers?"

"I have no idea. I don't know him very well, never have talked to him except to say hello. The bartender says Lister's not one to give up easily. If he does bring them back it would certainly mean a raise in pay and a free house to live in. He would be a shoo-in to replace the sheriff."

Sam stabled and fed his horse, then walked by the bunkhouse to inform the hands that Bud's condition was not nearly as bad as it could have been. He climbed the hill to his house, then ate a bowl of cornbread and milk and went to bed.

Early in the morning, he was back in Franklin. He had taken the buggy, hoping he might be allowed to carry Bud home. The hearty breakfast he bought at the cafe and carried to Bud disappeared quickly, and the youngster said he felt fine. The doctor had been standing at the window looking out into the street. Turning to Sam, he said, "Is that your buggy out there?"

"Yes."

"I guess you can take the boy home. Go slow and ride him easy, don't want to aggravate his wounds. Make him keep that arm in the sling and don't try to change the bandages. I'll do it myself in a few days."

"Yes, sir," Sam said, getting up from his chair. "I'll be back for him later, got some things to do first." He walked down the street to the sheriff's office. Several men stood outside, and one of them informed Sam that Lister had not brought back the killers. The deputy soon appeared in the doorway and beckoned Sam inside.

"Figured you'd want to know how the manhunt turned out," Lister said. "They were easy enough to follow, didn't even try to hide their trail. They stopped in

Calvert and bought three bottles of whiskey, then rode up and down the street in broad daylight yelling, laughing and shooting into the air. Marshal Pond was out of town, and it's probably a good thing. Somebody would have died if he'd been there, and it might very well have been Leo.

"Anyway, they finally crossed the Brazos. No use for me to cross the river, I have no authority over there. They headed west, and I've notified the U.S. marshal. Bill Chance is the whole problem, Sam. His stupid cousins just follow him around because they consider him a fancy gunfighter. It's true that he has killed a few men, but I hear that not all of them were sober, and none of them were men with know-how." Lister paused for a few seconds, then asked, "Do you intend to take up the chase?"

"No." Sam returned to the doctor's office and picked up his nephew. One hour later Bud was lying in his own bed.

The days stretched into weeks, then two months had passed. Bud's wounds had healed nicely, but he had little use of his right arm. He was learning to work the leather left-handed, and had retained his contract with the army.

The county commissioners' court had appointed Deputy Lister to finish out Pate's term as sheriff, and only yesterday Sam had been in Lister's office. The new sheriff seemed to have only one thing on his mind.

"I tell you I'm even having trouble sleeping at night," Lister said, handing Sam a copy of the *Fort Worth Democrat*. "Read this."

The sheriff pointed to a half-page editorial that blasted county, state and federal law enforcement officers for their apparent lack of concern in the case involving Bill Chance and the Streep brothers, who had gunned down Sheriff Wallace Pate and another man before the eyes of half a dozen witnesses in Robertson County. The trio had then traveled west, the article stated, harassing and robbing citizens randomly, and were even now brazenly walking the streets of El Paso daily. The editor closed the article by asking the following questions: Why is it so difficult for the authorities to find the fugitives when their whereabouts is common knowledge to everyone else? Could it be that our duly sworn and duty-bound protectors are simply afraid of them? Are the officers just waiting around, hoping a man named Sam Curtin will leave his ranch and do their job for them once again? Sam folded the newspaper and laid it on Lister's desk without comment.

"I have no idea where the editor got his information," Lister said, "but I do know that most of the wanted men eventually show up around El Paso because of its proximity to the Mexican border."

"Just a quick run across the border and they're legally safe," Sam said.

"I've been thinking about resigning this job," Lister said. "That way I'd be free to hunt them down. I could still run for sheriff in the next election."

"You could do that, Frank, but I think you should give the U.S. marshals a little more time."

"Maybe so," Lister said, He stared through the window for a moment, then turned to face Sam. "Hell, I'm surprised that you aren't already on Chance's trail. It was your nephew he crippled." Sam began to shake his head.

"He shot Bud in self-defense. Wally was already dead and Chance had holstered his gun when Bud drew and fired on him. Even though Bud's a lousy shot, it's just possible that sometime before he ran out of shells he might have managed to hit Chance. Chance had no choice in that part of the incident."

"Is that the reason you haven't gone after him?"

"That's it," Sam answered, and left the office.

Jeff Jordon had worked out very well, proving daily that he knew how to do other things just as well as he roped cattle. He had expertly trimmed and shod the hooves of every horse on the premises, including Sam's chestnut. He had turned the roan into an excellent cutting horse, usually saddling him before sunup and riding him during the coolest hours of the day. Sometimes he would sit on Sam's porch at night, sipping coffee or whiskey and listening to Red Jordon stories. Sam deliberately kept the stories light and humorous and Jeff obviously enjoyed them, for he always laughed in the right places.

The more time Sam spent around Jeff, the more he was convinced that the man was indeed the son of Joshua Jordon: the same deep voice, many of the same movements and the same sense of humor. Jeff had plenty of stories of his own, and had sent Sam into guffaws of laughter on several occasions. Tonight he told a short one that had been passed on to him by his father during the winter they spent trapping on the Platte. Red had not known if it was a true story or just a joke, but of course Red told it as if it were true: In a saloon out in Arizona Territory, two men were about to face each other in a gunfight. One of the men was very large and the other a runt. Sensing that he might be getting the short end of the deal, the big man halted the bartender's countdown, yelling loudly. "Wait a minute!" he said, pointing to the runt. "This ain't fair. He's got a bigger target than I do, look how little he is." The runt smiled, then spoke to the bartender. "Take a piece of chalk and draw a man my size on him, then if I hit him anywhere outside that chalk line it don't count."

Sam produced a bottle of whiskey and the two had a nightcap, which was their custom of late. Jeff said he enjoyed his job at Curtin Hill more than any he had ever held. He had gained weight, and now looked more like a thirty-year-old. Sam was well pleased with him, and so were the Halleys. He said good night to Jeff early so both could get a good night's sleep, for Sam himself had put in a twelve hour day. In the morning, he would be on the train to Hillsboro.

He drank a dipper of cold water from the spring and went to bed. He lay awake for a while trying to picture in his mind exactly what a running horse looked like. Jeff had told him that Rick and Mack had had an argument this morning. Rick had said that when a horse was running at a full gallop, sometimes all four of his feet would be off the ground at the same time.

"No, no, Rick," Mack had said, "a horse keeps at least one foot on the ground at all times; that's how he keeps his balance." The two had argued over the point for several minutes. Sam, who had been around horses all his life, and spent years training them, did not know for sure. He had never given any thought to the matter. Both the Halleys had laughed at Rick's imaginary observation. The youngster had gotten mad and stalked away, then came back later and renewed the argument.

"By god you can laugh if you want to," Rick had said, "but I know what I see. I was watching you ride across that meadow, Mack, and I could plainly see it. I saw all four of that horse's feet off the ground at the same time."

Jeff also thought that a horse kept continuous contact with the ground, but had stayed out of the argument. He had quickly succeeded in getting Rick's mind off the horse's feet and onto something else. The two bunked in the same corner, and almost every day Jeff would teach Rick something new about horses, or a new rope trick.

Sheriff Frank Lister arrived at Sam's house shortly after sunup the following morning. At Sam's invitation, he came into the kitchen and accepted the cup of coffee he was offered. As Lister sat down, he pushed a check across the table for Sam to read.

"It's made out for a thousand dollars," Lister said, "and the county fathers have authorized me to deposit it in your bank account. They want Bill Chance and the Streep brothers, dead or alive, and there'll be more money to come if you take the job.

"Seven merchants in Franklin have already pledged a hundred dollars each, and when word gets around that you're on the job I think every business in the county will contribute money. This thousand is just to pay you for your time and to cover expenses; the real money will be waiting for you when you get back. I feel certain that it will be the highest reward ever paid in Texas, for I will personally ask every merchant in the county for a contribution." Sam was silent for a while, then began to speak slowly.

"I made a decision a while back that I would not go after another man, Frank . . . not for bounty." The sheriff responded quickly.

"Hell, we won't call it a bounty. We'll simply call it letting the people of Robertson County show their appreciation by making life a little easier for you. We can't let those sons of bitches get away with the cold-blooded murder of the best sheriff this county ever had. The truth is, Wally Pate was your friend, Sam; he thought the world of you. He told me that himself, many times."

"You can lay off now, Frank," Sam said, raising his voice a little, "I'm thinking about it. Just take the check back to town. If I decide that you should deposit it, I'll let you know. Right now, I've got to get a few things together; I'm taking the train to Hillsboro at ten."

During the train ride he spent much time thinking about Bill Chance and the Streeps, for by now he had decided to hunt the men down. Wally Pate had indeed been his friend, and had risked his life for the citizens of the county on numerous occasions. Sheriff Lister had said that Sam was the only man around who could be counted on to win out over the outlaws if a showdown turned into gunplay.

As the train made its way north through the snowy cotton fields, he sat by a window thinking of things other than the wanted men. He was coming on to twenty-nine years old now, and began to ask questions of himself: Was he really the fastest gun in the Southwest, as many people were saying? How long before his quick hand-eye coordination deserted him? Was he already past his peak, and slowly going downhill? Would he be lying at the feet of a man with a quicker hand when the answer became obvious? No! he quickly decided. This would positively be his last manhunt. He would soon be a married man, and he owned the ideal place to raise a family. As he grew old and his skills eroded he would do as Red Jordon had done: use rifles and shotguns to protect himself if need be.

He spent the afternoon with Anita, who sensed early on that his mind was somewhere else. At her prodding, he retold the story of the shooting that had taken Sheriff Pate's life and wounded Bud.

"You are going after the killers, then?"

"Yes. I feel that Wally would have done it for me." She walked to the gate and stood staring down the street for a long time. Turning back to face him, she wiped at her eyes.

"Do you have any idea how long you'll be gone?"

"No, but I'll write to you often."

"Can you imagine how hard it will be for me to just sit here day after day, night after night, not even knowing if you are dead or alive?"

"Yes, I can, but you could go down to the ranch and stay with Lu till I get back, then we could be married in Calvert."

"No, sir, Mr. Sam Curtin. I want to be married by Reverend Moss right here in my own church, just like we planned. I don't want to go back to the ranch till I'm part of the family."

"I understand, honey. I'll bring my brother and his family up here for the wedding. Everything is going to be just fine." She put her arms around his waist and hugged him tightly, her eyes downcast.

"I'll wait right here for you, Sam, but you must promise that after we are married you'll stay home and help me raise the children we've talked about so many times."

"I promise," he said, taking her in his arms.

Although it was very late when Sam arrived home, he stopped at the bunkhouse and called Jeff outside.

"I want you to carry a message to Sheriff Lister early in the morning, Jeff, and I don't want anyone else knowing about it. If you don't find him in Franklin he'll be somewhere around Calvert. Just tell him I said to deposit the check."

"Is that all?"

"That's all."

Seventeen

It was now early October, and Sam sat in a railroad car headed west. The tracks ran all the way to El Paso now, with the line having been finished just this year. The drudgery of crossing the West Texas desert on horseback had been eliminated for those with train fare. Sam's chestnut rode in the stock car, along with Bud's black. Bud had insisted that Sam bring the animal along, saying, "Take Charley Horse, Uncle Sam. If you have to chase somebody down you'll be sitting on a sure winner."

"I know, Bud, thank you. I'll take Charley Horse."

Sam's first stop had been at the office of the *Fort Worth Democrat*. The editor refused to reveal his sources, but assured Sam that the information he had published had been both timely and correct. He remained steadfast in his belief that the wanted men were in or around El Paso.

"You have my respect, Mr. Curtin," the editor had said, "and judging from the mail I received after the article appeared, you have the respect of my readers. I wish you well, and I'm very pleased that a man of your distinction has stepped forward in an attempt to do something about such riffraff." Having no other lead, Sam had boarded the train for El Paso.

He sat in the rollicking passenger car, thinking of his quarry. He would recognize the men on sight, for from somewhere Sheriff Lister had obtained pictures of all three. Buck-toothed and ugly, the Streep brothers were very similar in appearance, with each man having an unruly mop of yellow hair that seldom saw a barber. Both were in their early twenties and of medium height. They had lived with their mother outside the town of Hearne until she passed away, then they had turned to lawlessness. When their cousin, Bill Chance, had been released from prison early this year, the duo had become a trio. Many honest people had suffered the consequences, for the three had traveled throughout Arkansas and East Texas taking whatever they wanted wherever they found it.

Bill Chance, said to be thirty-one years old, was considered by all to be the most dangerous of the three. He had recently been released from prison in Kansas after serving a five-year sentence for manslaughter. Chance was a handsome man, having hair as black as coal and dark eyes that were said to turn to fire when he was angry. He stood six feet tall and weighed about two hundred pounds. Sheriff Lister said it was highly unlikely that Chance would ever return to Kansas.

"Men don't like to live in an area where they've done time," Lister had said. "Besides, Chance likes whiskey too much. Back in February Kansas passed a law that prohibits the sale of alcoholic beverages." Sam doubted that prohibition would alter the drinking habits of Kansans to a noticeable degree, and said as much. Most men knew how to make their own whiskey.

Just before dark he ate supper in the dining car, deciding for the second time today that the food was ill prepared and terribly inadequate. Sam was a big eater, and used to good food.

During the day, the heat in the passenger car was uncomfortable, and the nighttime temperature was downright cold. He spent several of the daylight hours standing on the rear platform, where a strong breeze played between the cars. At night he curled up in his seat with his coat spread over his knees and shoulders, grabbing a few winks whenever he could. As the train neared El Paso he began to recognize the landscape. Nothing had changed, of course, since he and Red Jordon had ridden this same route on horseback. And as before, due to the train's continuous gain or loss of altitude, his ears had been popping all morning.

Arriving at the station, he led his horses from the train and to the livery stable. Registering at the nearest hotel, he once again became Mr. Sam Smith, and slept away the entire afternoon.

Darkness found him walking the streets, especially the area along the Rio Grande. He entered a few of the saloons to inspect the clientele, but most of the time just peered over the short swinging doors or through the windows. He gave up shortly after midnight, for though he had seen countless men of a seedy-looking nature, he saw no face that looked familiar.

He had no reason to believe that the men would recognize him on sight. Nevertheless, he took no chances, always staying near some kind of cover that could be gained quickly. At the hotel, he had cut the thong from his holster with his knife, making sure nothing would hamper the quick movement of his hand. Sheriff Lister had said he had no doubt that the killers would know Sam by name and reputation, but he did not believe they would recognize him on sight. Sam was unwilling to bet his life on such an assumption, and would make every effort to see before being seen. Knowing it was possible that the men could identify him from his days with the trade show, Sam had made a decision before he left Calvert. Hoping to disguise his appearance somewhat, he would not shave his beard until the hunt was over. The dark stubble had already hidden much of his face, and the endless itching had begun.

He walked the streets each night for more than a week, and last night he had ridden Charley Horse into Mexico. With the brim of his hat pulled down to his eyes, he rode back and forth through the town, looking through open doorways and inspecting the people along the street. Never once did he leave the saddle, for he knew that horse thieves abounded. Left unattended, such a fine animal as Charley Horse would disappear quickly. Late in the night, having had no luck in Mexico, he recrossed the river to El Paso.

He had been in town for two weeks when he finally struck a lead. In his frustration, Sam had begun to show the pictures when questioning people, and had hit pay dirt almost immediately. The owner of a shabby bar and restaurant had seen the Streep brothers. He said the Streeps had been in his place several times, and he was hoping he had seen the last of them.

"All they do is raise hell and run off the rest of my customers," the man said. "Never have bought more'n one drink apiece; just stand around talking about fighting and shooting."

"What time of night do they usually come in?" Sam asked.

"Never have been in here at night, it's always in the daytime. I tell you them bastards have cost me money, always insulting my customers till they get up and leave. Challenged me to a gunfight once when I tried to call them down. One morning they were standing out front waiting for me to open up; guess they'd had a hard night and needed a drink."

The owner of the establishment, whose name was Al Hipp, was also the bartender. When told of the Streeps' background and the crimes committed by them, he was eager to help.

"Sam Curtin, huh?" Hip said, after Sam had introduced himself. "Who'd ever believe that I've been standing here talking to the Judge?"

"I'm hoping you won't mention that to anyone," Sam said. "It could put me in a bad position."

"Of course it could, and I'm sworn to secrecy. It's a little darker over there on that corner stool against the wall. If you sit there long enough I believe you'll eventually see your men walk through that door." Hipp poured himself a drink of whiskey, then added, chuckling, "I just want to see the look on their faces when they see who they're up against." Sam ate his meals there and sat on the stool for the next three days, occasionally walking around to stretch his legs and keep his body loose. Then, on the morning of the fourth day, his search came to an end.

He heard the Streeps before they entered the building, then a moment later Clem pushed the door open with his foot, followed closely by his brother. As they walked to the bar both men were still laughing, apparently at some conversation that had been going on between them. In a tone of voice that was usually reserved for workhorses, Clem spoke to Hipp.

"Give us a bottle, barkeep, and don't be long about

it. Gonna git this day started off right." Taking a bottle from the shelf behind him, Hipp quietly obeyed.

Sam quickly decided that now was the time. Both men looked as if they had not slept last night, and he thought their reflexes might be a trifle slow. He would not give them time to steady their nerves with whiskey. Neither man had looked in his direction, and as they concentrated on opening the bottle and pouring drinks for themselves, Sam slid from the stool and walked out behind them, stopping twenty feet away. He made a loud coughing sound. Both men whirled, with Cooter moving to Clem's right. About six feet separated the brothers now. Sam spoke.

"I'm gonna be heading for Franklin this afternoon and I figured on you fellows coming along." Both men stiffened, but neither showed fear. Keeping his eyes on Sam constantly, Clem began to snicker, talking out of the side of his mouth to his brother.

"You hear that, Cooter? You hear that? Don't you reckin that's the Judge there tryin' to hide behind them whiskers?"

"Why, I shore do b'lieve it is," Cooter said, smiling himself now. "D'ya thank he aims ta take on both of us at th' same time?"

"Looks ta me like he's thankin' about it, he's tryin' to look as tough as he can. Too bad he didn't go by Tascosa first; Bill woulda done 'im in fer shore."

Sam spoke loudly, "Bill Chance is dead!" Though the statement was false, it produced the desired effect. As shock registered on the faces of both men, Sam made the quickest draw of his life. He fired two shots so close together that Hipp heard only one sound. Only when he saw both the Streeps fall to the floor did he realize that Sam had fired twice. The first shot had gone into Clem's open mouth, and the second tore into Cooter's heart. Each of the brothers had drawn his weapon, but neither had lived to fire it. The guns now lay on the floor, where the outlaws had dropped them.

Drawn by the sound of gunfire, a sizable crowd of men had gathered in the building. Hipp ordered them to stay away from the bodies, and to touch nothing. He had sent a young Mexican for the town marshal, who was on the scene quickly. The current marshal had been hired in April. He was a handsome man who stood well over six feet tall named Dallas Stoudenmire.

"Ain't heard much about you lately, Curtin," he said, pointing to the bodies. "Who you got there?" Sam handed him the pictures and wanted posters.

"The Streep brothers," he said. "They ambushed Sheriff Wallace Pate in Franklin; gunned him down in front of several witnesses." The marshal looked the dead men over, then studied the pictures.

"Well, you've sure got the right men. I knew about Sheriff Pate being killed; if I had known these were the men who shot him down I'd have taken them on myself."

Sam smiled at the marshal, all the while thinking: the hell you would, you big sonofabitch. You're just like ninety percent of the lawmen in Texas, riding a gravy train at the taxpayers' expense and you'd tremble in your boots at the thought of having to face a live gunman. To the marshal, he said, "I'd like to bury them here, and I'd appreciate it if you'd write a letter stating that fact." The marshal nodded.

Clem had involuntarily told Sam exactly where to find Bill Chance. After seeing to the burial of the Streeps and collecting his letter from the marshal's office, he returned to his hotel room and wrote a letter to Anita. He did not mention the shooting. He ate supper early, then went to bed. He must get a good night's sleep, for tomorrow he would begin the long journey to Tascosa.

The following day he rode the train east for two hundred miles, then unloaded his horses. Riding Charley Horse and leading the chestnut, whose back was burdened with bedding, camping gear and a sack of grain, he headed north. The ride to Tascosa might take as long as ten days. He had brought a heavy coat and warm clothing, for the weather in northwest Texas could sometimes turn treacherous in the fall.

Tascosa, situated in the northwest corner of the state, had been established when pioneer settlers built adobe huts and irrigation ditches along area creeks in the early 1870s. The village had become a supply and shipping point for several huge ranches, including the famed XIT and LIT spreads. The bustling town, known as the cowboy capital of the plains, became the seat when Oldham County was organized in 1880. The famous and infamous—from Kit Carson to Billy the Kid—had walked its rough plank sidewalks. The cemetery was an essential part of the area, having been set up even before the town was officially laid out, for in this riotous, wide-open cowboy town, gunfights were the traditional means of settling disputes. Bill Chance should feel right at home in Tascosa, Sam thought, as he rode north through a drizzling rain.

The rain ceased just before dark, and he camped alongside a deep ravine. Though he had managed to keep his bedding dry by wrapping it in his slicker, the clothing he wore was wet, and the strong wind now blowing from the north sent a shiver through his body. Having no way of knowing how much rain had fallen farther north, he resisted the urge to camp in the ravine where he would be sheltered from the wind. He knew that sudden flash floods had sent more than one sleeping man to his just reward. He fed a portion of the grain to each of the horses, then ate a cold supper from his pack, washing it down with water from his canteen.

Always on the lookout for renegade Indians who had kicked over the traces and fled the reservation, he rode the sparsely populated area for two days without seeing another human being. On the third day, he overtook two middle-aged men and their families who were traveling north in two covered wagons. They had camped for the night, and Sam was invited to join them for supper. He readily accepted, for he was hungry and the food smelled good. He ate a delicious meal with he knew not whom, for no one in the group had offered a name. The eldest of the men, whose beard reached the bib of his overalls, seemed to be their spokesman.

"Heading for the town of Canyon," he said, "been promised work on the big T Anchor Ranch, there."

"Big is right, from what I hear," Sam said. "They say some of the men who work there don't even know where it ends."

"Wouldn't know about that. Anyway, we've been promised year-round work and living quarters for our families, so that's where we're headed."

Sam sat around their campfire for close to an hour with no conversation between himself and the men. They spoke only to their scrawny wives and children, a teenage boy and a girl about seven years old. Finally, deciding that his name would mean nothing to people such as these, he introduced himself.

"By the way, my name is Sam Curtin." He watched the faces of the men closely, and saw no sign that either had ever heard the name before. Good, he thought.

"You can throw your bedroll under my wagon if you want," the bearded man said, offering no name of his own and continuing to stare into the fire, "looks like it might decide to rain before morning."

"No, thank you," Sam said, rising to his feet, "I'll just move out onto some good grass and camp with the horses."

"Well, don't go riding off nowhere in the morning till you've had a good breakfast."

His horses had eaten everything within reach of their picket ropes, so he moved them to new grass and spread his bedroll a few yards away. He slept well, and it did not rain. He ate breakfast with the travelers next morning and the clean-shaven man, who was much the taller of the two, was more talkative.

"Since we're heading in the same direction, I was thinking you might want to ride along with us," he said. "Can't offer you no money, but there's plenty of food and you'd have a place to keep dry." As he talked, the man had been raking a baked sweet potato from the hot ashes of the fire with a stick. "Truth is," he said, "we had a good scare a few days ago when a bunch of bad-looking characters followed us for a while. I guess they finally decided we didn't have nothing worth taking." The man went into a short coughing spell, but recovered quickly. He continued, "We'd sure feel a lot safer with a man like you along, good as you are with that gun."

"Good? How do you know that?"

"Well . . . it's sure what everybody says." Damn! Sam was thinking. Had his name and reputation actually traveled this far? The obvious answer was yes.

Knowing that he would be in the saddle for at least a week, Sam accepted the arrangement. Though Canyon was a day's ride out of his way, he would arrive in Tascosa in better condition, for it was rare that a traveling man came across three hot meals a day. As they cooked supper each night, the women would also cook the following day's dinner, then all they had to do was stop at noon and reheat the food.

Three days later, the bearded man's wagon broke an axle. His wife, who had been driving the team, let out a muted scream. Sam looked backward just in time to see the wagon bed hit the ground with an audible crash, as the rear wheels folded inward. The team stopped instantly, and the lady jumped to the ground.

"What on earth are we gonna do?" she asked, directing the question to her husband.

"Leave it here, I guess; nothing else we can do." The woman began to cry and beat one of the wheels with a tiny fist.

"Leave it here?" she asked. "Leave everything I own in this godforsaken country? Ma cooked on that stove there before I was even born." Sam slid from underneath the wagon, where he had been assessing the damage.

"No reason to leave it here," he said, "we can make a new axle." Then, turning to the man with the beard, he asked, "Do you have an ax?"

"Sure, I got an ax," the man said sullenly. "Got an adz too, but do you see anything around here to cut down for an axle?"

"No, but I see several horses," Sam said, becoming slightly irritated by the man's attitude. "Give me a harnessed horse and a singletree and I'll ride around till I find a mesquite tall enough and straight enough to make one." The man seemed perturbed at the thought of letting one of the horses out of his sight.

"You got two horses, there," he said, "why can't you use one of them to pull the tree back?" Sam fired his answer quickly.

"Look, fellow, both my animals are top saddle horses

and I certainly don't intend to confuse their little brains by putting a pulling harness on them." Then, out of earshot of the women, he said, "Do you want the damned axle or not?" The man slowly nodded, and began to unhitch one of the horses.

When Sam returned the following morning, he was dragging not a mesquite tree but a species of poplar known as black cottonwood. Sorry timber for the building of anything, but strong enough to make an axle for the wagon. He ignored the bearded man's complaints about him being gone so long, and went about hewing the axle. One of the women was quick to bring him a plate of hot food. The men had so far been content to merely watch as Sam did the hewing.

Both men seemed to be about as helpless as their women, and Sam wondered just how long they were going to remain on the T Anchor payroll. As he worked, he chuckled silently to himself. He was wondering how long a little thing like a broken axle would have held up the Halley brothers. The twins most likely would have been carrying an extra in one of the wagons, he thought.

Within a few hours, the new axle had been greased and the wagons were rolling. Neither of the men had bothered to thank Curtin, but when the bearded man's wife served Sam's dinner the plate was much heavier than usual. These people were a weird lot indeed, he was thinking as he ate the food. None of them ever spoke unless it was absolutely necessary. During the several days he had been with them, he had heard no one address another by a given name. Most people, including himself, simply made up a name when they did not want their true identity known.

The old proverb about children being seen and not heard certainly rang true here. Neither of the kids had spoken a single word since Sam had joined them, though he did hear them giggling and talking to each other at a distance. Were these people running from the law? Probably not. Were they leaving behind a lot of unpaid debts and did not want their whereabouts known? Probably so. He pushed the thoughts out of his mind, for in neither instance should it be of any concern to him. He would deliver them to Canyon in a few days and be on his way.

Three days later Sam stopped at Palo Duro, while the travelers continued on to Canyon, a short distance away. As their wagons faded from view, the women and children waved to him. He stood in his stirrups and waved his hat. "Good-bye," he said softly. "Whoever the hell you are." Then he walked his horses forward, peering down into Palo Duro Canyon.

Eighteen

On the tabletop expanse of the Texas high plains, a branch of the Red River had carved the incredible spires and pinnacles of Palo Duro. The walls plunged a thousand feet to the canyon floor, exposing brilliant multicolored strata. The view was almost breathtaking, and though Sam was not particularly a religious man, he had a feeling that a power much greater than that of the river had created the magnificent spectacle before him. He also knew that he was looking at the scene of Texas' last great Indian battle:

On a sweep across the high plains in 1874, the already famous Colonel Ranald S. Mackenzie, leading troops from the Fourth Cavalry from Fort Richardson, discovered a huge Comanche Indian camp in the canyon. The Indians had broken from their reservation and were menacing a wide area. How Mackenzie had accomplished the almost impossible task of approaching the Indians undetected was not generally known, but his troops had quickly overrun the village and captured more than a thousand horses, chasing the Indians deeper into the canyon. In a master stroke of tactics, and perhaps with a certain amount of compassion for the hapless Indians, Mackenzie did not try to dislodge them. Instead, he burned the village and slaughtered most of the horses. Without shelter, provisions or the vital mobility of their horses, the proud warriors of the plains had had no choice but to plod back to their reservation.

As Sam sat staring down into the enormous cavity, he was wondering what the battle had been like. Even from his limited vantage point he could see dozens of places in the canyon that could be defended easily, and with a minimum of strategy. He patted his horse's neck and whispered through clenched teeth, as if talking to the animal, "If the Comanches had been well equipped, old Mackenzie would have had one hell of a fight on his hands."

He rode partway into the canyon, where he shot a rabbit and camped for the night. The trip had been a tiring one for himself and his horses, and he intended to stay in the canyon till all were rested. He thought Bill Chance would keep; that he had surely found others of his own ilk in Tascosa and would not be going anywhere. Anyway, the town was only a day's ride from here.

After dark, he sat beside his campfire, eating the rabbit and drinking coffee. The fire could not be seen from more than a few feet away, for he had camped beneath an overhanging rock that was surrounded by huge boulders. After eating, he extinguished the fire and rolled into his blanket, for the night was growing cold. His thoughts immediately turned to home.

He was a fortunate man indeed, he was thinking. Not

yet thirty years old, he owned a fine ranch and a beautiful home, and he owed money to no man. Nor did he intend to go into debt, for he had watched his brother grow old before his time worrying about someone breathing down his neck for every dollar he could scratch out of the earth. He remembered that Hamp had once quit chewing tobacco for a year simply because he did not have the money to buy it. He had grown his own tobacco that year, but most of it stayed in the field because he did not like the taste. Today, Hamp chewed as much as he wanted, and had switched to a better brand.

And the beautiful, intelligent Anita Keeling. She was waiting to marry him and bear his children. Most men were not so fortunate, he thought. When his current mission was completed he would take her to Curtin Hill as his wife. He would buy another section of land and immediately begin to upgrade his herd. He had already spotted two more purebred bulls that were for sale in Dallas. Perhaps by the end of the first year, Anita would bless him with a child. As his eyelids grew heavier and the night turned colder, he added another blanket to his covering and was soon asleep.

He built a fire at sunup, for the northwest Texas mornings were downright cold this time of year. He sat by the fire, eating the remainder of the rabbit, enthralled by the dazzling brilliance of colors ricocheting throughout the canyon as the rising sun made its entry. Far below he could see cattle roaming leisurely about in their neverending quest for the few blades of green grass that remained among the brown. He supposed that they were T Anchor cattle, though none were close enough to read a brand. Sitting quietly, he decided that any man who could shoot a rifle would have no problem surviving here, for during the past couple hours he had seen enough wild game to feed an army.

He had moved out onto a rock outcropping where he had an unrestricted view of the area below. A few miles away he could see the town of Canyon, which had originated as T Anchor headquarters and was considered the gateway to Palo Duro. He could see two small buildings on the canyon floor that were probably used only when it was necessary for cowboys to remain there overnight. As he strained his eyes trying to locate some human activity, a man spoke from the rim of the canyon, no more than forty feet above him.

"Good morning, feller. Couldn't help noticing you up here, you stick out like a sore thumb." Sam looked up quickly to see a beady-eyed man who appeared to be about forty years old. His left cheek was puffed out of shape with the quid of tobacco in his jaw, and his head was pushed so far into a high-crowned Stetson that both his ears were bent downward.

"Well, I guess you're not gonna shoot me since you haven't done it already," Sam said, smiling.

"Ain't never shot nobody that weren't asking for it," the man said, never taking his eyes from Sam, "I coulda shot you from anywhere in the canyon." Sam knew that to be true, for in his right hand the man held an 1874 fifty-caliber Sharps rifle, probably the truest-shooting rifle ever manufactured. Accuracy was almost taken for granted, and direct hits from distances of well over a quarter mile had been authenticated many times. The rifles were so highly regarded by hunters and fighting men alike that most men had begun to refer to them as "Old Reliable." A few years ago the company had even begun to stamp the popular nickname on the barrels of the hard-hitting weapons. The Sharps sold for about fifty dollars, and in the hands of an expert marksman one shot was all that was usually necessary, regardless of the size of the game.

Around the man's middle, riding high in a worn-out holster, was a copy of the forty-four caliber Colt Dragoon: another fearsome weapon with unquestioned firepower.

"I guess it goes without saying that I'm glad you didn't shoot," Sam said, making his way to the top of the canyon. The man had never pointed the rifle in Sam's direction. He now stood with the muzzle of the gun resting on the toe of his boot. He doffed his hat to reveal a bald head, then spat a mouthful of tobacco juice at a rock.

"I work for the T Anchor," he said, his eyes taking in the Peacemaker and cutaway holster that was tied to Sam's leg with rawhide, "and it's part of my job to ask what you're doin' here."

"Just resting," Sam said, "I've been in the saddle for a week and a half." He offered a handshake, adding, "My name is Sam Curtin." The man's facial expression changed instantly as he recognized the name. Pushing his own hand forward, he began to speak nervously.

"My name's Cotton Overby. Folks named me Cotton back when I had some hair." Sam grasped the rough hand, giving it a firm shake. Overby continued to talk.

"I cain't stand here and pretend that your name don't mean nothin' to me; I've heard it plenty of times. Ain't never heard of you doin' nothin' that weren't honest, though. You can stay in the canyon as long as you want. I'll have some beef and beans about sundown, and there's a extry bunk in the cabin."

"I appreciate the offer, Cotton, but I'll be long gone before then."

Sam walked with Overby to a nearby tree where the man's buckskin was tied. Mounting the animal and shoving the Sharps into the boot, Cotton said, "Well, if you're after somebody I hope you ketch 'im, ain't never heard of you huntin' nobody 'less they'd done sump'm awful." Sam waved good-bye as Overby rode behind a huge boulder and back down into the canyon.

After watering his horses and moving them to a better grazing area, he built a small fire to reheat the cold coffee that remained in his pot. He sat on a log, rethinking his unspoken opinion of Marshal Dallas Stoudenmire. In his mind he had placed the marshal in the same category as some of the worthless lawmen he had known. By talking with some men in El Paso Sam had learned that Stoudenmire was indeed a man with sand in his craw. He had served with the Confederate Army and the Texas Rangers before becoming city marshal of El Paso. He had been on the job only three days when he shot John Hale and George Campbell, two members of the Manning sporting crowd. Stoudenmire had walked into the men with both of his Smith and Wesson forty-fours spitting flame. In less than ten seconds two more men had been added to the roster of undesirables who had fallen before his twin revolvers. Unfortunately, a third man had died, for one of Stoudenmire's wild shots had hit an innocent Mexican bystander, wounding him mortally. The men had told Sam that the marshal had quickly cleaned out many of the dives along El Paso Street, making many enemies among the criminal element. They also said that he sometimes walked the street drunk, shooting off his guns and bragging. Sam sat on the log sipping the last of his coffee, thinking that any man who mixed excessive amounts of whiskey with gunfighting would probably not live long in a hellhole like El Paso.

Shortly after noon, Sam left the canyon. He would cover most of the distance to Tascosa before camping for the night. Tomorrow might bring a showdown with Bill Chance and an end to Sam's life as a manhunter. Never again! he had decided. He thought often of the day the young boys had run alongside his horse, pointing and laughing—calling him a bounty hunter.

He skirted the town of Canyon and headed north across the high plains, riding the chestnut and leading the black. Though he knew that Charley Horse could probably run him into the ground, Sam still preferred to ride the chestnut. The animal was steadier of nerve, and not skittish. Only a few minutes ago when a covey of quail had burst noisily from the grass directly underneath the chestnut's feet he had remained still, while the black had fought his lead rope. The chestnut was a finished product of the Sam Curtin method of horse training, and with the exception of the day Bud had ridden him in the race with the roan, no rider other than Sam had ever sat on his back. The big horse seemed convinced that no harm could come to him as long as his master was near.

The year Bud was fifteen, Sam had taught him a few things about training horses. "You might be able to bully a dog or a cow into doing something, Bud," Sam had said to the youngster, "but it won't work with a horse. You can't force him to do anything. You have to make him *want* to do it by touch, voice and direct eye contact. And you have to make him think that you're stronger than he is. If you start on him early enough that's not hard to do.

"You should pick up a foal when he's twenty-four hours old and hold him in midair until he stops struggling and holds still. Do that every day for the first week or two and for the rest of his life he'll think you can still do it." Bud laughed loudly. Sam smiled, adding, "Even though he'll grow to be ten times as heavy as you and twenty times as strong, in his little mind he will always believe that anytime you're displeased with him you can simply pick him up and throw him away."

Sam's reputation as a horse trainer was well known at Fort Worth. Inside the barracks a memorandum had been posted on the bulletin board for the benefit of recruits, and had remained there for several years. It read:

> Always approach a horse on his left side, and never approach or touch a horse of any age without first speaking to him. Though the location of his eyes makes it difficult for him to see directly in front or behind, he will turn his head to compensate. His eyesight is excellent and his hearing is even better. Do not be surprised when he turns his head in the direction of a fallen leaf—he actually heard it hit the ground. A man would be wise to pay close attention to the ears of his horse. When the animal raises his head and begins to move his ears about independent of one another, he has heard something and is trying to pinpoint the direction of the sound. When both ears come together and funnel in the same direction, he has located the source. A rider should be wary, and proceed no farther until he has determined the nature of the horse's concern!
>
> Signed: Sam Curtin

Sam had written the memo at the request of Captain Fry, who immediately ordered it placed on the bulletin board. Sam only hoped that over the years the memo might have helped some young recruit to understand his horse's warning signals.

At ten the following morning, he sat in his saddle atop the highest hill in the area, looking down into the town of Tascosa. Beside him was the cemetery that was no doubt called Boot Hill by the locals. A few of the graves were so fresh that the grass had not had time to grow over them. Some had markers, but most did not. He supposed that the unmarked mounds contained the remains of gunfighters, drifters or other persons considered to be of small consequence. He noticed that one of the graves was widely separated from the others, perhaps signifying that its occupant had been something less than a well-respected citizen. Sam thought that most of the men here had indeed died with their boots on, having few if any friends when the end came.

The town lay a quarter mile below, with nothing between except prairie grass. Seeing no way to approach without being in full view of the entire town, he guided the chestnut down the hill to the livery stable, passing a few men along the street who seemed to pay him no mind. He ordered oats for his horses and sat on a bench watching as each animal ate its fill. Then he placed large buckets of water under their appreciative noses. Sam had never been one to trust the feeding of his horses to another man—he wanted to know what they ate and how much. The big hostler seemed to understand, and sat nearby working on a wagon wheel. Sam curried both animals, then put his saddle on the black. He thought that very soon he might be needing the fastest horse in the county, and he had no doubt that Charley Horse was it.

"Just leave my gear on the horses," Sam said, paying the hostler for the oats, "I might not be in town long." The man nodded, and Sam headed for the door. Then, having second thoughts, he turned back to the liveryman.

"Seen ol' Bill Chance lately?" he asked.

"See 'im 'bout ever' day," the man said, pointing to

a building across the street and a few doors down. "Thank he's over there in the saloon right now."

Sam had decided beforehand that Chance would never allow himself to be taken back to Franklin alive; that the outlaw was a man with little or no fear who definitely had enough sand to meet Curtin in the street for a showdown. With that in mind, Sam adjusted his holster and began to walk forward.

A log building stood beside the saloon, jutting several feet farther out into the street. Standing against the building to protect his back, Sam had a good view of the front door of the watering hole. He stood with his feet spread slightly apart, his hands hanging loose and natural at his sides. When a scrawny old man came from the saloon and started to cross the street, Sam called to him.

"Say, old-timer, is Bill Chance in there?" The man stopped quickly, nodding.

"Would you take a message to him for me?"

Nodding again, the old man asked, "What do you want me to say?" Sam pushed his hat to the back of his head, shifting his weight slightly forward.

"Just tell him the Judge is here," he said.

"Fight!" the old man yelled at the top of his lungs, then began to skip toward the saloon like a schoolboy. Had it not been for the seriousness of the moment, his actions would have been comical.

"There's gonna be a fight!" he shouted, as he neared the door of the saloon. "The Judge is here an' he's a-wantin' Bill Chance!"

Chance did not keep Curtin waiting long. He strolled from the saloon as casually as a man going on a picnic. His handsome face showed no fear as he continued to walk toward Sam. When he had cut the distance to forty feet, he stopped.

"Been expectin' you, Judge," he said, "you shore know how to keep a man waitin'."

"I had to take a trip to El Paso first."

"Guess you got Clem and Cooter, then." Sam nodded.

The fire he had been told about was creeping into Chance's eyes. Sam would wait no longer. He pointed to the man with the forefinger of his left hand, saying, "After you, Chance."

Still showing no sign of fear, Chance eased himself into a crouch, saying loudly, "Good-bye, Judge!"

Even as he spoke Chance went for his gun. His draw was fast, but he was just clearing his holster when he took a shot in the chest from Curtin's Peacemaker. Staggering into the street, Chance fired a shot that went into a log beside Sam's head. Curtin sent another slug into Chance that knocked him to his knees, but did not stop him. He was crawling toward Curtin now, and fired another shot that missed Sam's head by no more than an inch. Sam put a slug into the man's forehead that ended the fight. Though it seemed much longer, the encounter had lasted less than a dozen seconds.

The outlaw now lay on his back, staring at a cloudless sky through sightless eyes. Just as Sam had suspected, Chance had been game to the end. Several men had moved out onto the plank sidewalk, though they kept their distance and none of them spoke to Sam. In plain view of them all, he took a bank note from his pocket and stuffed it under the dead man's belt, shouting loudly, "I'm leaving money for his burial; any man who does the job can claim it!" Keeping an eye on the bystanders, he crossed the street at an angle and walked down the opposite side to the livery stable. Twenty minutes later he was headed south with two things on his mind: Anita Keeling and Curtin Hill.

Nineteen

He arrived in Hillsboro ten days later drenched to the bone. He had been wet for the past two days, and the rain was still coming down. Leaving his horses with the liveryman, he walked at a fast clip to Anita Keeling's cottage. At his first knock, the beautiful lady burst through the doorway.

"Oh, Sam," she whispered, jumping into his arms and smothering his face with kisses. "You're back . . . you're really back. It seemed like this day would never come." He held her tightly and returned her kisses, saying nothing. She pulled him through the doorway, taking his coat and hat.

"You're so wet," she said, "take off your clothes and let me dry them by the fire."

"Wet, cold, tired and hungry," he said, making no effort to shuck his clothing. "I haven't even had a campfire since it started raining two days ago."

"Well, I can fix all of those things," she said, "come on, take off those wet clothes." When he was slow to comply, she turned to face him.

"Have you changed your mind?" she asked. "Are we still going to be married?"

"Oh, yes," he said quickly, "just as soon as I can get Hamp and his family up here to Hillsboro." Without another word she was gone to another room. When she returned, she was stark naked.

"Now," she said, "give me those wet clothes!" With no further hesitation, he began to strip. She soon had his clothing hanging on two ladder-backed chairs in front of the fireplace. He sat by the fire watching as she moved about, seemingly unaware of her own nakedness. Though he knew that she had doffed her own clothing in order to make him feel more comfortable, he preferred not to dwell on that fact. Very soon he was neither wet nor cold, and a short time later, he forgot that he was tired and hungry.

He stayed in Hillsboro for two days, and on Saturday morning boarded the train for Calvert. As usual, getting the chestnut into the stock car had been a major problem. It had taken Sam and two other men more than twenty minutes to load the animal. The horse simply hated trains, and each ride seemed to make him harder to load the next time. Not so with Charley Horse, who always trotted on board easily, seeming to be eager for the ride.

The wedding was set for next Saturday afternoon, one week from today. Hamp, Lula and Bud had already agreed to make the ride to Hillsboro on the early-morning train. Reverend Moss would perform the ceremony at the First Baptist Church, and some of Anita's friends would attend both the wedding and the reception that was to follow.

* * *

Sam Curtin had been born in poor country during hard times, and had been raised in Texas under the same circumstances. Though he had had to fight his way through boyhood, and had faced and overcome more problems in the past three years than most men saw in a lifetime, nothing had prepared him for the situation he found when he reached Curtin Hill.

As Sam crossed the shallow creek, he could see that Jeff Jordon was standing beside the road, between Hamp's shop and the corral. He had never seen Jeff wearing a sidearm before. Today, he had a Peacemaker hanging on his right leg. Stopping beside the man, Sam smiled.

"Never saw you dressed that way, Jeff," he said, pointing to the Peacemaker.

"Been keeping it out of sight for more than a year, now," Jeff said, his green eyes staring out from beneath his wrinkled brow, "thought it was time to put it back on."

"Something wrong?"

"Go on up the hill and talk to Mrs. Curtin," Jeff said, taking the pack horse's lead rope, "I don't know that I'd be able to explain it to you." Sam kicked Charley Horse in the ribs and rode up the hill to Hamp's house. As he dismounted, Lula appeared in the doorway. She walked slowly to him, putting both arms around his neck.

"It's bad, Sam," she said chokingly, "I mean . . . it's awful bad."

"What is it?" he asked, shaking her gently. "Come on Lu, tell me."

"It's Hamp, Sam," she said, sobbing into his chest, "he's dead!" He led her to a nearby rocking chair, then fell to his knees beside her. Holding both of her hands in his own, he spoke softly, asking for the details.

"Somebody killed him down at the shop," she said. "Bud was over in Franklin getting a wagonload of supplies, then he found Hamp's body when he got back. Everybody said there was blood all over the place down there, but Bud wouldn't let me inside. He locked up the shop, and I don't have a key." She wiped her eyes, then looked at him pitifully, adding, "You have a key, don't you Sam?" He did not answer right away. He believed that Lula had every right in the world to see the spot where her husband died. He also knew that though she sometimes cried, and was usually more emotional than a man might be, deep inside she was the toughest person on the ranch.

"Yes, Lu," he said, patting her shoulder reassuringly, "I have a key. I see no reason why you shouldn't be allowed in the shop, and I'll take you down there in a few minutes. But first, I want you to tell me everything you know about it." She composed herself quickly, and began to tell the story:

Bud had gone to Franklin early Tuesday morning, and had found Hamp's body when he returned in the afternoon. Without telling his mother, Bud had locked the shop and mounted a fast horse, returning two hours later with Sheriff Lister. The sheriff had gone over the area meticulously till dark, then returned the following morning with his deputy and Dr. Vine. Their investigation had lasted till past noon.

It was established early on that Hamp had been killed with his own knife. Though the blade was no longer than two inches, Hamp had kept it sharp as a razor, for he used it in the precise trimming of leather. Though he had been stabbed and slashed many times, Hamp would probably have lived, the doctor said, had it not been for the stab wound to the neck that had severed the jugular vein. The short-bladed leather knife had simply not penetrated Hamp's husky body deep enough to puncture vital organs.

It was known to everyone at Curtin Hill, and probably a number of other people, that Hamp usually kept large sums of money at the shop. The small box in which he kept the money was found at his feet—empty. His pocketbook was also missing, as were two rifles and a shotgun that hung on the wall.

Sheriff Lister believed that the murder and robbery had been a spur-of-the-moment thing, completely unplanned, and considered only after Hamp had innocently displayed a large amount of cash. He reasoned that anyone planning the crime, and not wanting to risk the noise of a gunshot, would have at least brought along a knife with a blade long enough to do the job quickly.

Lula had seen two horses tied at the shop's hitching rail the morning Hamp died. She had been in the yard, hanging her wet wash on the clothesline, and had paid them no mind. Customers came and went at all hours of the day, she said. Though the distance was too great to make any kind of identification, she did remember that the horses were black, and that when she walked into the yard half an hour later the animals were gone.

None of the hands had seen anything. Jeff, Rick and both of the Halleys were busy working on the other side of the hill, far from the shop. None of them ever went in there anyway, especially Rick. Back during the summer Hamp had barred the boy, saying he was tired of straightening up behind him. Both of the Halley twins had put rifles on their saddles after Hamp's death, and Jeff Jordan had begun to walk around looking like a gunfighter, Lula said, adding that she believed that's exactly what he was. So did Sam.

Hamp had been buried on the hill beside Red Jordon,

three days ago. Lula said that she didn't know anywhere else to put him, since none of the Curtins had ever died before. Sam assured her that she had chosen the right place. Hamp and Red had been friends, and had sometimes sat up talking till past midnight.

When Lula had related as much of the story as she knew, Sam got to his feet and walked to the end of the porch. Lula followed, and continued to talk.

"I've prayed day and night, Sam, asking the Lord to treat Hamp good." He stood staring up the hill toward his brother's grave, a granite expression on his face. When he spoke again his tone of voice was like that of a stranger, with more than a little sarcasm.

"While you were praying did you mention the fact that we've had about enough problems lately?" he asked. "Did you ask Him how much more of this He's gonna put on us?"

"Oh, Sam, you shouldn't go talking like that. The Lord knows what He's doing. How do we know He ain't got a herd of horses, and needed a good saddlemaker?" Sam did not answer.

"Come on," he said, taking her arm, "I'll take you down to the shop."

It was obvious to any eye that Hamp had put up a good fight, for the shop was in complete disarray. The bloodstains started at Hamp's desk, where he transacted business, and ended in the far corner of the room, where a large puddle indicated that he had bled to death there. Lula held her composure well as she walked around the room, then announced that she was ready to go back up the hill.

"Just wanted to see it," she said. Sam walked her to the house, then immediately returned to the shop. He was just unlocking the door, when Bud came splashing across the creek and brought his horse to a sliding halt beside him. Jumping to the ground, he spoke breathlessly.

"Guess Momma's done told you what happened," he said.

"Told me all she knew."

"Well, don't nobody else know much more," Bud said. "I followed the trail of the horses Momma saw down here, and the tracks went straight to Calvert. That don't tell us a damn thing, though."

"Probably not," Sam said. "I'll look them over later."

The two walked around inside the shop, with Bud pointing out the overturned chairs, the bench that was lying upside down and the desk that had been pushed sideways. He said that everything was just as he had found it. Both of them knew that Hamp was a stickler for neatness, and that these things had been rearranged during the fight.

"Might not mean nothing," Bud said, reaching into his pocket, "but I found this lying on the floor between Pa's desk and the doorway." He handed Sam a small red button, the same size usually found on the front of a man's shirt. The thread on the button was gold in color, and was still wrapped tightly around its center. The thread had not broken, it had merely been pulled from whatever garment it had been attached to.

Sam turned the button over in his hand several times, then asked, "Did you find this before anybody else came in here?"

"Found it right after I found Pa's body, on my way out the door. I asked Momma about it. She said she sewed on every button Pa had, said he didn't own nothing like that. She said she ain't never had no thread like that, neither." Sam tossed the button from one hand to the other.

"I believe you've found more than you thought,

Bud," he said. "I think whoever wore this button had a hand in killing your pa. Lying right between him and the doorway, Hamp would have seen it, and picked it up. Besides, he swept this place at least once a day, sometimes more." Sam dropped the button into his pocket. "Don't tell a soul that you found this, Bud," he said, "nobody." Bud nodded, and followed Sam outside.

"Bud," Sam said, as they stood beside the shop's hitching rail, "I'm gonna ask you for a favor."

"Well, you know I'll do it, Uncle Sam." Taking money from his pocket, Sam handed it to his nephew.

"I want you to take the early train to Hillsboro in the morning. Tell Anita what happened, and ask her to come back with you. Tell her that Lu needs her, and . . . tell her that I need her." Bud listened as Sam gave him directions to Anita's cottage, then walked up the hill to prepare for his early-morning train ride.

Then Sam began the tedious job of reading the horse tracks around the shop. Though it had recently rained for several days farther north, the Calvert area had been dry for the past two weeks. Sam moved around the hitching rail slowly, bent over at the waist with his nose to the ground. Though there had been much traffic around the shop lately, it did not take him long to discover that two horses had left the rail in a hurry in the recent past, their hooves tearing large chunks of clay out of the dry earth. Their hind hooves had dug into the earth and twisted, as the animals had been whirled away from the rail and pointed toward the road. He knew immediately that the horses had belonged to the killers, for no customer would ever leave the shop at a hard run. He began to follow the tracks toward the creek, his eyes glued to the ground.

He lost the trail before he even got to the creek, and several times returned to the shop to start over. Dozens of horses had traveled the road since the last rain, many of them at a running gait. One set of tracks looked much like another, intermingling so much that it was difficult or impossible to separate them.

He crossed the creek on the foot log. He had cut the large oak down several years ago, allowing it to fall across the creek so that foot traffic would not have to wade the shallow water. He had left most of the limbs intact, so that the walkers would have something to hold on to.

Across the creek, he found that the tracking problem intensified, for the dripping wet hooves of the horses had slipped around considerably as they dug in for more solid footing. He walked up the road for several hundred yards, then retraced his footsteps to the shop. Although Sam knew that Bud had meant well, he also knew that the youngster could not have tracked the killers' horses to Calvert, or anywhere else. No more than a mile from the creek, the road came to a T, with a left-hand turn going to Franklin, and the right-hand going to Calvert. At least fifty and sometimes as many as a hundred horses a day traveled that road, and it would simply be impossible to track a particular animal. Sam would never mention that fact to Bud.

He walked to the bunkhouse, where he found Jeff putting the last simmering touches on a large iron pot of beef stew.

"Smells good, Jeff," he said, taking a chair at the table. "I think I'll have a bowl if you've got enough."

"Got more than enough," Jeff said. He dished up two large bowls of stew and joined Sam at the table. The two ate quietly for a while, then Jeff broke the silence.

"At least one of us should have been on this side of the hill, Sam."

"It probably wouldn't have mattered," Sam said, adding more salt to his stew. "Most likely it was a noiseless killing, and you'd have had no reason to pay attention to what went on at the shop. Your work was on the other side of the hill, so that's where you were supposed to be. None of us ever expected something like this to happen."

They were soon joined by Rick and the Halleys. Each man dished up his own supper, then sat down at the table. After offering a quiet hello to Sam, they all went about the business of eating.

With supper over, and darkness coming on, Sam walked to the bunkhouse door. Rick followed, looking as if he might break into tears.

"I'm . . . aw . . . awful sorry," he said. Sam began to pat him on the back, brushing the boy's hair out of his eyes with his other hand.

"Have you got any money, Rick?" he asked.

"Got twenty cents. Got it hid in a good place, too." Sam handed the youngster a few dollars.

"Hide this with it. Buy anything you want next time Mack lets you go to town with him." Laughing loudly, Rick grabbed the money and ran toward the barn, having no idea that he was revealing the general location of his secret hiding place. Knowing that having the money would occupy Rick's mind for the remainder of the evening, Sam climbed the hill to his own home. He soon had a fire going, for the evening was cool. Then, sitting in front of the fireplace, away from the eyes of everyone else, he broke down. He had not shed a tear since he was a child, but now he cried like a baby.

Hamp had been both father and big brother since Sam's early childhood, and though Sam had not always had everything he wanted, he had certainly had the things he needed. His mind went now to the time Hamp had almost come to blows with a neighbor on Sam's behalf. Eleven-year-old Sam had given the neighbor's son, who was two years older, a beating, blacking both eyes and knocking out one tooth. The neighbor had brought the boy to Hamp, pointing out the damage.

"I demand that he be punished," the neighbor had said, "look what he done. That tooth ain't gonna grow back in, neither." Hamp had shaken his head to the man, agreeing that the tooth was gone for good. Sam had stood by quietly, for he had already told Hamp the story.

"Well, are you gonna punish him?" the man asked.

"Nope," Hamp said sternly. The man was furious.

"I demand that you punish that boy!" he yelled. "Otherwise—"

"Otherwise what?" Hamp had interrupted. "Sam told me that your boy tried to take his kite away from him, and he don't lie to me. Boys have been fighting since the beginning of time, and you or me neither one ain't gonna be able to stop it."

The man bristled, taking a small step in Hamp's direction, repeating, "I demand—"

"You can demand all day, mister," Hamp had said, "but I'll stand with Sam. If you intend to make a man thing out of it, I figure you're gonna have about the same kind of luck your boy did!" Hamp moved half a step closer to the man, who began to back away toward his buggy.

"This ain't over!" he yelled. "I intend to see what the sheriff has to say about it."

"You do that," Hamp had said, relaxing from his rigid stance, "and ask him if he knows any way to keep boys from fighting."

That was the same year Hamp sold his brood sow to buy Sam's first rifle. He had made the transaction over Lula's objections. "He'll be a man before you know it,

Lu," Hamp had said lovingly, "and a man is expected to know how to use a rifle." The rifle had been presented on Christmas Eve. The brothers had then engaged in a long bear hug, neither of them yet knowing of the amazing hand-eye coordination with which young Sam had been gifted.

Hamp had allowed Sam to grow at his own pace, letting him learn from his own mistakes, and offering advice only when it was sought. He had always encouraged Sam to find his own way of doing things, saying that if people only did things the way they were taught by somebody else, nothing would ever change or get better.

Two hours later Sam was still sitting in front of the fireplace, but his eyes were dry. He shoveled ashes over the few remaining coals from his fire, then walked outside to relieve himself. He must get a good night's sleep, he was thinking. He would cry no more, for he had things to do. A few minutes later, he was sleeping soundly in his feather bed.

Twenty

The following morning, Sam tied his chestnut to the buggy and rode into Calvert with his nephew. Bud would leave the vehicle at the livery, then board the train to Hillsboro. Tonight, he would deliver Anita Keeling to Curtin Hill. Just thinking about it gave Sam a warm feeling, for he was deeply in love with the woman.

He saw Bud off on the train, then learned that Sheriff Lister had not been in Calvert during the past several days. Sam pointed the chestnut toward Franklin, and gave the animal its head. He arrived two hours later.

Riding down the street toward the sheriff's office, Sam passed several men with whom he was well acquainted. Though all of them spoke or waved a greeting, none made an attempt at conversation. He supposed that they all knew of Hamp's death, and simply did not know what to say. Neither did the sheriff.

"I don't know what to say, Sam," the lawman told him, after the two shook hands. "I don't know much more than I did before I rode over to the shop."

"Didn't expect you to," Sam said. "However, you might keep an eye out for his rifles and shotgun; somebody might be wanting to sell or trade them at a bargain price. The rifles are a Henry and a Winchester, and the shotgun is a double-barreled Greener."

"I know about them, Sam," Lister said, pouring two cups of coffee from a smoky pot. "I've already put out word with every gun dealer in the area."

They sat at the sheriff's desk drinking coffee, each man a little reluctant to talk about the grisly scene at Hamp's shop. Finally, the sheriff brought the conversation around to Sam's recent manhunt.

"I already heard about your run-in with the Streeps in El Paso," he said. "Did you have any luck in running down Bill Chance?"

"Got him in Tascosa." The sheriff jumped to his feet laughing, looking as if he might be about to perform a war dance.

"That's good," he said, continuing to smile. "I mean that's real good." He soon reseated himself at his desk and began to look and sound official again.

"I've made two deposits to your account in Calvert," he said, "and there's more to come. Some of the merchants were reluctant to contribute until after the fact. I'll be paying them another visit, now." Sam nodded indicating that he was pleased. Then he decided to put the question that had been nagging at him to rest.

"Did you notice anything unusual around Hamp's shop when you first arrived, Sheriff?"

"Noticed right off that two riders had put the spurs to their horses damn near in the front door, and I'd say that's unusual. I made several attempts to track the horses, but I lost the trail before I even got to the creek. It was worse on the south side of the creek, like hunting a needle in a haystack."

"I reached the same conclusion when I attempted it," Sam said. His question had been answered to his satisfaction. He now knew that Sheriff Lister was not stupid, and that he had actually made an investigation. Getting to his feet, and offering a parting handshake, he said, "I'll be getting on back to the ranch, now. If you get any good information I sure would appreciate knowing about it. Hamp raised me, you know."

"Of course I know," Lister said, following Sam to the doorway, "and I can understand you wanting to settle the score yourself. Even though I'm the taxpayers' sheriff, and it did happen in my county, I'll promise you one thing: if I do find out who the killers are I'll name them for you. Of course, that'll have to be just between you and me."

"Just between you and me," Sam repeated, and left the building. After having breakfast and several cups of strong coffee in the courthouse restaurant, he mounted the chestnut and turned the animal toward Calvert.

Once there, he headed for the livery stable, for he wanted to talk with the hostler. Finding that the man was not in, and the office locked, Sam sat down on an upended nail keg to wait him out. Since the time was shortly after noon, Arkansas had probably gone somewhere to eat, for he would never close the stable on Sunday, his busiest day of the week.

"I'll tell you th' same thang I told Sheriff Lister," Arkansas said to Sam, in answer to his questions. "Ain't nobody brought back no winded or lathered horse. I didn't rent out no horse last Tuesday, or no other day last week. Th' rentin' business died when th' weather turned cool." Sam thanked the man, then began to walk about town. He was soon talking with his favorite bartender.

"It's like I told the sheriff and his deputy," Les said, "I haven't seen any strangers in here or out on the street. The only talk I've heard has all been sympathetic. Everybody liked Hamp, Sam."

"Maybe not everybody," Sam said, "you know what happened."

"Yeah. Well, I didn't mean whoever killed him."

"I know," Sam said. "If you hear anything you think I should know about, I'll be around the ranch somewhere."

"Like I told Sheriff Lister, the first thing I hear that don't sound right, I'll come running. I knew Hamp Curtin for more than twenty years, and never knew him to give anybody the short end of the stick. I've known him to fix things for people knowing damn well he'd never see a dime for his work."

Sam questioned several other people during the afternoon, but everywhere he went, the sheriff or his deputy had been there before him. No doubt about it, he finally decided, Sheriff Lister was on the job.

He left Calvert at midafternoon, arriving at the shop an hour later. He noticed right away that someone had scrubbed the floors clean. The few faded pink stains that remained would be seen only if a person looked for them. Lu must have spent most of the day on her knees with a brush and bucket, he decided, for though anyone on the ranch would have done the job, none would have done it without being asked. He also noticed that the padlock was missing from the door's hasp, meaning that Lu did not intend to be locked out of the shop again.

Sam sat in Hamp's comfortable chair for the remainder of the afternoon, trying to imagine what had passed through his brother's mind as the scene played out. Had he yelled for help? Sam doubted it. Hamp had most likely fought like a tiger. Though he did not get around well on his peg leg, he was nevertheless a very strong man, and would have been hard to handle at close quarters. Sam supposed that the killers had discovered this fact early on, and had picked up the knife as a last resort. Hamp had kept the short trimming blade lying close to his elbow when he was at work, and though it was very sharp, it was hardly the instrument a man would deliberately choose to commit murder. The knife had been found at Hamp's feet, with both the blade and handle drenched with blood.

At least one of the killers would have had blood on his hands and probably his clothing, Sam was thinking. Where had the men washed themselves? The creek? Maybe. Washing blood from a man's hands in the cool creek water would have been easy enough. Getting the stains out of clothing would be quite another matter.

Hamp had many things in the shop that sold for less than a dollar. Sam believed, as did Sheriff Lister, that the killing had been a spur-of-the-moment thing; that the killers had made some small purchase, then spotted a large amount of money when Hamp attempted to make change. Lu had said that Hamp usually carried several hundred dollars on his person. She believed that after being dirt poor for most of his life, the carrying of large sums of money in his pocket made him feel more successful. Sam believed that the lady was correct.

Hearing a rider approach the barn, Sam poked his head through the doorway to see Jeff Jordon leading his horse into the corral. Sam called the man to him.

"You want to help me hunt Hamp's killers, Jeff?" he asked.

"Why, hell yes, Sam, you know that."

"All right," Sam said, "sit down and let me tell you

what I have in mind. First of all, Anita will be coming here before nightfall, and I can't just go running off. Starting at sunup tomorrow, here's what I want you to do: . . ."

He instructed Jeff to ride the creek for several miles in each direction, looking for tracks indicating that the killers had washed themselves there. Searching the creek's south bank was all that was necessary, for the men would never have stopped on the north side, putting themselves in plain view of anyone at Curtin Hill.

Next, Sam wanted Jeff to look over every saddle and bridle at the livery stables in Calvert, Franklin and Hearne, paying close attention to the reins, for he found it difficult to believe that a man with blood on his hands could ride a horse without leaving stains. Especially since the amount of blood had not been small. Hamp had bled a lot.

"Take this with you," Sam said, handing Jordon a small roll of bills. "Stay in hotels and eat in restaurants. Have a few drinks in the saloons and keep your ears open."

"Consider it done," Jeff said, shoving the money into his pocket. "It'll probably take a few days, but it'll be done right."

"I know," Sam said, then watched Jeff walk across the road and disappear inside the bunkhouse. Then Sam walked up the hill to his own home. He sat on the porch for a while, wondering where the worthless spotted dog had gone. It had probably moved over to Hamp's place when Sam had no longer been around to feed it. Then, when it turned out that Lu was not so free with the handouts, the mongrel had once again hit the road in search of greener pastures. Sam stepped to the end of the porch and kicked the pile of straw into the yard, fleas and all.

He was still sitting on the porch when the buggy crossed the creek. Even at this distance, and though daylight was fading fast, he could see that Anita rode on the seat beside Bud. As the mare trotted up the hill to Lula's house, Sam stepped into his yard and began to walk over. Bud helped the lady to the ground, then began to pile her baggage onto the porch. Lula stepped into the yard and the women embraced, as Bud drove the buggy toward the barn. Then Sam was on the scene, and Anita ran into his arms.

"I'm so sorry, Sam," she said, speaking just above a whisper, with tears running down both cheeks. "He was such a nice man, and I know you loved him dearly." He held her close for a long time, saying nothing. Lula broke the spell.

"I've got supper ready," she said. "Let's eat while it's still warm."

Bud joined them at the table shortly, and it was a quiet meal. Anita made several attempts at conversation, once asking Lula if she had dried the apples from which the pies were made. Lula replied that she had, and said nothing else. Bud poured himself a final cup of coffee, then reseated himself at the table.

"I'm gonna keep the shop open, Momma," he said.

"Of course you are, son. You've got to make a living."

"I've still got the army contract, but I want to do some of that fancy tooling like Pa done. Ain't never tried it, but I can learn it. Pa had to learn it." Lula began to smile for the first time in several days.

"Lord, I should say so, son," she said. "Don't reckon he made a single thing he was satisfied with for the first four or five years. Stay with it, you can learn it just like he did." She pushed her chair away from the table, exhaling loudly.

"Don't know what in the world I'm gonna do," she continued. "I've been depending on Hamp since I was fifteen years old." Anita began to pat Lula's arm, then Sam spoke loudly.

"You don't have to depend on anybody, Lu. Hamp had some money put by, and it's all yours. Half of that shop down there is yours." He poured some syrup over the butter that remained on his plate, then continued. "Besides, I've got some money these days, and your name is Curtin. You don't have to do anything that you don't want to do."

"Well, just the same," she said, "cooking for just Bud and myself ain't much of a job."

"Do something else, then," he said. "Go to town, ride around the country. See things, and buy yourself something pretty. There ain't much to do around the ranch at this time of year, any of the hands will drive you anywhere you want to go. I'll do it myself if I happen to be around."

"We'll see," she said, rising and beginning to clear off the table. A moment later, she turned to Anita, saying, "I put all of your stuff in that back bedroom, you can sleep there till after the wedding."

"Thank you," Anita said, beginning to stack the dishes.

She joined Sam on the porch half an hour later, and the two sat holding hands in the darkness. He was soon holding her close, running his hands over her shapely body. Each of his kisses became more passionate, then he whispered, "I need you real bad, honey."

She pushed herself away, saying softly, "We can't do that again, Sam, not until we're married. And especially not here; Lula would lose respect for both of us. I made a pledge to myself just this morning."

* * *

The pledge lasted for three days. Lula had just left in the buggy with Mack Halley, headed to Calvert, when Sam ambushed Anita in the kitchen. After a few kisses and much artful persuasion, she silently allowed him to lead her to the bedroom.

"When are we going to be married?" she asked later, as they sat on the front porch.

"Don't know exactly," he said. "I need to stay around here for a while; I've got lots of feelers out for information on Hamp's killers. Don't know when I can get back up to Hillsboro."

"Why can't we be married right over there on your front porch?"

"Hell, there ain't no reason not to. I could handle that before the day is out, but you said—"

"I've changed my mind," she interrupted.

They were married in Sam's yard two days later, with Lula's pastor performing the ceremony. Though it was a happy occasion for all concerned, no one seemed quite as delighted as Lula herself.

"I'm so proud and happy for both of you that I could just squeal," she said. "You two are gonna have the prettiest children in this county." Then, using sugar, water and whiskey, she surprised Sam by mixing herself a little toddy. A short while later, she crossed the hill to her own home. The ceremony had been attended by everyone who lived at the ranch, for Jeff Jordon had ridden in an hour before the wedding. He had been gone for almost a week, and Sam was anxious to talk with him. With the help of Mack Halley, Bud carried Anita's things across the hill to her new home. Then Sam locked the doors and spent the next three hours alone with his bride.

"Been in about every saloon and livery stable in the county," Jeff said, when Sam called him from the bunkhouse at sundown. "I didn't find any tracks along the creek, and I sure didn't learn anything at the stables. Every single one of the liverymen told me that Sheriff Lister had already been there, looking for the same thing I was." Though he was disappointed, Sam had to smile, for he knew that Robertson County's commissioners had chosen well in appointing Lister to finish Wallace Pate's term as sheriff. The man would no doubt be a shoo-in during the next election.

"I'll say one thing for Sheriff Lister," Sam said, "he sure as hell gets around." Turning on his heel, he walked back up the hill to finish what he had started earlier in the afternoon.

He was out of bed early the following morning, having rediscovered the truthfulness of the old proverb that a man could get farther behind and catch up quicker on his lovemaking than anything else. He saddled the chestnut and rode over the hill, for he had not ridden about his ranch in quite some time. He also wanted some time alone to think.

He rode along at a walk, racking his brain for answers. Had Hamp known his killers? It was very possible, for most of his business was transacted with repeat customers. Quality craftsmanship was Hamp's trademark, and word of mouth had advertised that fact throughout the county and beyond. Most of the area's ranchers and cowboys conducted business with him at least once a year, some of them several times. Sam doubted that the murder had been committed by a disgruntled customer, for satisfaction was guaranteed. Hamp had long had a policy of refunding any man's money who was not pleased. If he had any known enemies he had certainly never mentioned it to any of the family. All of which brought Sam right back to Sheriff Lister's foregone conclusion: that the murder had been a spur-of-the-moment thing brought on by Hamp's habit of keeping large sums of money on hand.

Riding along with his mind wandering, Sam had unconsciously ridden off his own property and onto Hank Warren's spread. He quickly decided to continue on, for he had not talked with Warren in more than a year. William Warren had started the ranch half a century ago, and it had passed on to Hank when his father died. The Curtin family had known the Warrens well for many years. When he rode into the yard, Sam could see Hank and his two young sons down by the barn, building what appeared to be a pigpen. He rode down and dismounted.

"Hello, Hank," he said, nodding to the two boys.

"Haven't seen you in a coon's age, Sam," Hank said, talking around a mouthful of nails. He spat the nails into his hand, and put the hammer aside. "Sure was sorry to hear about Hamp. He was too good a man to go that way."

"Me and my brother wuz over at his shop the same day he wuz killed," the oldest of the boys said.

"You were?" Sam asked. "What time?"

"Reckon it was purty close to dinner. Mr. Curtin put a new bit on my horse's bridle. Didn't charge me nothin', neither." Sam wanted to hear more. He walked closer.

"Did you see anybody else around the shop?" he asked.

"No, sir. Didn't nobody else come while we wuz there."

"What color horses were you riding."

"Both of 'em are blacks," the boy said, pointing, "them two right over there in the corral." Sam looked at the horses and nodded, then seated himself on a block of wood that would eventually be split for the fireplace.

"One more question," he said, "try hard to remember. When you left the shop, did you walk your horses or run them?"

"Oh, that's easy to remember," the boy said, chuckling. "We left there as fast as we could, 'cause we wuz racin' each other to the creek. I won, too." Sam thanked the boy, and stepped back into the saddle.

"It's been too long since we've seen you and the missus, Hank," he said, turning his horse toward home. "Come over when you can. I've built a new home since you've been over, and I became a married man yesterday."

"Well, congratulations," Warren said loudly. "Where'd you build the house at?"

"Up on the hill, just west of Hamp's place."

"Well, we'll be over to see you in the near future. You can expect us just any weekend."

"All right, good-bye to you." He rode south at a walk, for he was in no hurry. He now knew that Lula had not seen the killers' horses at all. The two blacks she had noticed at the shop's hitching rail had belonged to the Warren boys, who had visited the shop many times in the past. Hamp had been appreciated by the youngsters of the area, for he was always eager to help them with some small problem, rarely charging them for his services.

And Sam's concern about the scarred earth around the rail had been put to rest. The deep tracks had been made by the charging horses of the Warren boys, as they playfully raced toward the creek. Sam had done the same thing countless times when he was a boy, and more than a few times since.

He kicked his horse to a trot, for he was beginning to feel hungry. Besides, he was a married man now, and he had not kissed his bride since sunup. "A man ought to kiss his wife at least once a day," Hamp had once said to Sam, "maybe feel around on her a little bit. Don't hurt none to tell her how pretty she is every time you think about it, either."

Sam put his horse to a canter, and half an hour later loosed it in the corral. Remembering Hamp's words, he smiled, then began to walk up the hill at a fast clip.

Twenty-one

He stayed in bed later than usual the following morning, snuggled up to his bride, for he knew that the weather had turned very cold outside. Seeing that Anita was also awake, he kissed her nose and pulled her closer to him.

"Don't know how I ever got along without you," he said.

"You got along because you didn't know any better," she whispered, laughing and tickling his ribs. "I'll get some breakfast started if you'll build a fire." He was out of bed quickly, and soon had fires going in both the stove and the fireplace.

After eating, he walked to the bunkhouse to find that Jeff was also getting a late start on the day. He was sitting at the table drinking coffee, reading from an old edition of the Fort Worth newspaper. Sam poured himself a cup, then joined Jeff at the table.

"The Halleys and Rick are already up and at 'em, huh?" he asked.

"They always are," Jeff said, laying the newspaper aside. "Out hunting something to do, I guess. Same thing I was doing the day your brother was killed. I rode that west boundary all day, but there just wasn't anything that needed doing. I didn't even know Hamp was dead till I got back here, just before sundown."

"You didn't see Hamp's body in the shop, then?"

"No. Bud and the Halleys had already brought him out and up the hill by the time I got here. Mack said the shop was a mess, but I didn't want to see it. I never went in there when your brother was alive, didn't see any reason to go after he was gone."

"You've never been in there at all?" Sam asked.

"Went in there the first day I was on the ranch, but Hamp didn't seem to want to talk to me. I never went back after that, 'cause he never did invite me."

"Oh, that was just Hamp's way," Sam said, reaching for the pot to warm his coffee. "He liked you just fine, Jeff. He even said so to me."

"Well, that's good to hear, Sam," Jeff said, reaching for his heavy coat. "Anyway, now you know why I stayed clear of the shop." Heading toward the door, he added over his shoulder, "I'll be going now, gotta try to earn my keep." He walked toward the corral, his holstered Peacemaker hanging well below his coattail.

Sam watched from the bunkhouse door as Jeff roped and saddled the big roan. The man was a pleasure to watch, and Sam only wished that he himself could be half as good. Jeff's skill with a rope was of the quality usually associated with circus performers. He systematically threw perfect circle loops for distances of forty or fifty feet, right on target. And he could do it with either hand. Shaking his head, Sam walked across the road to the shop. Bud sat in his father's chair, trimming leather according to a pattern he had ordered through the mail.

"Making Momma a pocketbook," the youngster said. "I know she won't complain if the tooling ain't too good."

"No, she won't, Bud," Sam said, patting his nephew's arm, "because the tooling is gonna be good. Just follow the pattern, and keep reading your book."

Bud picked up what was obviously an instruction book, holding it high in the air. He then dropped it onto the desk noisily, saying, "Pa was a hell of a lot better than the people that put out this book, Uncle Sam."

"Sure, he was," Sam said, rising to his feet. "You just try to remember the things you saw him do, you'll be all right." He patted Bud's arm again, then climbed the hill to visit Lula.

He found her sitting beside the fireplace, knitting. She put her work aside quickly, but not before Sam saw that she had been knitting a bootee.

"What are you working on, Lu?" he asked, smiling. She did not answer, and covered her work with a piece of cloth.

"Huh?" he asked again. She exhaled loudly, then resumed her knitting.

"Well, if you must know," she said, keeping her voice low, "I thought I'd make a few baby things. The way you two take after each other, you'll probably need them about next fall."

"Maybe so," he said. "Are you all right? Do you need anything?"

"No, Sam," she said, "I'm fine. You take care of the things you've got to do, don't worry about me."

An hour later, Sam was talking with a friend of long standing named Lonny Ramsay. A dark-haired, dark-complected man of about forty, whose midsection was rapidly turning to paunch, Ramsay owned a general fix-it shop beside the Calvert road, and worked on everything from watches to wagon wheels. Like Sam, he had originally come from Mississippi, and had been in the Calvert area for a long time. Ramsay's shop was located no more than fifty feet from the road, so the man saw, or at least was in a position to see, anyone traveling in either direction. Especially someone coming to or from Curtin Hill, for the road came to a T almost at the side door of his shop.

"Ain't seen nobody but you and Hamp's boy, Bud," Ramsay said. "Of course, I saw him pass hauling a woman in the buggy a few days ago."

"How about the day Hamp died, Lonny. Did you see anybody that looked to be in a hurry?"

"Nope. A hard-running horse draws attention, Sam. Ain't nobody passed here lickety-split in a long time."

Ramsay was an avid hunter, and kept a pen full of hounds year-round. Though he sometimes hunted bigger game, his favorite activity was to sit on a stump waiting, as the beagles drove the rabbits to his gun. He had returned from the war with bad knees, and could not chase after the dogs the way he once did. Sam had joined him on more than one rabbit hunt in the past.

"I guess we'll have to put your dogs in the woods again before Christmas, Lonny," Sam said, getting to his feet. "If you get ready before I do, just let me know."

"Let's make it about the first of December," Ramsay said. "Got some things I need to catch up on around here, first."

"Well, while you're catching up," Sam said, taking a cheap pocketwatch from his vest, "see if you can make this thing run." Ramsay held the watch up to his ear, shaking it.

"Sounds like something's loose in there," he said. "I'll take it apart later today." They said their good-byes, and Sam stepped into the saddle.

He was soon at the livery stable in Calvert. He sat in the office, talking idly with the liveryman, who was busy working on a bridle.

"Sheriff Lister was in here all right," Arkansas said, in answer to a question from Sam. "Went over ever' damn piece o' leather I got." He squatted on his haunches to add another chunk of wood to the stove. "I shore ain't seen nobody named Jeff, though; don't reckin I know th' man."

Thanking the liveryman, Sam remounted and rode down the town's main street, his mind on Jeff Jordon. "Been in about every saloon and livery stable in the county," Jeff had said. Had he deliberately lied to Sam? Or had he skipped Calvert purposely, concentrating on places farther out? Sam tied his horse to a hitching rail and began to move about the town on foot. During the next hour, he talked with half a dozen bartenders, all of whom he had known for years. None of them had seen Jeff Jordon.

The ride to Hearne took more than two hours. Sam stopped first at the livery, then made the rounds of the saloons. He received the same reactions to his questions that he had in Calvert. Nobody in town knew Jeff Jordon, and when given a detailed description, all shook their heads negatively. The man had not been seen. Though he now knew that Jeff had lied to him, Sam decided to be thorough. He pointed his chestnut toward Franklin.

He arrived there after sundown, and the story was the same. Neither the liveryman nor the bartenders had seen Jeff. Nor had the clerk at the hotel, where Sam registered for the night. He lay on his bed wide awake for a long time, thinking of Jeff. Sam did not really know the man, nor did he know anyone who did. One thing was obvious: Jeff was, at the very least, a liar. And though Sam knew that the man had actually known Red Jordon, that in itself meant little. Red had been a big talker, and all any man had to do to learn his life history was listen.

Sam left the hotel at sunup. Though sleep had been slow to come, he had rested well, for he knew that his wife would not be worried. They had talked it over several days ago, and she had been very understanding. "I know you won't be spending much time at home till this thing is over," she had said, "and I also know that it is something you have to do. I just hope you'll let me know where you are as often as you can." He now headed for the livery stable, where he roped and saddled the chestnut. He said good-bye to the hostler, then rode out of town at a gallop. He gave the horse its head, for the morning was very cold and the animal was eager to run. He made the ride home in near record time.

Loosing the chestnut into the corral, he switched his saddle to Charley Horse, then rode up the hill. He kissed Anita several times, then informed her that he would be riding out again. He was soon feasting on steak and eggs, along with hot biscuits and strong coffee. A short time later, he rode over the hill, where he found Mack Halley and Rick cutting wood. Dismounting, Sam motioned Halley to him.

"Mack," he said, quietly enough that Rick could not hear, "I want to know where every man on this ranch was on the day Hamp was killed."

Halley took the glove from his right hand so that he might better scratch his head, saying, "Well, the best I remember, me and Rick were doing just what we're doing now, and my brother was off to the east there cleaning out and boxing up that sandy spring."

When it became obvious that Mack was going to say no more, Sam asked, "And Jeff?"

"He spent the day on the west boundary, chasing cows back onto Curtin property." Sam hesitated only for a moment.

"Do you know that for sure, Mack?" he asked.

"Well, I don't guess I do, but that's what he said he was doing. I don't see as much of him as I used to, he's been just kinda going his own way lately." Sam nodded his head, and put one foot in the stirrup.

"Whatever you do, Mack," he said, "don't let Rick know that I've been asking questions." Halley smiled, and returned to his woodcutting.

Like the chestnut, Charley Horse wanted to run in this cold weather, and Sam rode to the northwest corner of his property quickly. Once there, he turned the horse south, riding along at a slow walk. He followed a zig-zagging course for the next two hours, finally arriving at his southern boundary. Then he crossed onto his neighbor's property and rode north again.

At noon, he was back at the northwest boundary, and very disappointed. Jeff had lied about his whereabouts on the day Hamp was killed. No horse had traveled this boundary during the past two weeks. Not unless the animal had wings. Jeff had come on the hill lying, Sam had concluded, no telling where he had actually met Red Jordon. The story about him being Red's son had probably been made up on the spot, after he had learned that Red was dead. Jeff, or whatever his name actually was, had no doubt spent some time around Red Jordon in the past, learning enough of the man's background to make the imposter role an easy one to play.

And he had played the role well, for Sam had not only given him a year-round job, he had given him a good horse, money and Red's new saddle. Had even offered him the old man's Spencer rifle. Sam's mind went now to the many nights Jeff had sat on the porch drinking Sam's whiskey, telling stories about his depraved childhood in Virginia. And the one about his mother dying accidentally from a fall on a pitchfork was too good not to have happened to somebody, sometime. He had probably heard the story somewhere, then simply adopted it as his own. Sam sat very still in the saddle for a long time. He was staring at the ground disgustedly, for he now believed that Jeff had killed his brother. After quite some time had passed, he kicked Charley Horse in the ribs and pointed the animal southeast.

He bypassed his own home, and headed straight for the bunkhouse. Finding no one around, he walked to the corner where Jeff slept, seating himself on the man's bunk. A large box sat against the wall at the head of the bunk, and Sam began to go through its contents. He found what he was looking for in less than a minute: at the bottom of a small stack of neatly folded clothing was a flannel shirt with red buttons. Shaking the garment out, he saw that the third button from the top was missing. Taking the red disk from his vest pocket, he fitted it against the shirt. The match was perfect, even to the rough place on the shirt where the tightly wrapped thread had pulled through the flimsy cloth. And the thread on the remaining buttons was gold in color. Convinced now that he had found his man, Sam returned the shirt to its position at the bottom of the box, then left the building.

He was soon sitting on his own porch, weighing his

options. He had no idea where Jeff was at the moment, but felt sure that the man would show up before dark. Should Sam simply disarm Jeff and carry him to Sheriff Lister at gunpoint? He would surely be prosecuted for murder, but if he could concoct a good enough story, a jury might demand more evidence than a missing button. No, Sam decided, he would handle the situation himself. That decision made, he called his wife to him, for he thought that it was only fair that she know the truth: that he intended to kill a man before the day was over; that he had once again become the Judge. She was even more understanding than he had expected.

"I guess you've ruled out turning him over to the law," she said. It was more a statement than a question.

"Yes."

"Then you must do what you have to. Everyone says you're the best there is, but please be careful." She kissed him on the lips, then walked back inside the house. Sam did not see the tears that were soon flowing.

He was still sitting on the porch when he saw Jeff riding in an hour before sundown. Sam was off the porch quickly, walking down the hill to the bunkhouse. He stood in the yard next to the wellcurb, waiting, the small red button in his hand. When Jeff had fed and cared for his horse, he walked from the corral and through the gate, closing it behind him. Turning, he saw that Sam had taken up the unmistakable gunfighter's stance, thirty feet away. Jeff froze, but showed no signs of fear.

"Why did you do it, Jeff?" Sam asked loudly.

"Wha . . . what do you mean?"

"You've lied to me constantly, fellow," Sam said. "You must have thought I was even dumber than I am." He opened his left hand, allowing the red disk to show. "This button came off of that flannel shirt in your box. Hamp tore it off while you were killing him."

Jeff made no effort to deny the accusation, just spread his feet apart in his own stance of readiness. Then he said, "You've got it only half right, Judge." Judge! Jeff had never called Sam by that nickname before. "I was in the shop, all right," Jeff continued, "but I didn't kill Hamp. Johnny Suit took care of that."

"Johnny Suit? Who's he?" Sam wanted to learn more, and intended to let the man talk as long as he would.

"Gambler and gunman," Jeff said. "Hangs around Fort Worth."

A moment of silence followed, with the tension building. Sam spoke quickly, asking, "What is your name?" Jeff grinned widely, even chuckled a little.

"Well, it sure ain't Jeff Kirby, or Jeff anybody. My name is Will Brannon." Sam recognized the name as being that of a gunslinger from Kansas who had reputedly killed at least half a dozen men. "Guess we both know that there ain't but one of us gonna walk away from here," Brannon continued. "If that happens to be you, you'll find half of the money in my pocket. Suit's got the other half. He took the guns to Fort Worth; gonna sell 'em there. He—" Sam made his play! One shot rang out, and the third button was now missing from another one of Will Brannon's shirts—probably resting somewhere near his backbone. Brannon bounced off the gatepost and fell on his face, still holding on to his gun. He had cleared his holster, but had not lived to raise his shooting arm. Sam kicked the gun away and stood watching, as he listened to Brannon cough out his last breath.

Sam was trying to understand the reason for Brannon's confidence—or overconfidence. He had been nowhere near the fastest gun Sam had ever faced. And why had he volunteered so much information? He had obviously believed that he himself would be the one to walk away from the showdown, and that the information would die with Sam Curtin.

As Bud walked over from the shop, Rick and the Halley brothers rode into the yard. None of the men spoke, just stood staring at the body, waiting for Sam to explain the situation.

"His name is Will Brannon," Sam said to no one in particular. "He's one of the men who killed Hamp." The stunned look on the faces of the men was understandable. Jeff Jordon was the last man any of them would have ever suspected.

"Jeff?" Bud asked, a tone of disbelief in his voice. "I never woulda—"

"As I said before," Sam interrupted, now holstering his weapon, "his name was not Jeff. He was a gunman from Kansas named Will Brannon. He admitted his part in the killing once he realized that I was on to him. Take your pa's money from his pocket, Bud. Give it to your momma; it's hers now." Bud's quick search produced a large roll of bills, which he shoved into his own pocket.

"He sure didn't earn that kind of money around here," Mack Halley said, which reminded Sam that the Halleys were due for a raise in pay.

"Do you want me to go get the sheriff, Uncle Sam?" Bud asked, glancing at the corpse and shaking his head.

"If you're not too tired, Bud." The youngster saddled a horse and headed for Franklin.

Across the road, well away from the others, Rick stood holding his horse's reins, the strain plainly written on his face. Sam walked to him now. Rick's whole body stiffened when an arm went around his shoulder.

"I know that Jeff treated you good, Rick," Sam said in soft tones, "and I know that you liked him. But people are not always exactly like they seem. . . ."

Twenty-two

Sheriff Lister had carried Brannon's body to Franklin, and Sam had paid the undertaker to bury it. Lister had said that as far as he was concerned the matter was over and done, that there would be no further investigation. The lawman knew nothing of Johnny Suit, though he did believe that he had heard the name somewhere.

Brannon had been in the ground for a week. Today, Sam was loading Charley Horse onto the train for Fort Worth. He had left the chestnut in the corral, for he had long ago grown weary of fighting the animal at each boarding. Besides, Charley Horse was stronger, and Curtin never knew when he might need the exceptional speed and stamina. He was carrying no pack animal on this trip, intending to use the rails as much as possible. He was soon sitting comfortably in the passenger car, as the train rattled out of Calvert headed north.

Less than a dozen others were aboard, and Sam spoke to no one, just sat quietly by the window, watching the farms pass fleetingly by. Some of the fields had already been plowed under, but most still held on to the decadent brown cotton stalks, now devoid of the snowy fruit that had been picked and sold weeks ago. The cotton farmers had enjoyed an exceptional year, and the economy of the area was at an all-time high. And it had been a good year for local cattlemen, himself included. He was expecting an excellent calf crop, and next year he would have steers to sell on the open market.

Today, he was beginning what he expected to be the last manhunt of his life. Distasteful though it was, he could do no less, he must play the cards which he had been dealt. He had only to close his eyes to vision his brother fighting for his life, finally being overpowered and cut down years before his time by conscienceless thieves. Will Brannon had been a scoundrel of the worst kind, and Johnny Suit was no doubt of the same stripe.

He had no idea what Johnny Suit looked like, though he felt that he would have little difficulty in locating a lead. Gamblers and gunmen were usually well known. Perhaps Brannon would have described his accomplice if Sam had asked, but Curtin had expected the man to be faster than he was, and it had long been his policy to take care of business while his opponent was busy talking.

Anita had said little about the bunkhouse shooting, for Sam had prepared her beforehand. Lula, however, said that she had never trusted Jeff because the man had a certain look in his eye. She had always believed that he was up to something, she said. She also cautioned Sam about hiring every drifter who lumbered up the hill, the fact that Sam had known the Halley twins for years before putting them on the payroll notwithstanding. Lula was Lula, Sam was thinking, as he stared through the window of the moving train. A lady with a strong opinion on almost everything, and he loved her dearly.

He disembarked at Dallas, then saddled Charley Horse and headed west to Fort Worth, a distance of perhaps thirty miles. There were a few watering holes between the towns, and he would be asking questions.

An hour before nightfall, he came upon the small settlement of Grand Prairie, which had been established on the Texas and Pacific Railroad at the close of the Civil War. It had originally been called Deckman, but had been renamed in 1873. Several saloons rested alongside the tracks, and Sam had already spotted the livery stable and a small hotel. He decided very quickly that he was through traveling for this day. A few minutes later, with his horse fed and in a warm stall, he approached the rough, unpainted counter at the hotel.

"I need a room for the night," he said to the clerk, who appeared to be at least seventy years old.

"Ain't got but one left, mister," the old man said, "an' it ain't very good. Ya'll have ta take it or leave it."

"Does it have a bed and a blanket?"

"Of course it does," the old-timer laughed.

"I'll take it."

Moments later, Curtin quickly decided that the old man had described the room aptly. The bed, which appeared to have been built of green lumber that had now shrunk out of shape, had been pushed against the wall, its legs resting on wooden blocks sawed from two-by-fours. A ladder-backed chair that looked as though it might be dangerous to sit in was beside a rickety-looking table, near the opposite wall. A coal-oil lamp was on the table, along with a pitcher of water and one glass. A large sheet of cardboard covered the lower portion of the room's only window, the panes of which had been broken or removed. Rags and cotton had been stuffed beneath the edges of the cardboard to turn back the cold wind. If Curtin had ever paid money to sleep in a sorrier place, he could not remember it. He sat on the bed lightly at first, then put his full weight on it, surprised that it had not fallen down. Finally deciding that the bed was much sturdier than it appeared to be, he headed for the street. He was hungry.

The beefsteak and potatoes he had at the first restaurant he saw were very good, made more so by the fact that he had not eaten since breakfast. The same middle-aged lady who took his order cooked it and served it. With a foreign accent that Sam took to be German, the lady said her name was Hilda, and thanked him for coming to her restaurant. Smiling generously, he thanked her for the well-prepared meal. His gratuity was also generous when he left the building.

Turning up his coat collar against the chill, he began to walk the street, looking for just the right saloon in which to have a drink. He chose a wide, false-fronted building at the end of the block. No name was posted above the door of the establishment, only a sign stating that whiskey, wine and gambling could be found inside. Curtin took a seat at the far end of the thirty-foot-long bar, close enough to the potbellied stove that he could feel its warmth. Unbuttoning his coat, he ordered whiskey from the thick-chested bartender, who appeared to be a few years younger than himself. Tall and uncommonly muscular, Sam suspected that the young man had been hired at least partially for his ability to deal would-be troublemakers a rough hand.

The saloon was not nearly as large as it appeared from the outside, for a large kitchen and dining room occupied half of the building, separated from the drinking and gambling area by a flimsy, six-foot-high wall with swinging doors. Though no more than a dozen men were present in the room, Sam knew that the crowd would increase in size as the night wore on. However, he did not intend to wait around. He held his empty glass up for the bartender to see, and the man was there quickly.

"Do you happen to know a man named Johnny Suit?" Curtin asked, as his glass was being refilled.

Putting the cork back in the bottle and replacing it on the shelf, the bartender returned to face Sam. Bending over and speaking quietly, he said, "Yeah, I know him. Haven't seen him in more than a year, though." The man continued to stand with his elbows on the bar, clearly expecting Curtin to say more. Sam obliged.

"I've never met the man," he said, "a fellow just told me that I should look him up. In fact, I don't even know what he looks like."

The bartender straightened his body, but did not back away from the bar. With a smile playing around one corner of his mouth, he said, "Now, let me get this straight. A fellow told you to look Suit up, but didn't tell you what he looks like?"

"Didn't have time," Curtin said, taking a sip from his glass. "Somebody killed him before he could tell me." The man moved to the opposite end of the bar to serve some new customers. Afterward, he stood staring down the bar at Sam for a long time. Then, nodding once and beginning to smile broadly, he returned.

"I've got it, now," he said, snapping his fingers. "You're Curtin. I used to watch you doing all them shooting tricks with the medicine show when I was fifteen years old. I still ain't figured out to this day how a man can get so good with a six-gun." He refilled the glass, waving away Sam's offer to pay. "I never have seen you since them days," he said, a look of admiration on his face, "but I've sure heard plenty. Everybody calls you the Judge, nowadays." Neither confirming nor denying the man's conclusion, Sam sipped at his whiskey.

"You want to describe Suit for me?" he asked.

"I'll bet you're the one killed that fellow before he could tell you what Suit looks like, ain't you?" When Sam did not answer, the man leaned forward again, speaking slowly. "You bet I'll describe him for you. He's somewhere around thirty years old, and about the same size as you. In fact, he looks a little like you, 'cept his hair's a little darker. It's real wavy, and he keeps it trimmed nice and neat. Wears glasses when he's playing cards, but I never saw him with them on no other time.

"Anybody hunting him who ain't friendly had better be damn good, because Suit is. I don't mean that he could stand up to a man like you, Mr. Curtin, I just meant that he's a lot better with firearms than most folks." The bartender walked down the bar to check on the drinkers, then returned.

"Is your visit with Suit gonna be friendly?" he asked.

"No."

"Good," the man said, "then I'll tell you some more things about him. He's a damn crook, Mr. Curtin, and he don't care which side of the deck he deals from. If he can't take a man's money with the cards, he'll do it with a gun.

"I whipped his ass right here in this saloon last year, and I've been walking on eggshells ever since. He pulled a gun on me, and the only reason I'm still around is that some of his friends disarmed him. He swore he'd be back after me.

"If you don't find him around Fort Worth, try Parker County. That's his old stomping ground." He looked over his shoulder to check on his drinkers once again, then continued. "Yes, sir, if you put his ass in the graveyard I'll hear all about it, then maybe I can sleep a little better." Finishing his drink, Curtin thanked the man and left the building.

He was walking the streets of Fort Worth before noon the following day, having already spoken with Tarrant County sheriff Bain. The lawman said that he knew Johnny Suit as well as a sheriff was expected to know a crooked gambler, but had not seen him in months. He did not believe that Suit was in Fort Worth at this time, and suggested that Curtin travel to Weatherford, in Parker County. Sam intended to do exactly that. He would spend the night here and get an early start in the morning. The trip to Weatherford would be a good day's ride, and not having a pack horse, he was ill equipped for spending the night on the trail.

He registered at one of the town's better hotels, then spent the afternoon wandering about. The area had changed much since his days with the medicine show. Crowded streets, businesses and expensive homes now occupied land where nothing existed ten years ago. He visited the stockyards and sat through part of a cattle auction, surprised at the prices being bid for the animals. The day when a man could buy a sizable herd for a few hundred dollars was long gone, and stocking a cattle ranch had become an expensive operation. He left the auction feeling somewhat smug in the knowledge that he had stocked his own ranch at precisely the right time.

After a supper of pork and applesauce, he returned to the hotel. His accommodations were a marked improvement over the place in which he had roosted last night, and he slept well in the comfortable bed. He visited none of the town's saloons, for he must get an early start tomorrow.

Weatherford originated in the 1850s when it was selected as the seat of Parker County, and was named for Jefferson Weatherford, a member of the Texas senate when the county was created. At that time, it was the last settlement on the Western frontier, on the route of wagon trains traveling between Fort Worth and Fort Belknap.

The town was also the final resting place of Oliver Loving, known as the "Dean of Texas Trail Drivers." Loving came to Parker County from Kentucky in 1855. Wounded by Indians during a drive with Charles Goodnight, he died at Fort Sumner in 1867 after traveling in secret and without food for five days. With the help of Goodnight, Loving's son returned his father's body to Weatherford for burial, traveling a distance of more than six hundred miles by wagon.

Curtin arrived in Weatherford an hour before sundown. In the center of town, he sat his saddle for a while gazing at the flimsily constructed courthouse. He believed that the structure was an oversized firetrap, that one careless spark would probably reduce the building and all county records to ashes in a matter of minutes. And "careless sparks" were not always accidental, there were plenty of men around who did not want records of their activities kept. There were also plenty of men around who would quite happily turn the records into a bonfire in exchange for a few dollars. Sam believed that all courthouses should be built of something other than wood, especially since there were so many fire-resistant building materials to be had.

Having an hour of daylight left, he turned his horse and began to ride around the town. The south side boasted many beautiful Victorian-style homes, with several more under construction. Half a dozen young men were out working on the landscape with hoes and shovels, as Curtin rode past the school of higher learning. And though they might have been improving the grounds out of a sense of pride, Sam thought it more likely that they were working their way through college out of necessity.

At sunset, he deposited the grateful Charley Horse at the livery stable. Then, with his Winchester in his hand and his saddlebag slung across his shoulder, he walked up the street to the hotel. He passed several saloons on the way, knowing that when darkness fell he would be visiting most of them.

A look of reverence mingled with awe passed over the hotel clerk's face as Sam signed his true name to the register. An act that he quickly regretted, for he knew immediately that he had been recognized.

"Don't advertise the fact that I'm in town, old-timer," he said. The man nodded. Walking down the hall to his room, Curtin promised himself that he would never again sign his true name to a hotel register. The name had simply become too well known in recent years. Though it was possible that the old man had recognized him on sight, Sam doubted it, for it had been more than ten years since he had last appeared in Weatherford with the medicine show. Besides, he had not shaved his face in more than a week, and the heavy beard already hid his facial features to a great extent.

It was three nights later that Curtin learned for sure that he had missed his quarry, that signing his name to the hotel register had cost him an appointment with Johnny Suit. For three nights now he had moved in and out of the saloons and gambling dens, lingering in some for hours. Everywhere he went men sidled away from him in an obvious attempt to avoid conversation. Though Sam had attempted to question a few men, he had received curt answers from all, and each man had quickly decided to be somewhere else.

It was well past midnight when he sat down on a barstool beside an old man who was nursing a glass of whiskey shakily. Ordering a drink for himself, Sam motioned the bartender to refill the old man's glass. Seeing that he was about to gain a free drink, the old-timer greedily gulped the remainder of his whiskey, then pushed the empty glass toward the bartender.

"Name's Upjohn," he said, offering a handshake, "and I sure do thank you for the drink."

"Smith," Sam said, taking the man's hand, "and you're welcome."

"Well, I guess a fellow can use any name he wants to," Upjohn said, taking a sip from his glass. "But it won't do you much good around here, Mr. Curtin, everybody knows who you are."

"Is that a fact?"

"Reckon it is, and I'd say that everybody knows why you're in town. At least Johnny Suit seemed to think he knew; he cashed in his chips and shot out of here like a bat out of hell, when Ben Jones announced that the Judge had just registered at the hotel."

Whatever Curtin was about to say was interrupted by the bartender, who yelled loudly, "Drink 'em up, men, it's closing time!" Sam bought a bottle of the most expensive whiskey in the house, carefully turning it so the old man could clearly see the label.

"Guess I'll have to do the rest of my drinking at the hotel," he said, pushing himself off the stool. "You're welcome to come along if you want, Mr. Upjohn." The old man sat quietly for a moment, staring at the bottle.

"Guess I could stand a couple more drinks," he said,

getting to his feet. "That brand goes down mighty easy." He followed Curtin through the door and up the street to the hotel.

Offering his guest the only chair, Sam seated himself on the bed, then handed the bottle to Upjohn.

"Here," he said, "take the poison off of this." Taking a sip, then licking his lips, the old man took a stronger pull, then handed the bottle back to Curtin.

"Like I said before, that stuff goes down a little smoother than what I usually drink. I used to buy it all the time, but I can't afford the stiff price these days." Sam said nothing, and lifted the bottle to his own lips. He took only a small sip, for he was in no mood to drink. He wanted to listen, and quickly handed the bottle back to Upjohn. Sam did not have to wait long, for after a few long pulls at the bottle Upjohn began to speak freely. Running his fingers through his gray hair, his brown eyes staring at the wall, he said, "Me and the wife used to have a good little spread up on the river, and we could buy most of the things we wanted. She liked a taste of good whiskey every now and then, herself. She died three years ago, and I lost it all within a year. A deck of cards and a bottle of whiskey, Mr. Curtin, that was my downfall. I didn't even learn how to play good poker till after I'd gone broke.

"I can usually get enough out of the games nowadays to eat and drink. That is, if I'm patient, and don't bet on nothing but cinches. Of course, after you do that for a while people quit calling your bets, 'cause they know you've got 'em beat. That's when you have to start eating light and drinking cheap whiskey.

"I've been broke for three days, now. Ain't even had enough money to get in a game. Johnny Suit cleaned me out just before he learned that you were in town."

"Then you think Suit left town because of me?" Sam asked.

"Know damn well he did," Upjohn said, tipping the bottle again. "He got shakier'n a pregnant nun the very second he heard your name, couldn't even hold on to his money. He dropped a dollar on the floor when he was stuffing his winnings into his pocket, didn't even stoop to pick it up. When he asked Ben if he was sure you were in town, and Ben said that he had seen your name on the register himself, Suit was out of that place at a trot.

"He saddled his horse at the livery and was out of town five minutes later, headed west. I learned all this from Hank Blue—he's the liveryman, you know. You see, I sleep there at the stable; got me a nice little bunk set up in the tack room. The bunk was Hank's own idea, and it's helped me a lot. I give him a little money when I can, though." He took another sip from the bottle, then set it on the table.

"I've had enough for tonight," he said. "I don't drink to get drunk nowadays, just try to keep a little in me so I won't get sick. That's the way it is, you know. If you drink every day for a long period of time, you'll get sicker'n a dog if you try to just up and quit." Sam nodded, indicating that he understood. He pointed to the bottle.

"Take the rest of that with you when you leave, then you'll have something to help you get started in the morning."

Seeming to take Sam's statement as a hint that he should be on his way, the old man got to his feet. Shoving the bottle into his coat pocket, he asked, "Was Johnny Suit right to assume that you're looking for him?"

Curtin thought carefully for a moment, then said, "He was right. He cut my brother's throat for no better reason than to steal his money."

"Well, I'll be damned," Upjohn said. "I guess you know that for sure, huh?"

"Right," Sam said, as the old man reseated himself in the chair and began to scratch his head. Curtin took this opportunity to speak his mind. "I believe we can help each other, Mr. Upjohn. You can help me get a lead on Suit's whereabouts, and I can put you back in the poker game." Upjohn's face brightened at the very thought of once again having the money to make a decent bet. Getting to his feet, he walked around the room quietly, obviously busy with his own deep thoughts.

"Might be that I could find out a few things," he said finally. "I don't give a damn what happens to Johnny Suit, mind you, I wouldn't be broke today except for him. I always knew he was cheating me, but I never could catch him at it. Of course, there ain't no hell of a lot that I could have done about it if I had caught him. I'm an old man, already ate up with arthritis." Sam nodded sympathetically once again.

He sat quietly for quite some time, a plan slowly evolving in his mind. Finally, he said to the old man, "Are you game, Mr. Upjohn? Do you want to earn some money?"

"If it has something to do with putting Johnny Suit away, I'm game. And I can't rightly say that I wouldn't appreciate getting another toehold with the gamblers." Sam was on his feet quickly. Taking some money from his pocket, he handed it to the old man.

"Get yourself something to eat after a while," he said. "Get another bottle if you have to, but don't drink any more than you need. Find out everything you can about where Suit might have gone, then meet me right here tomorrow night after dark. The reason I have to ask you to do this is because nobody in this town will talk to me." He walked to the door, waiting to let the old man out. "You'd better go now," he said, "it'll be getting daylight pretty soon." As Upjohn stepped into the hall, Sam added, "And be careful who you talk to." Upjohn nodded, and walked down the hall.

Curtin slept till late in the morning, and awoke very hungry. On his way to breakfast he walked past the desk clerk, and could not resist the temptation.

"I didn't appreciate you spreading the word that I'm in town, old-timer," he said.

"I didn't say nothin'," the man said defensively, "jist tol' a coupla friends that know how ta keep their mouths shet."

"Oh, yeah," Curtin said over his shoulder, and kept walking. He didn't feel like arguing with a man who must be pushing eighty. He crossed the street to the restaurant, where he ordered a platter of ham and eggs, along with buttered pancakes, syrup and coffee. The waitress had assured him that the "Workingman's Special" contained as much food as any man should eat at one time. Sam was convinced a few minutes later when she placed the platter on the counter. At least half a dozen eggs, he decided.

A middle-aged man who was having nothing except coffee sat on the stool beside Curtin's. After an exchange of greetings, Sam spoke to the man again.

"Would you happen to know a man named Upjohn?"

"Travis Upjohn?" the man asked, then continued to talk. "Known him about all of my life." The man took a sip of his coffee, and offered nothing else on Sam's question.

"I just met the man," Curtin said, trying again, "and I was just wondering what kind of fellow he is."

"He's as good as a man needs to be," the man said, getting to his feet. "The gods ain't been smiling on him much lately, but he's all right." The man paid for his coffee, and walked out the door.

When Curtin finished his breakfast, he walked next door and bought a quart of whiskey for Mr. Travis Upjohn, then returned to his hotel room. He slept till late afternoon, then returned to the restaurant for an early supper. Afterward, he bought a copy of the *Fort Worth Democrat* and retired to his room for the night.

He was reading the newspaper by the light of the coal-oil lamp, when he heard a light tap on the door. Bracing himself for anything, he eased the door open.

"Talked to a lot of people," Upjohn said, entering the room. "Most of them, including Hank, think Suit would have gone west at least as far as Palo Pinto County." Curtin needed no further explanation. He was ready to put his plan into action.

"How well do you know Hank Blue?" he asked. "And how well do you trust him?"

"Why, we grew up together," Upjohn said, "and I trust him completely."

"All right," Sam said. "Do you feel up to riding with me for a few days?"

"Sure. Takes me a little longer to get in the saddle these days, but I can ride good enough. Don't have a horse, though."

"No problem, Travis," Curtin said. "Here's what I want you to do: . . ." He instructed the old man to rent a fully rigged pack horse from his friend Hank Blue, along with a saddle horse for himself. He was to outfit the pack horse with any and everything they would need for the trail, and meet Sam half a mile west of town at ten tomorrow morning. Reminding him to bring plenty of bedding and warm clothing, Curtin placed a roll of bills in his hand.

Upjohn nodded, saying, "It'll be done right." A moment later, he was gone. Sam had smelled whiskey on his breath, but Upjohn was sober.

Twenty-three

Upjohn rode out of Weatherford the following morning at half past nine. Aboard a broad-chested black, he led a small roan mare whose pack was fully loaded. Both animals appeared to be in prime condition. He had just topped the hill and left the town behind when Curtin rode out of the trees and joined him.

"Looks like you've got about everything we'll need," Sam said, pointing to the pack animal. The old man smiled.

"Got everything I'll need," he said, "and I reckon you ought to be a lot tougher than I am." Curtin offered a rare smile of his own, and turned his horse toward the Palo Pinto Mountains.

They rode west for the remainder of the day, meeting only a couple wagons and one man on horseback. The area was sparsely populated indeed, and neither man believed that Suit would linger in such country. Upjohn expressed the belief that the man would not even slow down until he had ridden at least as far as Breckenridge.

They camped beside a small stream an hour before sunset, only a few miles south of the mountains. Sam had noticed that Upjohn had taken only one drink during the day. The old man tipped his bottle again now, taking a long pull. He then set about gathering dry wood for a fire. He turned out to be much sprier than Curtin had expected. Sam sat on the ground with his back against a boulder, watching as Upjohn snapped the limbs across his knee like a much younger man.

When the flames had begun to lick at the dry wood, the old man took two new bedrolls from the pack and spread them beside the boulder. Then he was gone to the creek with the coffeepot. A short time later, with the coffee brewing on the fire, he began to prepare supper. Chewing on a piece of straw, Sam had sat idly through it all. The work would give Mr. Upjohn something to do besides drink.

"Thank you, Travis," Curtin said, as the old man dished up a meal of smoked ham, warmed-over biscuits and strong coffee just before dark.

"Think nothing of it," Upjohn said, joining Sam beside the rock. He chuckled, then added, "It ain't every day that a man gets a chance to ride with the Judge." They ate their meal in silence, after which Upjohn produced the bottle. Sam joined him in a drink, then the whiskey was put away for the night. They sat with their backs against the huge rock, listening to the sound of the crackling fire. Finally, the silence was broken by Upjohn.

"That horse you're riding is one of the best-looking animals I've ever seen," he said.

"He's just like he looks," Sam replied. "Fellow

named Red Jordon died on my ranch, and left the horse in the corral."

"Red Jordon?"

"Yeah, did you know him?"

"Lord, yes, been knowing him for over twenty years." Upjohn began to shake his head, adding, "I sure didn't know he was dead, though."

"According to the doc, it was some kind of blood disease," Sam told him.

"Sure sorry to hear that," Upjohn said. "Me and Red go back a long way. I tried to get him to join the Confederate Army with me, but he said he didn't give a damn who won that war, said he had fish to fry in the mountains." Sam smiled, knowing that those had been Red's exact words. They talked for a while longer, with the old man saying that Red Jordon used to stop by the Upjohn spread and stay for a week at a time.

"Said he always stopped by just to get the free food and lodging," Upjohn said, "but he was all the time joking."

"He was serious," Sam said. The old man walked to the dying campfire and banked the remaining coals.

"Maybe so," he said, crawling into his bedroll, "but I still hate hearing about him dying. I'll tell you one thing, sure didn't nobody mess with Red. He'd send a man to the graveyard quicker'n a cat could lick its ass." Upjohn said good night, and was soon sleeping soundly.

Curtin was soon in his own bedroll, but sleep was slow in coming. He was thinking of his beautiful Anita, and longing for her touch. Even Hamp had said that she was a knockout, and he had been a man not known for lavish compliments. Her beauty aside, she was the most intelligent woman Sam had ever been around, and he knew that she would teach their children well. The thought that she might in the not-too-distant future give him muscular sons and beautiful daughters was pleasing indeed. Perhaps the first child was already in the making; maybe Lula's decision to make up some baby things had been timely. Sam hoped so.

Then, as he had done many times since the bunkhouse shooting, he began to think of Will Brannon, alias Jeff Kirby. The man had been the most convincing liar imaginable, and Sam had believed every word. Even now he could almost believe some of the long, drawn-out stories Brannon had told while sitting on his porch, obviously making them up as he went along.

Brannon had been a good actor, all right. Did he have some reason other than money for wanting Hamp dead? Sam would never know. It was plain enough that the murder had been planned beforehand. Otherwise, why would Johnny Suit have been on the premises? Only a few days ago Mack Halley had told Sam that Jeff often spent the night away from the ranch, and was sometimes gone as long as two days. Halley said that he did not report the man's absence to Sam because he knew that Sam liked Jeff. Besides, he said, Jeff always performed his duties well, and worked hard enough to make up for the time spent somewhere else. Sam had accepted Halley's explanation, but made it clear to the man that he expected to be apprised of such things in the future. After all, Mack was drawing an extra fifteen dollars a month for knowing what was going on at Curtin Hill.

The big roan that Sam had bought from Dan Brewster now belonged to Rick, and the youngster was overjoyed. Though he could not always be counted on to use the best judgment in the world, the kid had developed into a good enough cowhand, and was exceptionally strong. Unable to understand why Sam had shot Jeff, Rick had been devastated. It was not until after

Sam and others had painstakingly explained that Jeff had been an imposter, that he had deceived them all and helped to kill Hamp, that the youngster seemed to grasp the situation. He had then taken Jeff's box to the road and dumped it on the ground. Striking a match, he stood idly by while the fire reduced the box's contents to ashes. No one questioned Rick's action, it was understood by all.

When Curtin finally went to sleep he slept soundly till around midnight, at which time he became conscious of subtle movement nearby. He opened one eye and watched as Upjohn crawled to the saddlebag and extracted the bottle. The old man took a strong pull, swallowing several times, then returned the whiskey to the bag. Then he returned to his bedroll and lay very still. But sleep would not be coming any time soon; the whiskey must have time to settle his nerves. Then he would relax, and maybe go to sleep again.

Things had not always been this way with Travis Upjohn. Though slightly stooped at the shoulders and on the frail side nowadays, his six-foot frame had once stood as straight as a fence post, and weighed more than two hundred pounds. He had never been known as a gunman, but had been an excellent scrapper to whom most men gave a wide berth. Even to this day a knowing man could read the story from the scars on Travis Upjohn's knuckles. A story that had been read by Sam Curtin on their first meeting.

Upjohn had come west from Georgia in 1855. Accepting the first job he was offered, he stayed on the ranch for more than six years, eventually working his way up to foreman. When Texas cast its lot with the South during the Civil War, he had enlisted, following General John Bell Hood through hell and high water.

After the war he returned to Parker County, where he

married his beloved Victoria Blankenship. Within a year he had built a log home and established his own small spread, using money lent by a wealthy Union officer whose life he had spared in battle.

The Upjohns had steadily prospered, eventually having four hired hands on the payroll. Their happiness had never been complete, however, for though Vickie had twice given birth, the couple had reared no children. A daughter had been stillborn, and a son had died before his first birthday. And though the lady had fervently hoped to conceive again, it was not to be.

Victoria had died of pneumonia three years ago. Unable to deal with his grief, Upjohn had turned to the bottle. His fortunes had quickly taken a downturn, for he had neglected his business woefully. He soon became a fixture at the poker tables, sometimes playing when he was so blinded by alcohol that he could scarcely see the cards. On one occasion he lost a hundred head of cattle in a single night. Within a year he had been reduced to sleeping at the livery stable. Taking a drink wherever he could find it became a daily routine, and through the generosity of his friends, he could usually acquire a stake in a poker game. With patience and his newfound knowledge of the game, he could most times win enough money to supply food and drink.

Upjohn had long known that he must stop drinking or die. And he had tried on several occasions, but had given in after only a couple days of shaking and vomiting and gone in search of a bottle—and relief. Only yesterday he had made himself a promise that he would try again. Though he had brought along several bottles of whiskey, he did not expect to drink all of it. He would drink a little less each day, cutting down, down, and out.

The following morning Upjohn awoke sick, as usual. Mornings were the worst time. He hit the bottle immediately, then sat back to await its effect. Half an hour later, he had a fire going under the coffeepot and was busy slicing ham for breakfast. Curtin had awakened and walked away from camp to relieve himself. When he returned, he said, "Did you have a rough night, Travis?"

"Not as rough as some of them have been in the past," Upjohn said, "because I drank less than usual yesterday." He served up breakfast, then continued, "I'm gonna kick that damned whiskey, Sam. Lord knows it's been kicking the hell out of me for a long time."

"You can do it, Travis," Sam said, sinking his teeth into a slab of ham. Then, talking around the food, he added, "I'd bet a million men have done it."

"Make that a million and one," Upjohn said, heading for the creek to wash the skillet.

Curtin grained the horses while Upjohn broke camp, and the men were soon riding west again. They skirted the Palo Pinto Mountains to the south, wanting to save the horses. A cloudless sky and the bright sunshine did little to warm up the day, for it was the time of year when the cold north wind blew relentlessly. Both men were bundled in thick clothing and heavy coats, and were fairly comfortable. They held the horses to a brisk walk, though the animals showed every sign of wanting to run on this cold morning.

They stopped for coffee at noon, then continued west till one hour before sunset. They camped for the night at a small spring, three miles east of Breckenridge. This time Sam helped with the camping chores, then picketed the horses where they had access to good grass and the runoff from the spring. He then built a fire and put on the coffeepot.

"Why don't you have a drink from your bottle, Travis," Curtin said, "and sit down for a while." Sam had noticed that Upjohn had not taken a drink since early morning, and had begun to look sickly during the past few hours. The old man did as Sam had suggested, then leaned his back against a stunted oak.

Curtin prepared the remainder of their ham and biscuits, then, opening a small can of tomatoes, dumped half of its contents on each plate.

"This should perk you up a little," he said, handing a plate to Upjohn. They ate in silence, then Sam spread the bedrolls. Then, after washing the plates and the skillet at the spring, he joined the old man beside the fire with a cup of coffee.

"Good place for camping," he said, waving his arm toward the spring. "From the looks of things, we're not the only ones who thought so." The blackened earth and ashes from many campfires could be seen around the spring, a few of them recent.

"Oh, no," Upjohn said, "that spring's what makes people stop. Good water's what everybody's looking for."

At sunset, Curtin walked into the woods, searching for suitable fuel for the fire, as all of the dead wood near the spring had been used by earlier campers. When he dropped an armload by the fire at dusk, he noticed immediately that the old man looked healthier, color had returned to his face. He had no doubt been after the bottle again.

"Want me to ride into Breckenridge after a while and have a look around?" Upjohn asked, holding his hands over the fire then rubbing them together.

"That's what I had in mind from the start," Sam said.

"Well, it's a damn cinch that you can't sneak up on anybody," Upjohn said, reaching for the coffeepot, "you're too well known. Every man in these parts who don't know the Judge on sight has most certainly heard the name." Curtin said nothing, and Upjohn continued. "Even if Suit does happen to see me I don't believe it will unnerve him; men who play poker move around from one town to another all the time. Of course, he ain't gonna see me if I can help it."

"I like the sound of that," Curtin said. Taking some money from his pocket, he offered it to the old man, saying, "If it turns out that you have to get in a game, use this."

"Don't need it," Upjohn said, " 'cause I ain't gonna be getting into a game. Might need to buy somebody a drink, though, you know how that is. In that case, I've got enough money left from what you already gave me. You just get yourself some sleep. I'll probably be late getting back."

"Just be sure to sing out before you come into camp," Curtin said. "I sleep mighty light."

Upjohn saddled his horse and rode away into the night so quietly that Sam did not hear him leave. The old man had taken one last pull at his whiskey, then pitched the bottle to Sam. Curtin tipped it to his own lips, then stretched out in his bedroll.

The settlement had been named for John C. Breckenridge, vice president under Buchanan. It had been established in 1876, and though still little more than a wide place in the road, it was the major retail and shipping center for Stephens County ranchers.

When Travis Upjohn rode into town two hours past dark, lights were burning in only three buildings—all watering holes. The first saloon contained only two customers, and Upjohn did not even linger for a drink. Back outside, he began to lead his horse down the street. He passed the second saloon by, for he could already see that a dozen horses stood outside the third, with twice as many tied to rails across the street. He had found the action.

He entered the building and stepped to the side quickly, for he did not want to linger near the lighted doorway. A circular bar that employed two bartenders stood in the center of the large room, with stools all the way around. On the east side and to the rear of the bar, several card games were in progress. On the west side, Upjohn bought a beer and moved off among the dimly lit tables, where he could observe the games without being seen.

The strongest concentration of light in the room was over the gaming tables, and Upjohn seated himself just outside the glow. He knew that any man who was himself sitting under those lights could not see him in the semidarkness.

From his position at a small table the old man could see every gambler in the house, and Johnny Suit was not among them. Nor had Upjohn expected him to be. Serious gamblers waited till later in the evening, when stakes were usually raised and betting became reckless. Upjohn was in no hurry. He had all night.

And he waited most of the night. It was now only one hour till closing time, and Suit had not appeared. Rising from his chair, the old man slid onto a barstool on the west side and ordered a beer. He was served quickly, for the crowd had already begun to thin out.

"Seen Johnny Suit lately?" he asked the bartender.

"Pretty lately," the man answered. "They say he took a bundle outta that stud game over there two nights ago. He ain't the kind to hang around once he makes a killin'. I'd say he's already over in Albany doin' unto others what they'd like to do to him. Albany's where the action is, now that Fort Griffin's folded."

"Yeah," Upjohn said, nodding, "I guess he'd be doing exactly that."

"Makes sense to me," the bartender said, picking up the old man's beer and wiping the bar beneath it. "Like I said, that's where the action is." Upjohn slid off the stool and headed for the door, leaving his beer untouched. He had some stronger medicine in his saddlebag.

He reported to Curtin two hours later, then picketed his horse and crawled into his bedroll. He did not awaken till long after sunup, when Sam called him to the fire for bacon and fried potatoes. For the first time in months, the old man ate his breakfast without first having a drink of whiskey. Nor did he tilt the bottle afterward, a fact that did not go unnoticed by Curtin.

"Do you feel all right this morning, Travis?" he asked.

"Not exactly," Upjohn answered, "but I sure can remember times when I've felt a lot worse. I expect to be sick, Sam; that's all part of the price you pay when you switch your nervous system from alcohol to water. I'll be all right in the long run, though."

Curtin led the horses into camp, then extinguished the fire. Wordlessly, they loaded the pack animal and saddled their mounts. Albany was an eight-hour ride to the west.

Twenty-four

It was already getting dark when they camped on the creek just east of Albany. They had gotten a late start this morning, and the days were short this time of year. While Upjohn rested himself on a fallen log, Curtin set up camp in the fading light. He unloaded and picketed the horses by starlight, then returned with an armload of wood.

Supper consisted of more bacon and fried potatoes, along with some cheese the old man had bought. Afterward, the men sat beside the fire, chewing on jerky and sipping coffee. Sam assured the old man that tomorrow he would shoot some kind of game animal, so they could prepare a decent stew.

Curtin knew that he could neither walk nor ride into Albany without being recognized, and explained as much to Upjohn.

"I hear that a lot of men who used to hang around

Fort Griffin are down here, now," he said. "Some of them would surely know me." He also explained that he had once punched Ben Hatch in the jaw in front of a dozen men who would still remember.

"Hatch owns the livery stable," Sam said, "and probably several other things."

"Guess you had a good reason for punching him."

"Good enough," Curtin said, pouring more coffee for both. "He beat up a teenaged boy who's mentally retarded. The kid lives on my ranch, now." The old man blew air into his cup to cool the hot liquid, then began to sip.

"You should have killed the sonofabitch," he said. Sam said nothing else on the matter. On his hands and knees, he began to remove sticks, stones and other debris from a small area for their bedrolls. Then, folding his heavy coat for a pillow, he lay down to rest.

"Guess it's time I got going," the old man said, getting to his feet. A few minutes later he led his horse into camp, saddled it, and mounted. He had not taken a drink since last night. Nor did he take one now. Raising his hand in a good-bye gesture, he rode off into the night.

Upjohn had not been gone twenty minutes, when Curtin walked into the woods away from the glow of the campfire. As he had done numerous times in the past, he began to limber up his shooting arm, making his fast draw and pointing the gun at a make-believe target with the quickness of a viper. After a while, satisfied with his speed, he returned to the fire and kicked off his boots. Crawling into his bedroll, he was soon sleeping soundly.

It seemed that Curtin had no more than closed his eyes, when Upjohn helloed the camp. Rising to one elbow, Sam beckoned him in. Without dismounting, the old man began to speak in excited tones.

"He's there, Sam!" he said. "Sitting there just as pretty as you please, playing stud." Curtin pulled on his boots, but did not leave his bedroll.

"Thank you, Travis," he said, "it looks like the hunt's over." Upjohn continued to sit his saddle.

"Well, are you going in after him?" he asked.

"Not tonight," Sam said, stoking up the fire, "he's not going anywhere. Tomorrow's Saturday, and there'll be lots of poker money in town. I want you to spot him for me again tomorrow afternoon, then I'll ride in." The old man unsaddled his horse, then picketed it with the others. A short time later, he rolled into his blanket.

Shortly after daybreak, Upjohn awoke to the sound of gunfire several hundred yards down the creek. Glancing at Curtin's empty bedroll, he smiled, then slipped on his boots and began to restart the fire. When Sam walked into camp half an hour later with a hindquarter of venison, the old man was waiting with a sharp knife.

Curtin washed his hands in the creek, then sat back and watched Upjohn slice steaks and peel potatoes. Coffee was soon boiling, and Sam filled his cup. Reseating himself on his bedroll with his legs crossed, he spoke to the old man.

"I've been thinking, Travis," he said, burning his lips on the rim of the cup, "now that you've decided to give up the bottle, what are you gonna do?"

"Don't know," the old man said, turning the steaks in the skillet, "figured I'd cross that bridge when I get to it. Why do you ask?"

"Because I think we could use another man on the ranch."

Upjohn began to chuckle softly, raking a bed of coals away from the fire. Placing the skillet upon them, he said, "Sure don't know what you think I could do to be worth a payday. Can't keep up with the young bucks these days."

"You can do the same thing you're doing right now," Sam said, getting to his feet and beginning to walk around. "My hands have to do their own cooking, and that cuts into their working time."

"Guess I could do that," Upjohn said quickly, dumping the potatoes into the skillet with the steaks, "but cooking for three ranch hands sure ain't much of a job."

"There'll be other things," Curtin said. "There's always some kind of errand to run in the buggy, or the supply wagon. If you run long on time and short on work, you can surely find something to do around the barn."

Upjohn nodded, and said nothing. He soon placed steaks on tin plates and topped them with heaping piles of brown potatoes. Handing a plate to Curtin, he spoke again.

"Guess you just hired yourself an arthritic old man," he said. "Guess I've cooked most things that people eat at one time or another. If the hands'll tell me what they want, I suppose I can handle it."

"I'm sure you can," Curtin said. He began to chuckle, adding, "Anytime you really want an honest answer about your cooking, just ask the youngest of the hands. His name is Rick."

Immediately after breakfast, the old man set about preparing dinner. After chopping up venison and onions, and pouring in a can of tomatoes, he placed the six-quart iron pot on the fire to simmer. He would wait a couple hours before adding the potatoes, salt and pepper.

Bundled up in his heavy coat, and wearing warm

gloves, Curtin soon dropped another armload of wood beside the fire.

"That bright sunshine sure is pretty," he said, "but I don't believe it's gonna warm this day up much. Had to break the ice in that ditch over there so the horses could drink."

"Be no more good weather till spring," Upjohn said, stirring the stew and adding more wood to the fire. "All of the nights and most of the days are gonna be cold for the next four months. Christmas'll be here before you know it."

Christmas! Though Sam intended to buy nice presents for all, he knew that it would be a sad day at Curtin Hill. Hamp had always been in charge at Christmastime, boosting the spirits of everyone else as he cut, trimmed and decorated the tree himself. He had always presented every member of the family with a nice gift, somehow seeming to know exactly what they needed most.

Even during the old days, when Hamp seldom saw a dollar, he had always had something nice for everyone—usually something he had made with his hands. And those had been the gifts most appreciated by the recipients. Sam still remembered the year he was ten, and the handmade whistle. At least Hamp had started out to make a whistle. Somewhere along the line he had decided to turn it into a musical instrument. Boring holes into the long, slender tube, he had then filled them with metal rings of different sizes, so that a different pitch could be obtained by blowing air through each hole. As a ten-year-old learned which holes to cover with his fingers, and which to leave open, a simple melody could actually be played. Sam still owned the whistle, or whatever it should be called, to this day.

Though he had his own woman to buy pretty things

for nowadays, Sam would also be concerned about getting Lula through her first Christmas without Hamp. She was a lady who accepted the day for its true meaning, and placed little consequence on the exchanging of gifts. And her wish list had always seemed to be nonexistent. Of the hundreds of times Sam had heard her speak to the Almighty over the years, never once had he heard her ask for anything. She was simply too busy thanking Him for the things she already had. Sam had no idea what kind of gift he would slip under her tree this time around, but he knew what he would place in front of it: himself and all the inhabitants of Curtin Hill. He would plan a big feast, and put Lula in charge of preparation. He would also buy her a bottle of good wine, for she liked the taste.

Upjohn rode out of camp shortly after noon headed for Albany. His assignment was to spot Johnny Suit as inconspicuously as possible, then return. The old man had saddled his horse and departed eagerly, for he had long held a strong dislike for the gambler.

Alone now, Curtin walked into the woods again. Easing into his gunfighter's crouch, he ripped the Peacemaker from his hip and brought it into firing position with lightning speed. Twenty times he made his fast draw, seeming to gain a little speed with each pull. Then, adding a sixth shell to its cylinder, he reholstered the weapon. The next time the Colt came out it would be spitting flame.

He led Charley Horse into camp and cinched down the saddle. He left the pack mare on her picket, for they would be returning by this same route. Shoving his Winchester into the boot, he tied the black to a low-hanging limb. Then, refilling his cup from the blackened coffeepot, he sat down on a log to wait.

His wait was not a long one, for Upjohn was back within the hour.

"He's sitting right where he was last night," the old man said breathlessly, dismounting slowly. "He can't see the front door from where he's sitting, so I'd say you can get as close as you want before he knows you're around." Getting to his feet, Curtin began to kick dirt over the fire.

"Thank you, Travis," he said, his voice taking on a businesslike tone. "I guess it's time."

They rode into Albany an hour later, with Curtin a few steps in the lead. With his eyes and ears alert for any kind of surprises, he headed straight for the saloon's hitching rail. They dismounted quickly, and tied their animals. Never one to postpone the inevitable, Curtin nodded to the old man, saying, "Now."

Upjohn stepped into the doorway first, with Sam close on his heels. The idea was that, with both men being of the same height, Curtin would have a chance to scan the room with his eyes before being noticed by anyone. Upjohn walked straight ahead toward the bar, while Curtin veered off to the right among the dimly lit tables. He did not stop until he reached the wall, where he stood long enough to allow his eyes to adjust.

He could see the poker game from his position, for the light was stronger where the players sat. A four-handed stud game was in progress, and Johnny Suit was busy dealing out a new hand, calling out the value of each card as it fell faceup on the table. Fearing that someone might become aware of his presence at any moment, Curtin moved quickly, while Suit's eyes were glued to the table. He stopped fifteen feet away from the game, shouting loudly, "Everybody except Johnny Suit move away from the table!" When a couple men were slow in moving, he shouted again, "Now!" Sam recognized Ben Hatch, who was the last to leave his chair.

"That's the Judge, Johnny," Hatch said to Suit, as he slowly moved away from the table. The place was eerily quiet, with Hatch's words seeming to reverberate off the walls. The name and reputation was known by everyone in the room, and each man knew what was about to happen. Within two seconds every man had scrambled out of the line of fire. Suit remained seated, with both hands on the table. Never taking his eyes from the man, Curtin shouted for all to hear, "Listen up, men, and I'll tell you why I'm here!" He nodded toward Suit, then continued. "This sonofabitch walked into my brother's shop recently and robbed him. Cut his throat and left him on the floor to strangle in his own blood." Sam could hear voices mumbling throughout the room. He spoke directly to Suit, now.

"I'll give you a better chance than you gave Hamp Curtin, fellow; get on your feet and make your play!"

Suit sat very still, all color drained from his face. Finally, with a shaky voice that was barely above a whisper, he said, "I'm not gonna draw against you. I'd be crazy to do that."

"You'd be crazy not to!" Curtin blasted. "It's the only chance you've got. I'll kill you if you don't!" Suit thought it over for only a moment, then began to ease himself out of his chair. He had not fully regained his feet when he jumped sideways, pulling his gun at the same time. All of which bothered Curtin not in the least, for he had been shooting moving targets most of his life. His first shot went into Suit's mouth, spraying the wall behind him with gray matter. Curtin sent another shot into the man's throat, then holstered his weapon. He walked sideways for several steps and spoke to the bartender.

"Tell your local lawman why I was here," he said. "If he wants to push it I live at Calvert, and I'm easy to find."

The bartender nodded, saying, "Will do." Curtin laid a sizable bank note on the bar.

"This should pay for the mess I made over there," he said. The bartender nodded again, and Curtin headed for the front door. He was joined at the hitching rail by Upjohn.

"Beats all in the hell I've ever seen," the old man was saying, "I bet if I live to be a hundred years—"

"Let's get Hank Blue's horses back to Weatherford," Sam interrupted. "We'll take the train from there to Calvert."